Ike spread a map on the hood of a Humvee and studied it for a moment. "There is absolutely no way to tell which direction Ben might take," he said. "He might head straight east, he might go north or south, he might circle around and come up behind Bottger's men."

"You're sure they were Bottger's people?" Lamar Chase, the chief of medicine, asked.

"Yes. The bodies are stretched out over there." Ike pointed to a row of bodies laid out by the side of the road, covered with ground sheets.

"Any taken alive?"

"Two. One of them is badly hurt and won't live out the rest of the day. He's been talking some. Ben has at least a hundred men, maybe twice that number, chasing him." Ike waved a hand toward the east. "Out there in all that thousands and thousands of acres of wilderness. I did some training out there years back, Doc. Skilled trackers and experienced woodsmen have gotten lost in that wilderness. Some of them were never found."

"Were there any signs of Ben's being injured?"

"No traces of blood. Scouts say he's limping some."

"Hell, yes, he's limping. He's probably bruised from head to toe. Might have cracked a bone or two. I don't see how he survived at all."

"He's lucky, Doc. Ben is the luckiest man I've ever known."

Lamar grunted. "You know, Ike, Ben's on his own now. No decisions to make, no paperwork to wade through, no one breathing down his neck. And you know what else?"

"What?"

"He's enjoying every damn minute of it!"

JUDGMENT
IN THE
ASHES

WILLIAM W.
JOHNSTONE

PINNACLE BOOKS
Kensington Publishing Corp.
http://www.kensingtonbooks.com

PINNACLE BOOKS are published by

Kensington Publishing Corp.
119 West 40th Street
New York, NY 10018

All Kensington Titles, Imprints, and Distributed Lines are available
at special quantity discounts for bulk purchases for sales promo-
tions, premiums, fund-raising, and educational or institutional use.
Special book excerpts or customized printings can also be created
to fit specific needs. For details, write or phone the office of the
Kensington special sales manager: Kensington Publishing Corp.,
119 West 40th Street, New York, NY 10018, attn: Special Sales
Department, Phone: 1-800-221-2647.

Pinnacle and the P logo Reg. U.S. Pat. & TM Off.

ISBN-13: 978-0-7860-2082-9
ISBN-10: 0-7860-2082-2
First Printing: October 1997

10 9 8 7 6 5 4 3

Printed in the United States of America

Book One

Duty is the sublimest word in our language. Do your duty in all things. You cannot do more. You should never wish to do less.

—Robert E. Lee

Prologue

Many citizens believed the collapse of America was inevitable. Just before the total breakdown, voter participation in national elections dropped to less than half of all registered voters taking part. Candidate campaigning had deteriorated into nasty name-calling and finger pointing, with real issues taking a back seat. For several decades, it seemed that Americans just could not find a middle ground in politics or in the enforcement of laws. Morals and values plummeted to new lows.

And the government began snooping into nearly every aspect of citizens' lives.

The IRS—which had become the most hated of all government agencies—knew to the penny what every citizen had in his or her bank account. The government had begun to view each citizen's income as not belonging to them, but to the government, especially since the percentage most American citizens had to pay the government had soared to over fifty-five percent of their gross income.

In many respects, America had become a socialist nation.

And the liberals had finally gotten their wish: legislation had been rammed through Congress effectively disarming American citizens, leaving those who wished to be armed with only bolt-action hunting rifles and double-barrel, single-shot, or pump shotguns. No semi-automatic rifles or shotguns and absolutely no pistols in the hands of private citizens.

Ammunition was heavily restricted and always registered. Government agents could enter a citizen's home at any time without warrant or warning. And did, often, with great enthusiasm.

And then the world seemed to go crazy, with brush wars popping up all over the globe, and spreading rapidly. Finally the bottom dropped out. One by one, governments all around the world began collapsing as citizens revolted. Then came a limited germ and nuclear war that quickly spread, leaving Earth without a stable government anywhere.

But there were those in America who had long predicted such an event. They were called many names: militia, survivalists, nuts, kooks, gun-freaks, conspiracy-freaks, paranoid—and those were some of the kinder names. But they had been correct in their thinking and far-sighted in their planning. America was in trouble, and a long, hard fall did indeed happen.

One of those who had predicted such terrible times for America was a young ex-soldier/adventurer named Ben Raines. It would be safe to call Ben a survivalist, but not a practicing type. That is to say he did not belong to any group who trained in the woods and conducted live-fire exercises. But Ben did believe in being ready, and when the fall came, he knew what to do.

After prowling the nation for almost a year, Ben began to organize people who shared his philosophical views of how a government should be run, and how it should conduct itself. En masse they moved to the Northwest, taking over three states as their own.

They called themselves Tri-Staters.

One

Where once there were only a few hundred, now there are thousands, Ben thought, as he stood outside a building at the old Tucson International Airport that was serving as his quarters and HQ and looked at the hustle and bustle of Rebels going about their work.

Part of his command was billeted a few miles away at the old Davis-Monthan AFB and 16 Batt, under the command of Mike Post, was stretched out just north of the city as a first line of defense in case that religious nut, Simon Border, decided to attack.

The campaign to rid the western part of America of punks and thugs was over, and the back of the punk empire had been broken and the head cut off. That much, at least, had been a success.

But now Ben faced a religious war with the hundreds of thousands, perhaps millions of Simon Border supporters and followers, and that was something he most definitely did not want.

But Ben could see no way out of it.

He had tried to talk some sense with Border, but the man was having none of it. He considered Ben to be the great Satan, and was determined to destroy him and anyone else who followed the Tri-States political philosophy of a common-sense form of government.

And when Simon tried that, just as the nation was strug-

gling to its feet, the country would be plunged into a religious war . . . a war'that might not have an end, for even
after all that had happened, factions were still fighting in
Northern Ireland.

Ben turned and went back into his office. With a sigh of
resignation he sat down behind his desk and looked at the
pile of paperwork facing him. Ben hated paperwork, but
knew he had to do it. He picked up a pen and went to work.

Hundreds of miles to the north, in one of his mountain
hideaways, the spiritual leader of millions of people, the
Most Reverend Simon Border, stared out the south-facing
window and thought of Ben Raines.

He would not make the mistake of hurling untrained and
untested troops against Ben again. That was foolish and
very arrogant on his part and had cost the lives of hundreds
of good men. Even as he pondered the situation, thousands
of his people were undergoing intensive field training,
learning as much as possible about the art of warfare.

Simon leaned back in his chair and smiled at the thought
of the nation, under his spiritual rule. What a glorious day
that will be.

Ben pushed aside the stack of paperwork and leaned back
in his chair. He could not concentrate on the seemingly
endless details of running a huge army. Besides, something
else was nagging at him: why was Simon Border waiting?
Why didn't he attack? The so-called religious leader had
made his brags, but nothing came of them.

"We've been here for six weeks," Ben muttered. "Growing stronger each hour. Still the man does nothing."

"Anything from Mike?" the ever-present Jersey asked.

The very pretty and diminutive Jersey was Ben's self-
appointed bodyguard. Wherever Ben was, you would find
Jersey shadowing him.

Mike was the Rebel chief of intelligence.

"Not in a couple of weeks," Ben replied.

Corrie the radio tech, had left her radio in the hands of

a relief operator and was relaxing with a cup of coffee. "High-level recon flights is still showing nothing. We're still getting reports that Simon's army is training, but they're in small units and it's a big area to cover."

Beth, the statistician, laid aside her journal and looked up from her desk. "And all action by Border's people east of the Mississippi River abruptly stopped about three weeks ago and no fighting has been reported since."

Cooper, the driver, said, "It just doesn't make any sense, boss. They start an offensive all over America, then just stop. Why?"

Ben shook his head.

Anna, Ben's adopted daughter, whom he had found as a dirty-faced little waif in Eastern Europe, turned her head with her close-cropped blond hair and cut her pale eyes toward him. Young/old eyes that had seen far too much for their age. "I am Catholic. Not a practicing Catholic, but Catholic nonetheless. I will never bow to someone such as Simon Border. If Simon does not want to bring the fight to us, we take the fight to him."

"I'm trying to avoid a religious war, Anna," Ben told her. "Not start one."

The young lady shrugged her shoulders. "Can't be avoided. You know as well as I, Border is up to something dirty—all in the name of God, of course. Personally, I think God turns His head and closes His eyes when wars start."

Ben grunted. Personally, he believed the same way. "Perhaps, Anna. But I'm not going to be the one to start this war."

Anna stood up, picking up her CAR as she did. "Did you ever consider that you just might not have any choice in the matter, General Ben?" She walked out the door.

"What did she mean by that?" Cooper asked. He shook his head. "Sometimes that girl spooks me."

"It's the Gypsy in her," Ben said with a smile. "It's said

that some Gypsies are born with the ability to see into the future."

"The same is said of our medicine men," Jersey, who was part Apache, said. "Personally I think it's all a bunch of shit." She walked outside to join Anna.

Ben chuckled and returned to his paperwork. But in the back of his mind he wondered what Simon Border was up to.

Simon was having some trouble of his own in his so-called paradise. Hundreds of people who adamantly rejected his dictatorial type of religion were making plans to clear out of Border's territory. These men and women did not necessarily embrace the Tri-States philosophy, but they certainly didn't want to live under Simon Border's rule.

Only problem with their leaving was that Simon had sealed his territory tight; no one in, no one out.

"Then we have to fight," one leader of a small resistance group told his followers.

"With what?" a woman asked. "Shovels and axes?"

Simon had disarmed any person who did not attend his churches and swear lifetime allegiance to his rule.

Disarming a population and declaring the ownership of nearly all types of firearms illegal is one of the most effective methods of stilling dissent.

"We make bombs," Glenn Waite told his people. "We start blowing up army barracks and police stations and local politicians."

"I can make bombs," another of Glenn's followers said. "It's really pretty simple. With all of us working, we can make dozens. If the other teams go along with it, we can have hundreds of bombs ready to go in a very short time."

Glenn nodded his head. "I'll contact them. Most, if not all, will go along, I'm sure. Get cracking on it, Martin. I'd rather die fighting as a free man than live under the rule of Simon Border."

"Everything is calm back here, Ben," Cecil Jefferys, the president of the SUSA and Ben's long-time friend reported. "We had a few minor flare-ups here in the SUSA with some people who feel that Simon's way is the best way, but they were quickly shown to the border and kicked out. I'm sure we have others, but they're keeping a low profile and their mouths shut."

"Then they're up to something, Cec."

Cecil sighed over the miles. "Yeah, I agree, Ben. And it worries me. But we can't polygraph or PSE the entire population."

"No," Ben returned the sigh. "And I wouldn't want things to come to that, anyway."

"Any word from Mike?"

"Not a peep. He's found him a woman up in Utah, I think. She's with a guerrilla team, so Mike joined them."

"Ol' Mike's in love, huh?"

"Looks that way."

"Good for him."

"Everything is quiet here, Cec. And I still refuse to take the offensive in this matter."

"I think you're doing the right thing, Ben. But if Simon's people start slaughtering dissidents in his territory, you might be forced to change your mind."

"You know something I should know, Cec?"

"No. But I wouldn't put something like that past the lunatic."

"Nor would I. All right, Cec. I'll bump you in a few days."

Ben returned to his desk and sat down, propping his boots up on a stack of paperwork he just simply quit on. "Corrie, when is Thermopolis and his 19 HQ Batt scheduled to pull in?"

"Sometime tomorrow."

Ben pointed to the paperwork. "When they get here, give all that crap to them. That's what HQ is supposed to do, not me."

"Right, boss. Boss?"

Ben cut his eyes.

"Some of the people were wondering about Simon Border. They know that Border's country is based, sort of, on his weird philosophy, but other than that, what kind of government does he have?"

"Socialistic, for the most part. Everything is state run. Collective farming and so forth; everything that anyone does is for the state, not for the individual. The state, of course, being Simon Border and his inner circle and friends." Ben smiled. "I think the people can have tiny gardens all their own."

"Well, that's damn charitable of Nutbrain Border," Cooper said.

"It didn't work in Russia," Beth said, laying aside an old paperback novel she had found along the way. Ben took note of the author, Linda Howard. He had known her back before the world erupted into war. "It was beginning not to work in China—according to what I've been able to read. Capitalism is the only form of government that's worth a damn."

"Thank you, Professor Beth," Cooper said.

"You're welcome, Coop." Beth stuck her nose back into the book. *Mackenzie's Mountain,* Ben observed.

"What is so great about that type of government, boss?" Coop asked.

"Nothing, as far as I'm concerned," Ben replied. "Personally, I think it stinks. And Simon and his followers could have it, if they'd just back off and stay away from us."

"Message coming in from Mike," Corrie said, holding up her hand.

Ben took the mic. "Go. Mike."

"I'll keep this short, Ben," the chief of intelligence said. "Simon is just about ready to make his move against you. In addition, there are hundreds of people living in his territory who are ready to fight him just as soon as you give the word. I'll give Corrie the map coordinates for air drops. We need weapons and ammo in the worst way."

"You'll get them, Mike. There is no hope Simon will back off?"

"No, Ben. None. But what difference would it make if he did back off? He's sealed his borders and refused to allow dissidents to leave. He's using force to coerce people to worship his way. He's preparing to kill any who oppose him. Make virtual slaves out of those who survive the purge."

Ben sighed and shook his head. He had noticed today that the gray was spreading rapidly among his once dark brown hair. Well, hell, Ben thought, it was time for him to gray. "Then I guess that does it, Mike. His armies have been training hard, right?"

"Right, Ben. We've got twenty battalions to field, he's got a hundred and twenty and more in reserve. They won't be making the mistakes they did at first. Count on that."

"I'll never understand how he got so many people to go along with his nutty plans."

"Long story, Ben. I'm still piecing it together. Someday we'll sit down over a pot of coffee and talk it out. But for right now, you'd better get ready for the fight of your life."

"Okay, Mike."

"Good luck." Mike broke it off.

Ben turned to find his team looking at him. "Get the Batt Coms in here, Corrie. Let's start making plans."

"Are we going to carry the fight to Simon's people, boss?" Cooper asked.

"I guess so, Coop," Ben's words were softly offered. "I don't see that we have any choice in the matter."

Two

The battalion commanders began assembling. Ben had reshuffled some of the battalion designations and eliminated a few others. Ike McGowen, a man who had been with Ben since the beginning, was the commander of 2 Batt. Ike was an ex-Navy SEAL and only a few years younger than Ben. Ike struggled with his weight, but no matter what he did, he still resembled a big teddy bear. The Englishman, Dan Gray, commanded 3 Batt. Dan was a former British SAS officer. West, the ex-mercenary, was the commander of 4 Batt. Georgi Striganov, the former Russian airborne commander, commanded 5 Batt. Rebet was the commander of 6 Batt. Danjou, the Canadian, commanded 7 Batt. Buddy Raines, Ben's son, was the commander of 8 Batt, the special operations battalion. Tina, Ben's daughter, commanded 9 Batt. Tina and West were engaged and would someday be married. Someday, when the fighting was over. Pat O'Shea, the wild Irishman, was the commander of 10 Batt. Greenwalt commanded 11, and Jackie Malone, a very pretty lady who was pure hell when it came to discipline, was the commander of 12 Batt. Raul Gomez commanded 13 Batt; Jim Peters, the Texan, 14 Batt. Buck Taylor was the commander of 15 Batt; Mike Post of 16 Batt; Paul Harrison commanded 17 Batt; and Nick Stafford commanded 21 Batt. Thermopolis, the ex-hippie, was the commander of Headquarters Battalion, designated 19 Batt. 18 and 20 Batts had been incorporated into other battalions. Each battalion in the Rebel army carried its own large contingent of tanks and artillery and heavy mortars. Each had an additional platoon of Scouts, a group of cold-eyed young men and women who had undergone some of the most brutal training ever devised by humankind. The Scouts were used for all sorts of dirty jobs, and were not happy unless they were taking incredible chances, usually working behind enemy lines, cutting throats. The battalions that made up the Rebel army were over-sized, several times larger than conventional battalions, about half the size of a regiment, so companies were larger, platoons were larger, squads were larger.

"Looks like we're into it, gang," Ben announced, after everyone had pulled mugs of coffee and taken a seat. "Against my better judgment," he added.

The batt coms sat silently. To a person, the news came as no surprise. They knew that while Ben had been agonizing over this decision, he would never tolerate any threat toward the SUSA.

Ben brought the batt coms up to date, laying out every piece of intelligence he had received over the past seventy-two hours. When it was all added up, there was no doubt in anyone's mind but that Simon was going to attack.

"We know Simon has little in the way of heavy artillery," Ben continued. "But that he has plenty of mortars. And one hell of a lot of warm bodies to throw at us. We can certainly expect suicide charges. And we all know how unpleasant those are," he said, very drily.

"We're going to be all over the map, aren't we, Ben?" Ike asked.

"Yes. Sometimes we're going to have to operate as guerrilla units, other times standing and slugging it out with Simon's people."

"How many small guerrilla units does Mike report operating in Simon's territory?" Paul Harrison asked.

"No firm count, Paul. Mike just said there were dozens

of them. We've been dropping them supplies for weeks, so they should be ready to go."

The Russian, Georgi Striganov, stood up and walked over to a huge wall map, staring at it for a moment. He shook his head. "We could very easily be bogged down here for months, even years," he said.

"Months is very likely, almost a certainty, but years is not going to happen," Ben told him. "I'll pull out and bunker in back home if I see signs of that happening."

"Placement of the battalions, General?" Raul Gomez asked what was foremost on all the batt coms' minds.

Ben moved to the wall map. "I'll be taking my 1 Batt and heading west in the morning. Ike will follow seventy-five miles behind me." Ben smiled. "Approximately, that is. The rest of the battalions will stretch out behind Ike, running west to east at seventy-five mile intervals, in numerical order, with the exception of Therm's 19 Batt, which will be in the center of the line. At El Paso, those remaining battalions will turn north, maintaining the mileage intervals. That will be approximately ten battalions stretched out between San Diego and El Paso. That will leave eight battalions, not counting 19 Batt, to make the turn north, stretching out some six hundred miles. That should put them almost to Dodge City. I have spoken with various militia leaders and they have agreed to plug the gap between Dodge City and the Canadian border. The southern front pushes north, the eastern front pushes west. That will include the militia. And they have agreed to come under my command, so we will supply them whenever they request it, with whatever they request. We've stockpiled enough supplies for a sustained campaign, so we're going to be loaded, and therefore not able to make much time on these bad roads. That will make us very susceptible for ambush and Simon's people will be lying in wait for us, bet on that. So heads up all the way. Get your people ready to roll. That's it."

After the batt coms had left, Ben sat outside for a few minutes, smoking a cigarette, Dr. Lamar Chase with him. Lamar had been with Ben since the beginning of the dream of a new form of government, a government whose laws were based on common sense. Lamar gave the cigarette in Ben's hand some disapproving looks, but kept his mouth shut about it.

"You're getting too old for the field, Lamar," Ben brought up the subject he knew he had to address. "You should sit this one out."

Lamar surprised Ben by saying, "I know it."

Ben looked at the older man. "Well?"

"Well, what?"

"Are you going to sit this one out? It's going to be a rough one."

"Of course not. I'll think about retiring from the field when you quit smoking."

"You mean I'm going to have to put up with you for the next twenty years?"

Lamar smiled. "If you persist in sucking on those damn cigarettes, yes."

"I don't smoke that many a day, Lamar."

"That's what they all say, Raines."

"Nothing worse than having to listen to the preaching from a reformed smoker, a reformed drunk, or a reformed whore," Ben grumbled.

Lamar laughed at Ben's expression.

"Seriously, Lamar. This campaign could turn out to be a bad one."

"All the more reason you need me along. Besides, my doctors expect to be here. And speaking of old . . ."

"I'll leave the field when I can no longer cut it, Lamar. And you know I will."

"Yes, I do know that, Ben. And I do think—hell, I know, I'm your doctor—you're good for a few more years. But

I'm still in pretty good shape for a man my age. I'll tag along for this campaign."

Ben knew to argue more would be futile. "All right, Lamar. That's settled then."

Lamar started to tell Ben his coming along was never in doubt, but he curbed his tongue on that. Besides, there was another reason he stayed behind. Others had been to see him and had convinced him that he should be the one to tell Ben.

"What's really on your mind, Lamar?" Ben broke into the moment of silence.

"I wish you'd stop doing that, Raines," the old doctor said sourly. "Sometimes you spook me."

Ben smiled. "Doing what, Lamar?"

"You know perfectly well what. Getting into peoples' heads as you do. Look, Raines, I might as well get this over with. He's been seen again."

Ben experienced a slow, cold chill creep up his backbone. He cleared his throat. "Who has been seen again, Lamar?"

"You know who, Ben. The old man with the robes and the staff."

"The *prophet?*"

"Yes."

"Where?"

"Right here. Out at the Air Force Base. Back at Base Camp One. He almost scared the shit out of the Secretary of State."

"When?"

"Two nights in a row, Ben. Just before midnight. All places at once. You know the drill."

"What the hell was Secretary Blanton doing up at midnight?"

"Getting a drink of water, so I heard. He turned around from the sink and there the old geezer was."

Ben chuckled and the ominous sensation that had crawled

up his spine slowly faded. "Why do I get the impression the old boy wants to see me?"

"If he's real, Raines."

"Oh, he's real, Lamar. He's no figment of anybody's imagination. I can assure you of that."

Lamar stood up and stretched. "I guess you'll be outside about midnight, then?"

"You bet. Lamar? Why were people afraid to come to me with this?"

"Because of who you are, Raines. Hell, you should be used to that by now. And speaking of spooking people: where is that damned old Thompson you carried around for years?"

"Close by."

"You retired it, I hope."

"In a manner of speaking."

"Whatever the hell that means." Lamar stared at Ben for a moment. "See you on the road, Raines."

Ben lifted a hand and watched as Lamar walked away. So the bearded old man dressed in robes and carrying a walking stick was back. Ben couldn't recall exactly the last time the man called the prophet had shown up . . . years, at least.

Ben looked up as Jersey stepped into view. "Did you know about the Prophet, Jersey?"

"Just rumors, boss. You know how the troops shut up around us."

Ben knew she meant his personal team. He nodded his head. "I'll be right here around midnight, Jersey. Alone."

"All right, boss. I'll pass the word. Boss, you think this old man is, well, real?"

"Yes, I do, Jersey."

"Where does he come from? What does he, I mean, what is he?"

Ben shook his head. "I don't know. All I know is he's

been showing up at various times for years, making predictions. Usually about me."

"But he shows up at several places at the same time!"

"Yes, I know."

"That means he's a . . . well, you know."

"Yes."

"That's got Cooper really spooked, boss."

Ben smiled. "I can just imagine."

"You want me to be out here with you tonight?"

"No, Jersey. But thank you."

"Okay, boss. I'll tell the others you said to stand clear."

"Thank you, Jersey."

At eleven forty-five that evening, Ben stepped out of his quarters, taking a wood and canvas camp chair with him. He placed the chair in the shadows, away from the building he was occupying. He went back into his quarters, poured a mug of coffee, walked back outside, and sat down in the chair. He rolled a cigarette, lit up, and leaned back and waited.

A few minutes later, a voice came out of the darkness. "Are you afraid, Ben Raines?"

Without turning his head, Ben said, "No. Should I be?"

"Aren't you going to look at me?"

"I've seen you, remember?"

"Your cause is a noble one, Ben Raines. At first I had my doubts. But you are not fighting for personal gain or power. And I have to admit I am impressed."

"Whoever you are."

A chuckle sprang out of the night. "What do you think I am?"

"I honestly don't know. Except you are no longer of this earth."

"I was never really of this earth, Ben Raines."

Ben had always suspected that. "How's God's mercenary, Michael, these days?" Ben tossed the question out.

Again, that chuckle. "He sends his regards."

"Good to know that ol' warrior is on my side."

"From the beginning, Ben Raines."

"Are you anywhere else right now?"

"No. Ben Raines, Simon Border is not at all what he seems. He is an evil man using God's name to satisfy his perversions. God will not frown when that man is destroyed. You must not allow Simon Border to spread his filth across the land. He must be stopped, and stopped now."

"Perversions?"

There was no reply. Ben twisted in the chair, first one way then the other. But he was alone in the night. "Perversions?" Ben again spoke the word aloud.

"Did you say something to me, General?" a guard called from some yards away.

"No, son. Just talking to myself. You seen anything strange this evening."

"No, sir. Nothing moving at all. Everybody is sacked out."

"Good. Thank you. Good night."

"Good night, General."

The guard walked on. Ben waited until he had faded into the night, then muttered, "Prophet, you just put my mind at ease about this campaign. But I wish I knew what perversions you were talking about."

The night wind sighed. But if it brought an answer, Ben could not read it.

In her bed, Jersey sat straight up, sweat pouring from her body. She threw back the covers and slipped from the cot. She'd just had a vision. Her ancestors had been speaking to her. But what had they been trying to tell her? It had all been so jumbled and vague. Except for the screaming. The screaming of children, Jersey was sure. But why were they screaming? And there had been an evil man in her vision, but a man without soul.

"Now how do I know that?" Jersey muttered, turning to the open window and letting the cool night wind dry the sweat on her body. "How do I know he had no soul? And if he had no soul, what happened to it?"

She caught a glimpse of a tall shadow in a clearing between buildings and knew it was Ben Raines. He was just standing there, gazing up at the starry sky. She wondered if he had met the Prophet and if he had, what had they discussed. Suddenly, she shivered as a chill crawled over her body. She quickly slipped into fresh nightclothes and stretched out on the cot, hoping that sleep would take her dreamless into a few hours' rest.

Ben stood for several moments after the sentry had faded from view. He never knew quite how to feel after an encounter with the prophet. He wasn't sure if he should feel honored, or whether he should put on a dunce hat and go stand in the nearest corner for acting a fool and really believing the old man was real.

But Ben was sure in his guts the old man known as the Prophet was very real.

"A noble cause," Ben muttered, as he walked back to his quarters. "I guess we'll just have to see about that."

Ben pulled off his boots and stretched out on his cot to catch a few hours' sleep. He was asleep within five minutes. Outside, a young sentry shook his head in disbelief at what he had just seen—or thought he'd seen.

It was a shooting star. But instead of falling *toward* the earth, the shooting star appeared to be traveling upward, toward the heavens.

But that was impossible.

Wasn't it?

Three

Ben and his 1 Batt pulled out at dawn, heading west on interstate 8. Scouts had reported no signs of impending trouble between Tucson and Yuma in the over two hundred miles of highway between the two cities. When the Rebels had moved into Southern Arizona in force, those who supported Simon Border moved north, most of them out of the state. Rebel intelligence had intercepted radio transmissions from Simon ordering his people out. Simon controlled a huge chunk of real estate; there was plenty of running room and plenty of land for resettling.

The old interstate was in reasonably good shape, probably due in part to the dry climate, but the convoy still could not maintain any speed: thirty miles an hour was about average. On their first day out, the convoy settled in for the night about fifty miles east of Yuma.

"Scouts report we're clean all the way down to the Mexican border and for fifty miles north," Corrie reported.

"West?" Ben asked.

"We're going to start running into trouble at the California line."

"Punks or Simon supporters?"

"Both. Intell reports large gangs of punks have supposedly changed their evil ways and accepted Simon Border as Lord on Earth."

"Repented their evil ways, eh?"

"So we are supposed to believe."

"And Simon Border is now Lord on Earth, eh?" Ben said with a smile.

"That's what a number of people are calling him."

"Among other things," Ben said drily.

Beth held out an old tourist pamphlet. "It says in here that the sun shines more in Yuma than in any other city in the United States."

"We won't be there long enough to enjoy it," Ben said. "Unfortunately."

"How far from Yuma to the California coast?" Anna asked.

"Several days, the way we're traveling," Ben told her. "But don't expect to see much in San Diego. We pretty much left that city in ruins."

"And when we hit the state line, we can expect the ambushes to begin," Cooper said.

"Right. That's why I gave the orders for everyone to be in full body armor. About noon tomorrow, I figure it's going to get real interesting."

The first ambush came on the outskirts of El Centro, a town that, before the Great War, had boasted a population of about thirty-five thousand. It came first in the form of mortar rounds that did little damage, for the crews were using the old walk-in method of sighting, and that told the Rebels Simon's people did not have modern sighting systems.

The column immediately spread out, the trucks putting more distance between them, and Rebel tanks wheeled about, main guns ready to fire.

"Put us right over there," Ben told Cooper. "Among those ruins."

"Yes, sir." Cooper knew better than to argue. Ben liked to be right in the middle of things.

Cooper just barely had the big wagon stopped before Ben bailed out.

"Here we go," Jersey muttered, jumping out right behind Ben and running to catch up.

Ben and his team spread out along what was left of a wall, about chest high, Corrie calmly radioing their position.

"I saw movement dead ahead of us," Ben told Jersey. "And that's too close in to be the mortar crews."

Gunfire ripped the afternoon, the machine-gun rounds chipping away at the wall, sending bits of concrete block flying.

"Now we know," Ben said with a smile.

"Convoy coming under attack at a dozen locations up and down the line," Corrie said. "The road is blocked about ten miles ahead. Scouts in a heavy fire-fight."

"Are they in trouble?" Ben asked.

Corrie smiled her reply to that.

"Right," Ben said. "Tell them to try to take a few alive, will you?"

"Ten-four, boss."

The one problem with using CAR's is that the barrel is too short for a bloop tube and grenades must be tossed by hand. The distance between Ben and his team and the ambushers was too long for that.

A young Rebel lieutenant came sliding in on his belly and looked at Ben. "Sir, if you had stayed with the main column you would be out of harm's way now."

"Yeah? And if your aunt had balls she'd be your uncle." Ben looked at him. "You're new."

"Yes, sir. I joined your battalion two weeks ago, replacing Weintraub."

"How is Bernie?"

"He's okay. But he's out of the field. Assigned to the home guard battalions back at Base Camp One. Ah, sir? This is sort of a strange time to be holding a conversation, isn't it?"

Ben chuckled. "What is your name?"

"Hardin, sir. Mitch Hardin."

"How many Rebs with you, Mitch?"

"A squad, sir. We came to get you out of this mess."

Ben's team all looked amused at that.

"What mess, Mitch?"

"You're pinned down, sir!"

"Oh," Ben said. "Well, not really."

"You could have fooled me, sir."

Ben laughed at the serious expression on the young officer's face. "Cecil told you to look after me, didn't he?"

"Cecil, sir?"

"President Jefferys."

"Ah . . . well, yes, sir. He did."

A burst of machine-gun fire cut short the conversation for a moment. "Corrie? Are the tanks in position?"

"Yes, sir."

"Tell them they may neutralize the enemy position whenever they are ready."

"Right, boss."

Two Rebel tanks cut loose with their main guns and all unfriendly fire from the ambush site stopped. Ben smiled at Lt. Hardin. "You see, Mitch. I told you we weren't pinned down."

But the Rebels took a few casualties that day, and Ben halted the column and told everyone they would stay the night. One Rebel later died after surgery, and several had to be flown back to Base Camp One for a lengthy hospital stay.

The Rebels buried quite a few of Simon's followers and took a number of prisoners. They were, for the most, sullen and defiant as Ben approached the small group of officers, held away from the other prisoners.

"No one is going to hiss, point, draw back in horror, and call me the great Satan?" Ben asked the group, sitting on the ground.

"The name fits you, Ben Raines," one older man with colonel's eagles on his shirt collar said.

Ben squatted down in front of the ranking officer. "Are you so stupid you've bought Simon Border's line of bullshit hook, line, and sinker?"

The colonel's face reddened. "I am not a stupid man, General."

"You must be, Colonel. If you believe all that crap Simon Border is spoon-feeding you."

"He's a good man, General. Sometimes he goes off on a tangent, but our way of life sure beats anything your political philosophy has to offer."

"So you personally don't believe that Simon is actually Lord on Earth?"

The colonel smiled. "It doesn't matter whether I do or not. Millions of others most certainly do believe it."

"You're about a half-assed mercenary, aren't you?"

The colonel's smile widened. "I am a professional soldier who has finally found his salvation, General. I am fighting for the Lord."

"Along with how many others of your, ah, chosen profession?"

"Enough."

"Enough of you to lead hundreds of thousands of lambs to the slaughter, Colonel?"

"The men and the few women under my command came willingly, General. They were not forced. They came because they believe our way is the best way. And with that, our conversation has ended. From now on, you will get my name, rank, and serial number, and that is all"

"You've told me quite enough, Colonel. Thank you." Walking away, Ben muttered, "Mercenaries. Simon's hired mercenaries. Now it's going to get interesting."

"How so, boss?" Corrie asked.

"Regardless of what preconceptions people might have of mercenaries, many of them are good fighting men, with a solid grasp of tactics. That's what Mike was talking about during one of our conversations. It was only a rumor, and Mike didn't go into it to any extent. But that's what he was talking about."

"That's why he waited all these weeks before attacking," Jersey said.

"That's it, Jersey. Corrie, bump Mike and tell him about this. I want to know how many mercenaries, where they're from, the whole nine yards. Tell him to bleed his sources dry, but get that information to me. It's important."

"I'm on it."

"Bruno Bottger," Ben murmured. "Has to be that son of a bitch. He's buying time."

"What, boss?" Cooper asked.

"The Nazi, Cooper. Bruno Bottger. I'll bet you a steak dinner with all the trimmings that Bruno contacted Simon and offered his assistance. Of course, with no strings attached. And Simon jumped at it."

"But of course there are strings attached," Beth said.

"Sure. But Simon, unless I'm badly mistaken about the man, doesn't realize that. Or if on the remote chance that he does realize it, probably thinks his army can handle Bruno's men. Which is laughable."

"Boss, that means Bottger is getting a toehold here in North America," Cooper said. "Or has already got one."

"That's right, Coop. And it just might be a solid one. You can bet that bastard has been busy setting up little Nazi cells all over America. Damn!"

Ben walked around in small circles for a moment, then paused and motioned for a Rebel captain to join him. He quickly told the captain about the mercenaries and about Bruno Bottger's linking up with Simon Border. "Polygraph all the prisoners, Captain. Carefully. Any that are suspected of being part of Bottger's army are to be sent back to Base Camp One for confinement."

"And the others, sir?"

"We'll turn them over to local resistance groups as we make contact with them."

"That's probably a death warrant for them, General," the captain pointed out.

Ben nodded. "Yeah. It probably is, Captain. But we've learned how those who resisted Simon's rule are treated— very badly. And besides, a very famous general once pointed out that war is hell."

The column was on the move at dawn, moving very slowly, due to the increasingly terrible condition of the highways. Ben had spoken with all batt coms and with Cecil back in the SUSA, advising them of this new development. He had not yet heard back from Mike Richards. Mike was probably out in the field, recruiting volunteers for resistance groups . . . or killing Simon Border supporters. The roads were so bad the column only made twenty-five miles the first day out of El Centro.

"Simon never intended to settle this part of his territory," Ben said, after chow. "My guess is he was going to let the punks and gangs and the dopers have it."

"Nobody's worked on that damn road in years, that's for sure," Cooper said.

Ben laughed. "The roads back home have spoiled us all."

"For a fact, boss," Beth said.

Ben had received more intel about Simon from Base Camp One late that afternoon. It was troubling, but not terribly surprising . . . more importantly, now more of the pieces of the puzzle were beginning to fit together. It had been confirmed by several people who had managed to break out of Simon's tight security around his territory that Simon was a practicing pedophile. And if that wasn't disgusting enough, Simon had been getting increasingly inventive with his sexual appetites toward young boys. He still liked females, the escapes told the Rebel intelligence officers, but only if they were girls . . . young girls. Grown women, they said, intimidated Simon.

And both the girls and the boys were getting younger.

Ben had not shared that information with anyone in his command—yet, for he knew what their reaction would be. First it would be outrage, and then that outrage would turn to cold, murderous fury. For as far as Ben knew, about 99.9 percent of the Rebels were quite normal with their sexual desires; normal being defined as conforming to the standards of the majority.

Ben would wait for a time before telling his batt coms about this latest development about Simon Border.

· And there was more in the coded communiqué from Cecil. There was trouble in the SUSA. Simon's people—and Cecil was certain now their numbers were greater than first thought—were rising up and making themselves heard in the form of terrorist acts. So far no one had been killed and only a few residents of the SUSA wounded. But Cecil felt the terrorism would intensify as the war in the west dragged on.

"You're quiet tonight, Ben," Ike McGowan's voice came out of the quickly gathering night.

Ben smiled and turned his head. Ike might be a bit over-weight, but he could still move like a ghost. "What are you doing up here with 1 Batt, Ike?"

Ike waved one hand and Ben's team rose and walked off a few meters, leaving the men alone. Ike sat down in a camp chair beside Ben. The camp chair creaked and groaned in protest and Ben chuckled.

"No smart-assed remarks about my weight, Ben."

"I didn't say a word, Ike."

"No. But what you thought. Listen, Ben, I've heard some pretty disgusting rumors about Simon Border. I wanted to know if they're true. Any truth to them?"

"There's trouble back home, too, Ike," Ben hedged the question.

"Cecil can take care of himself, and you know it. Besides, the citizens won't put up with terrorism. What about the rumors?"

What Ike said about the residents of the Southern United States of America was very true. They wouldn't tolerate Simon's supporters and their terrorist acts for any length of time before they retaliated, with or without approval by President Cecil Jefferys. The first child that was hurt in a terrorist bombing or shooting and Simon's supporters—and they were known—would quickly show up hanging from a tree limb. The SUSA was definitely not a place for those who wanted to buck the system, so to speak. Crime was virtually unheard of there . . . because it simply was not tolerated. The penalties for felony crimes in the SUSA were very harsh.

"I heard the rumors about Simon, Ike. Heard them several days ago. Now they've been confirmed."

"He's molesting children in the name of God?" Ike's voice was thick with ill-disguised anger and disgust.

"That's the word I get."

"You know what's going to happen when this news reaches the troops?"

"I can imagine."

"And? . . ."

"And what, Ike? There is nothing I can do to prevent rumors from spreading. Especially when the rumors are true. But the one thing we don't lack in this army is discipline. And discipline will be maintained."

Ike raised a big hand. "Don't concern yourself with failing discipline, Ben. That won't happen. What I'm saying is when the troops find out about Simon's, ah, kinky side, so to speak, they're not going to treat his followers very gently . . . male or female. Many of them have to know about this."

"Or at least suspect."

"Yes."

"And have done nothing about it."

"That's what I'm talking about. Our people damn sure don't need any more initiative to fight, Ben."

Ben sighed and leaned forward in his chair. He rolled a cigarette but did not light it. Turned his head and looked at Ike. "We'll sit on this news as long as we can. But once it becomes widespread among the troops, we won't lie to them. We'll confirm it."

"All right, Ben."

"You have anything cheerful to tell me, Ike?"

Ike smiled, wiping years from his face. "Thermopolis has agreed to look after Emil Hite and his people."

"Thank God!"

"That ex-hippie has really turned into a full-fledged Rebel."

"Oh, I knew several hippies before the Great War, Ike. Whole families of them. Most people had a gross misconception of hippies. Some were peace and love and wouldn't step on a bug. But most were just people who wanted to be left alone to enjoy their lifestyle as much as current mores would allow. Mess with them, and they'd go to fist-city just as fast as anyone else."

"You're a strange conservative, Ben," Ike said with a chuckle. "You actually liked most hippies."

"I sure did." Ben frowned. "Of course, I thought their music sucked."

The two old friends enjoyed a good laugh at that. Whatever tension there was between them melted away as quietly as twilight creeps in to darken the day. After a moment, Ike sobered and said, "You think we're in deep shit with Bottger's entrance in this fight, don't you, Ben."

"I think it's going to be the toughest fight we've ever faced. Not necessarily in terms of actual combat—even though that's going to be bad enough—but in its long-term effects."

"You think there is a chance we could lose this one, Ben?"

Ben lifted his eyes and stared for a moment at Ike before replying. "Yes, Ike. In the long run, I sure do."

Four

"Did you know," Beth said, reading from one of her tourist brochures. "That the San Diego Zoo was founded in 1916 by a doctor, Harry Wedgeforth?"

"Beth," Ben said, twisting in the seat to look at her. "Where do you get these pamphlets? And where do you keep them?"

"I've been gathering them for years, boss. I keep them in trunks in one of the supply trucks. I like to know about the places we visit."

"I don't like to think what happened to many of the animals in zoos," Anna said. "I know what happened to many of them in the old country."

"Sea World was also in San Diego," Beth continued. "I'd forgotten much of this. Seems like ages ago when we were there."

"It was a few years back," Ben conceded.

There had been no more trouble along the old interstate since the failed attack by Simon's people in El Centro. Flyovers showed hundreds of troops moving north, and they were digging in hard just north of Los Angeles, stretching west to east for miles.

"Get your rubbernecking done while you can," Ben warned. "Which won't be much because the city is in ruins. For when we hit what's left of L.A., it's going to turn rough."

"How far from San Diego to Los Angeles?" Anna asked.

"About a hundred and twenty-five miles," Beth told the young woman.

"Hollywood and Beverly Hills—where all the movie stars live," Anna said softly, the kid in her surfacing, something that rarely occurred. "Used to live," she corrected, her voice changing, becoming harder, more mature. "What happened to all the movie stars?" she asked. "With their fine homes, expensive cars, and millions of dollars?"

"We all became equal," Ben replied. "Trying to survive in a world gone mad. To tell you the truth, Anna, I really don't know what happened to all the movie stars and popular singers and so forth. I'm sure many of them were killed during the few hours of the gas attack. Probably more were killed in the rioting and looting and savagery in the days that followed. It was a wild time in America, I can tell you that for sure." Ben smiled in remembrance. "I roamed this nation for a year or more; started out with the intention of writing a book about how Americans were coping with this tragedy. And I can tell you firsthand, most were not coping with it very well at all."

"Americans had grown fat and lazy," Anna said. "I know many things about Americans from reading old journals and magazines and newspapers. They would spend hours sitting in front of their expensive televisions letting their brains rot watching the most stupid of games."

Ben chuckled. "I can't argue with you on that point, Anna. For the most part, you're correct."

"It was very bad in my country, too," Anna said. "But I think Americans suffered much more. For any number of reasons."

"Even though I really don't remember much of it," Beth said. "I have to agree with Anna."

"You blocked it out, too, Beth?" Cooper asked, a surprising gentleness behind his words.

"I guess so, Coop," Beth replied. "All of us did, except for the boss, that is."

"I was older," Ben said. "I'd seen the terrible bloody face of war many times. Besides, I predicted the world's governments would collapse; especially the government of the United States. I would have taken bets the government of the United States would be the first to fall. I'm glad that you all have blocked out the horror—most of it, that is. It was . . . well, very unpleasant."

"I remember some of it," Jersey said. "I've told you about wandering around and seeing all the dead and bloated bodies, with the carrion birds eating on them. I remember the vultures so bloated with human flesh they could not fly. They just waddled around on the ground, unable to take off."

"I remember being hungry," Corrie said. "But as far as accurately recalling actual events, I can't."

"I wonder if we ever will remember it?" Beth questioned softly.

"I hope not," Jersey said. "Well . . . maybe it would be good if we did. Maybe that would help us all to make certain something like that never happened again, right, boss?"

"It might, Jersey. But I don't think there are any guarantees. Hell, look at us. We've been fighting for years to restore at least a part of this nation, and we're still fighting." Ben didn't add that they would probably continue the fight for years to come. He really didn't have to vocalize it, for Beth said . . .

"I don't think the fighting will ever stop. I think we'll all die fighting for what we believe in."

"Oh, wonderful thought, Beth," Cooper said. "Hooray for our side."

"I agree with Beth," Jersey said.

"Yeah, me too," Corrie said. "I don't see any end to it. Boss?"

Ben sighed heavily, the long bloody years weighing hard upon him. "I don't see an end to the fighting," he replied. "Even though all we really want to do is live in peace in our own society. I've got kids I scarcely know. I'd like to play some baseball with them. I'd like to see them in a school debating society. I'd like to discuss philosophy with them. Hell, I'd like to get to *know* them." He laughed. "Maybe I'm just getting parental in my advanced years."

His team broke up in laughter at that. For even though Ben was middle-aged and could be deadly serious, he was, most of the time, a very young-at-heart middle-age, and in great physical shape.

The laughter died away and the team fell silent as they rode along in the big wagon. The truck carrying their personal gear followed a few dozen yards behind.

"Scouts report the old national forest east of the city ruins is clear of ambush," Corrie said. "As least as far as they could tell. But fly-overs with heat seekers show many warm bodies in there. What do you think, boss?"

Ben smiled and Cooper cut his eyes and groaned, knowing what that smile meant. "Now that you asked, I think we should stop and take a look."

Jersey gave him a very dirty look. "Why doesn't that surprise me?"

Ben struggled to put an innocent expression on his face. "Why, Jersey . . . whatever in the world do you mean?"

"Shit!" Jersey muttered.

The convoy stopped several miles deep into the old national forest. More Scouts stepped out of the brush and immediately surrounded Ben's vehicle.

"Lots of folks in these woods, General," a lieutenant said. "It isn't safe for you."

"The people living in there tell you that, Lieutenant?"

"In a manner of speaking, sir." The Scout held up a piece of cardboard with a crudely drawn picture of Ben on it. Under the drawing, the words: TEN FINE-LOOKING WOMEN OR TEN YOUNG BOYS PLUS ALL THE DOPE YOU CAN CARRY FOR THE HEAD OF BEN RAINES.

Ben's expression was bleak as he stared at the homemade

wanted poster. Then he whirled around and walked to the supply truck. He returned with his old M-14 and a full magazine pouch over one shoulder. The Rebels gathered around exchanged glances. They knew when Ben got out his old Thunder Lizard, things were about to get nasty. "I hate child molesters and dopers. Let's clear out these woods."

Ben assigned guards for the convoy, then spread the oversized battalion out along the interstate, facing both north and south, Scouts and other special operations people that traveled with the battalion spearheading the drive.

"Let's clear it out," Ben ordered, and moved forward, his team doing their best to keep him as far behind the spearheaders as they could . . . which was no easy task, for Ben liked to be right in the middle of things.

They had not gone a hundred yards into the timber before a Scout threw up his arm and halted forward movement. Ben started forward and Jersey and Cooper stepped in front of him. Neither of them said anything, but Ben got the message and smiled, nodded his understanding. He stayed where he was.

"Trip wire," a Scout called. "Attached to a homemade bomb. It's crude, but damned effective."

The explosive deactivated, the Rebels moved slowly forward, deeper into the forest.

"Down!" a Scout called, and hit the ground just a half second before the woods exploded in gunfire from an ambush.

Ben dropped immediately, without thinking, acting instinctively, from long years of combat experience, his team with him. Low limbs and leaves were cut by the raking gunfire from automatic weapons. Ben heard the unmistakable and unforgettable clatter of an M-60 machine gun and the heavier boom of high-powered hunting rifles, followed by the rattle of a few M-16's.

"Somebody on the other side has some experience in setting up ambushes," Ben said. "They're pretty good. Dug in and camoed well."

"They have us in a box," Corrie called, after affirming a transmission. "It's almost a full semicircle, working from about ten o'clock over to two o'clock."

"Grenades," Ben calmly ordered. "Everyone with bloop tubes use them. Let's give these asshole perverts—no play on words intended—something to think about."

Several dozen bloop tubes were loaded and fired, the forest erupting in a ring of explosions.

"Keep it up," Ben ordered. "Pour it on."

When the ambushers saw that the 40mm grenade barrage was not going to cease, many of them broke and tried to run. They were cut down by Rebels waiting for them to do just that.

Ben lined up several running together in the sights of his old Thunder Lizard and let her roar. On full auto the M-14 is a man-sized weapon to handle, hard to control and punishing if one is not familiar with it. Ben was very familiar with the old weapon. The heavy 7.62 rounds chopped the dopers down. They lay still on the forest floor.

"Flankers in position?" Ben asked.

"Left and right," Corrie told him.

"Tell them to do their stuff."

The teams of Rebels that had swung around and flanked the enemy positions opened up with 40mm grenades. The fight ended moments later with what dopers remained waving handkerchiefs tied to the ends of their rifles.

"We yield!" one called. "Jesus Christ, man. We give up. Stop shootin' at us."

"Cease fire," Ben ordered.

Ben moved to a small depression in the ground just to the left of his original position and sat down on the lip of the natural cup in the earth, unscrewing the cap on his canteen and taking a pull. He rubbed his shoulder where the M-14 had pounded him firing on full automatic. He ejected the half-empty magazine, stowed it in his magazine pouch and slipped home a full one.

Rebels marched two of the ambushers over to him and both of them sat down across from Ben.

"Stand up, you sons of bitches!" Ben barked at the pair. "No one told you to rest."

The two men, both looking to be in their mid to late thirties, jumped to their feet.

"You be Ben Raines, right?" one asked.

"That's right." Ben held up the cardboard wanted poster. "Which of you is responsible for this?"

Both thugs exchanged quick, furtive glances and remained silent.

"Names?" Ben asked.

"Big Jim," the larger of the pair said.

"Highway Harry," the other said.

Jersey laughed at the nicknames and both the thugs gave her hard looks.

"Are those looks supposed to frighten me?" Jersey asked.

"You be wise to watch that smart mouth, bitch," Highway Harry said. "You folks ain't clear of these woods yet."

"I am so frightened I might have to sit down," Jersey said scornfully. "My knees are trembling from fear." She looked at Beth. "Aren't yours, dear?"

"Oh, my, yes," Beth said. "I really believe the last time I saw anything that even remotely resembled this pair was when we watched that old movie about two turds that attempted to take over earth. How about you, Corrie?"

"Oh, definitely," Corrie replied. "Anna, dear, are you frightened?"

"Fear has all but stilled my tongue. Just the sight and sound of these two cretinous ass-wipes is almost too much to bear. I will try my best to curb my first inclination to run screaming into the woods. However, I might puke at any moment," she added sarcastically.

Ben and Cooper laughed at the expressions on the faces of the thugs. Rebel women could be as feminine as any women on earth—when they wished to play that role. But they could also be as salty and randy and profane and tough-as-nails when they chose to be.

Big Jim and Highway Harry stood speechless, jaws hanging open. They were not accustomed to being spoken to in such a manner by women.

"Close your mouths, shit-for-brains," Beth told the pair. "You might swallow a bug."

Ben waved at a group of Rebels standing close by and listening to the exchange . . . and smiling. "Get these two out of here before I turn my team loose on them."

A Scout walked up just as the pair was being led away. "This was a bunch of former outlaw bikers, General. The real West Coast bad boys. We found a bunch of old newspaper clippings in their hooches. They've been involved in everything you might care to name. Rape, murder, assault, dope, pornography . . . you name it. Most of them started as teenagers and never looked back."

"Find any prisoners they were holding?" Ben asked, in a very deceptively low voice.

"Some grown men they use for barter. Slave use, mostly. Women they trade back and forth between gangs. And some little kids, boys and girls, average age about ten. Both boys and girls telling some horror stories. Medics say they've all been sexually abused. In just about every way possible."

Ben's team stiffened in anger at the words.

"Nice bunch of people living in these woods," Ben muttered. "Are the children up to identifying their attackers?"

"Oh, yes, sir."

"Have them do so."

"Yes, sir. Anything else, sir?"

"When the attackers of the children have been positively I.D.'d, dispose of them."

"Yes, sir."

"Thank you."

That would take several days, for the Rebels would not rely on just the word of the victims. Eye-witnesses were notoriously inaccurate . . . although in this case, probably not. But there would be polygraph tests, and in the event of any doubts, chemicals would be used. If there were still lingering doubts, the accused would often be turned loose. Rebel justice was harsh, but in many ways getting there was fairer than the system of old. And if the criminal did live long enough to stand trial, the facts of the case were presented, both pro and con, and manipulative antics by defense attorneys were not permitted. The facts of the case on trial were presented, not a witness's past life. The Tri-States philosophy of justice was based on common sense.

"We're going to be in these woods for a while," Jersey said, not posing it as a question.

"Several days," Ben said. "And that might be very optimistic on my part. I've got spec ops people jumping in on the southern end of the park, and helicopters and fixed wing aircraft up and heading this way to plug that section. If we're going to clear this area, we might as well do it right."

"Several of the outlaw leaders want to talk to you, boss," Corrie said.

"They're being held at that old reception station close to the highway."

"All right. Let's go see what they have on their minds."

Jersey, Corrie, Beth, and Anna all responded with some very unladylike words.

Ben chuckled. "Come on, ladies. Keep it clean."

"Those snake-headed ass-wipes don't have a mind," Beth said, which was very much unlike her, for she was usually reserved in her comments and did not use profanity lightly.

"Cut open the top of their heads and all you'd find is a bunch of little pussies."

"Damn, Beth!" Cooper muttered.

Ben waited, for he knew the ladies were not yet through venting their spleens. No Rebel took child-molestation lightly, and in the SUSA the penalty was usually death. But unless the molester was actually caught in the act, there were few cases of vigilante action, for that was frowned upon in the Southern United States of America.

"I think we ought to cut off their equipment," Jersey suggested. "With a dull knife."

Cooper shuddered at the thought.

"Brand them on the forehead," Anna suggested.

"And on both cheeks of the ass," Corrie added.

"Whoa!" Cooper said.

"You people have seen cases of child-molestation before," Ben said, puzzled at their lingering hot anger. "What's so different about this one?"

"Have you see the kids yet, boss?" Beth asked.

"No."

"Perhaps you should," she said shortly.

"That bad, eh?"

"Worse than anything I've ever seen," Jersey answered.

Ben left the MASH tent as shaken as he had ever been. He had never seen kids so badly abused. Several of the youngsters were still in surgery, getting private parts of their anatomy repaired and stitched up from long abuse at the hands of adults.

Ben sat down on the ground, his back to a tree, and slowly rolled a cigarette. Several of the doctors had told him they had doubts about some of the kids ever recovering mentally from the abuse they had endured. They would be flown back to Base Camp One and the doctors there would try to heal their young minds.

Ben was just thankful that Lamar Chase was not rolling with his One Batt, for after seeing what had happened to the kids, Lamar would have taken a gun and killed the outlaws himself.

Ben was tempted to do that very thing. But of course he wouldn't. He'd wait until all the evidence was in.

Then he'd personally shoot the outlaws.

Five

Ben walked over to the clearing where the outlaws were being held and stood for a moment, staring at them. Ben noticed with a small amount of amusement that whoever had assigned the guards, had assigned all women Rebels to guard the outlaws, and the women were very grim-faced.

"Them damn kids lie, General!" one outlaw called. "We ain't abused nobody."

"Yeah, General," another shouted. "Them kids had already been buggered out good when we got them."

One of the women guards slowly lifted the muzzle of her M-16 with white-knuckled hands, then got control of her temper and lowered the muzzle.

A Rebel interrogation officer walked up to Ben's side and stood for a moment. "General, I honestly believe this is the most worthless gathering of human trash I have ever encountered."

"They've all been tested?"

"Every one of them. They're the biggest pack of liars we've ever tested."

"I thought we had more prisoners than this?"

"They're beginning to turn on each other, trying to save their miserable lives by ratting each other out."

"You've talked to the kids?"

"Oh, yes, sir. Those that are capable of talking, that is. Some just point to their tormentors."

"Are these men and women all ex-bikers?"

"No, sir. Actually, only a few are. The rest are just plain old-fashioned scum."

"I see. The women with them, they took part in the sexual abusing, too?"

"Yes, sir."

"Well . . . I mean, *how?* Women aren't exactly equipped for that sort of thing."

"Artificial means, sir. If you know what I mean."

Ben sighed. "Son of a bitch!"

"Yes, sir. General, some of the prisoners wish to talk with you."

"I suppose I owe them that courtesy."

"If you say so, sir."

"Very well."

"We've set up a squad tent over there, sir." He pointed.

Ben walked over to the tent and sat down behind a portable field desk. Jersey stood behind him and to his right, Beth behind him and to his left. Both of them were stony-faced. Cooper and Anna elected to remain just outside the tent. Corrie was busy with her radio.

Ben had a file on each prisoner in front of him, placed in alphabetical order. He opened the first file, read the first few paragraphs, felt queasy in his stomach, and closed the file. "Send the first son of a bitch in," he called.

The man stepped in and stood defiantly in front of Ben. "If you have something to say, say it," Ben told him.

"I'm a prisoner of war and I demand to be treated as such," the man said. "I know my rights and them kids lie!"

"A prisoner of war," Ben repeated softly. "I know of no declaration of war that exists between our two groups."

"Don't have to be none. You and your army invaded our state. We got a right to defend our sovereign territory."

"Really?"

"That's right."

"I suppose you are going to tell me you never sexually abused any of the children?"

"That's right. I never done no such of a thing."

"You're a liar! Some of your own people have rolled over on you."

"Them kids wanted it, General. They ain't nothin' but a bunch of lyin' little faggots. Some of 'em's goofy in the head, anyways. They ain't never gonna be good for nothin'."

Ben wrote two words on the first page of the file, then signed his name below that. "Cooper!"

"Boss?" Cooper stuck his head into the tent.

Ben handed him the file. "Give this to the interrogation officer, please. And take this walking piece of shit out of here."

"Yes, sir."

"What'd you write in that file, Raines?" the outlaw demanded.

Ben opened the file and held it up so the hulking oaf could see it. Just above his signature he had written, in capital letters: HANG HIM.

The battle for the old national forest fizzled out after only one day of fighting, with the dopers and the outlaws and the various other human scum and crud turning themselves in by the droves. Some of them were tried and hanged, but most were merely disarmed and turned loose, after being photographed and blood samples taken for DNA identification . . . should they ever again screw up in Rebel territory.

"You can bet they'll screw up in somebody's territory," Jersey opined.

"Just as long as it isn't in the SUSA or any town or settlement who subscribes to our philosophy," Ben said.

The Tri-States philosophy was becoming a real problem for newly elected mayors and governors all over the divided nation. There were thousands of people in all sections of

America who wanted to live under the banner of the Tri-States doctrine, but did not want to leave the place where they were born and reared. So they decided to stay right where they had lived for most of their lives and adopt the Tri-States system of justice . . . which was not at all to the liking of anyone who subscribed to the hanky-stomping, sobbing-sister, take-a-punk-to-lunch-bunch, it's-not-the-criminal's-fault, give-me-something-for-nothing liberal crowd who were once more surfacing in hand-wringing, snot-slinging whiny bunches outside of the SUSA.

They knew better than to cross the borders into the SUSA with their bullshit.

Unknown to either Cecil Jefferys or Ben Raines, the governors of a dozen Northern and Eastern states had agreed to meet secretly to discuss how best to deal with those people who insisted upon living outside the SUSA but still refused to recognize any law other than the common sense laws as set forth in the SUSA charter . . . . known halfway around the world as the Tri-States philosophy, and practiced in many foreign countries.

But what really irked the governors and mayors and other elected officials was while they were battling apathy and high crime in their areas, in those areas that subscribed to the Tri-States philosophy, neighbor helped neighbor to rebuild, and crime was practically nonexistent.

It was all very irritating to those officials who adamantly rejected the Tri-States philosophy . . . and they were determined to smash the movement before others could adopt it.

"Attempt anything like that," one newly elected governor said, "and we're going to have Ben Raines and his Rebels breathing down our necks. I don't want that."

"President Altman has pledged his support," another governor said.

"It will be years before Altman has an army of any size,"

the mayor of a rebuilding small city said. "And Altman is weak; he's afraid of Ben Raines and the Rebels."

"And you're not?" a governor questioned with a smile. "I can tell you all I am, and I'm not ashamed to admit it."

"The problem is," Governor Bradford, a newly elected governor from the northeast region of the separated nation spoke up, "those who subscribe to this Tri-State philosophy are well-organized and well-armed." He grimaced. "Ben Raines has seen to that. And they seem to have no respect for anyone who doesn't agree with them."

Governor Willis, a newly elected governor also from the northeast, but a moderate in his political views, shook his head. "I have to disagree with that, Brad. It isn't that they don't have respect for others. I've found Tri-Staters to be, for the most part, a very law-abiding, hard-working, and respectful group of people . . ."

Bradford snorted in derision.

Willis ignored him and continued, ". . . They have agreed to pay their fair share of taxes, they certainly are willing to help each other rebuild—we've all observed many shining examples of that. It's just they . . ." He paused and reflected for a few seconds; smoothed back his thinning and graying hair. ". . . won't tolerate crime or people who refuse to work and want something for nothing. In many ways, ladies and gentlemen, they personify the spirit of America of three hundred years ago."

"That is pure nonsense," Ellen Simmons, the governor of another Northeastern state and liberal from head to toe snapped. "They're outlaws and rebels. Their society is built on gunsmoke. My God, they've *hanged* people in those areas."

"But they have no racial prejudices, no crime, full employment, and a simple, workable set of laws," Willis pointed out. "What is the very first thing those people did? They rebuilt the schools . . ."

"And they're teaching things that should not be taught,"

Ellen persisted. "They're teaching morals and values and their concept of what is right and wrong. I wouldn't doubt but what they secretly have *prayer* in school. We just can't have that. I won't tolerate it. I will not tolerate it."

Governor Willis leaned back in his chair and hid his smile. He knew that the Tri-Staters, at least those in his state, did not have prayer in school. They had a moment of silence, during which the kids could pray silently if they wished, or they could think about homework or the boy or girl across the aisle from them, or whatever they chose to think about. And as far as teaching morals and values and right and wrong . . . what the hell was so wrong with that?

"And they also teach the kids warfare," Mayor Danbury said with a frown as he wriggled in his chair. "I find that most repugnant."

"They have their equivalent of Junior ROTC," Willis corrected patiently. "For both genders, with no discrimination. What is wrong with that?"

"They're homophobic," another mayor said.

"Oh, they are not," Willis said, more of an edge to his words than he intended. "In many ways they're much more tolerant than we are."

"I resent the hell out of that!" Ellen Simmons shouted. "Don't you dare cast me in a dimmer light to that bunch of right-wing gun-nuts."

"Me, either," Mayor Danbury said, then tightly compressed his lips into a bloodless pouty slash.

Willis sighed. "Don't move against these people. I warn you all. Don't do it. They'll fight, and believe me when I say, they're experts at it."

"Thanks to Ben Raines and his Rebels," Ellen said. "I just hate that man!"

Willis started to say that it was common knowledge that Ellen hated *all* men, but curbed his tongue just at the last second.

"These people have to be made to toe the line," another

governor said. "We simply cannot have little breakaway colonies all over the nation."

What's left of the nation, that is, Willis thought. And it appears to be growing smaller each time I look around. And speaking of looking around, he mused, looking around at this gathering I can see why so many free-thinking and God-fearing men and women don't want to have anything to do with us. What a bunch of ninnies.

"And once we stamp out these little pockets of anarchy," Governor Bradford was saying, "we can turn our attentions toward rebuilding the army and then once and for all defeat Ben Raines and the Rebels."

Governor Willis couldn't contain himself. He started laughing at that ridiculous statement. He was laughing as he stood up and pulled a handkerchief from his pocket and was wiping laughter-tears from his eyes as he walked out the door.

"Where are you going, Ed?" a mayor called after him. "And what is so damned funny?"

But Ed merely lifted a hand and kept on walking. Damned if he was going to be part of any group who declared war on Ben Raines and his Rebels. And Raines would hear about it; Ed had absolutely no doubt about that.

All the ramshackle huts and hooches and shacks in the national park were torn down and the materials used were stacked and burned. Ben knew it was only a stop-gap measure: others would soon inhabit the woods. But perhaps they would not be outlaws and thugs. The Rebels could only hope.

The column moved on, and the other west-bound columns moved out as well, for when the lead battalion stops, the others must stop as well to maintain the ordered distance.

Even though neither Ben nor Ike had so much as whispered the rumors about Simon Border and his sexual appetite for young children, the talk was spreading rapidly among the troops. Ben and the other batt coms could sense the tension growing among his people, for the talk was that if Simon was a molester, it was only reasonable to assume that so must be others in the hierarchy of his organization. At the very least, Simon's people knew of it, and were doing nothing to stop it.

When the column was only a few hours away from the ruins of San Diego, bivouacked for the night, Jersey came to see Ben as he sat alone in his mobile HQ.

"I gotta talk to you, boss," Jersey said.

Ben waved her to a chair. "What's on your mind, Jersey?"

"Simon Border being a pedophile."

"The talk is spreading, right?"

"Right."

"And the troops are getting restless and angry about it?"

"Right."

Ben nodded his head as he toyed with his empty coffee mug. "Okay, Jersey. It's been confirmed. The rumors are true."

"And Simon's followers know of it?"

"Well . . . some of them, sure. But I don't think the knowledge is widespread."

"How could it not be, boss?"

Jersey had a point and Ben knew it, but he just refused to believe that once good decent people (before Simon filled their heads with verbal nonsense) would allow such a monstrous thing to happen, and keep on happening, without doing something to stop it.

He said as much.

Jersey shook her head and frowned.

"Say what's on your mind, Little Bit. We've never held back from each other."

"It can happen, boss. It has before. We've all been reading some of Beth's books and journals. . . ."

Ben had to smile despite, or perhaps because of, the seriousness of the charges against Simon. Beth had half of the bed filled to overflowing with her research material, and was forever collecting more. Well, that was part of her job. Hell, it looked as though Ben would never get the chance to write his final book about the Great War and the changes in the world thereafter, so perhaps Beth would do it. She certainly had the talent and the material.

"I've been hearing more and more about Beth's gathering of material, Jersey."

"She's doing it for you, boss," Jersey said softly.

Ben looked up. "What?"

"She knows you want to write one more book about how the nation was ripe for trouble before the Great War, and how the people coped with the collapse of government and the rebuilding and all the trouble after the Great War. We all help her collect every scrap of information we can find. We've been doing it for years."

Ben was filled with a sudden very warm sensation of deep feeling for his team. Hell, he must be getting old; he should have seen what was happening. He turned his head away quickly and cleared his throat.

Jersey, sensing what was happening, jumped up and grabbed his coffee mug. "I'll just refill this cup for you, boss."

"Thank you, Jersey."

Ben turned in his chair for a moment, until he heard his coffee mug being placed on his desk. He swung his chair around. "I'll address the troops soon, Jersey. I've just been putting it off, hoping against hope the talk about Simon wasn't true." Ben frowned. "But . . . I just received work by messenger not thirty minutes ago that pretty much confirms the rumors."

"Two points to consider, boss: Maybe the followers of

Simon just don't believe the rumors. Or maybe the people think that Simon is such a God that they'll forgive him for it."

"I think it's the former, Jersey. My God, I hope it is."

"I hope it is, too, boss. 'Cause if it's the latter, God help his followers as we roll north."

Six

"Creepies," Ben said, lowering his binoculars. "Miserable damn creepies." His voice was filled with disgust.

One Batt was ready to roll past the old city limits sign of San Diego, on the south side of the once second largest city in California.

"Elegant shopping malls, a world-famous zoo, and seventy-mile-long coastline," Beth read from a tourist brochure.

Ben smiled at her.

"The average temperature is seventy degrees." She folded the creased brochure and put it in a cargo pocket of her BDUs. "Ain't that sweet?" she said sarcastically. "Now look at it."

Ben and the team burst out laughing. Cooper said, "And the ruins crawling with rats and creepies. What do we do, boss?"

"By-pass it," Ben replied. "We've got bigger fish to fry."

"What about the creepies, boss?" Cooper asked.

"Scouts report only a small concentration of them. It would take us weeks, maybe months, to flush them all out of the rubble. It isn't worth our time and effort."

"Creepies breed like rats," Anna said. "Better to take the time to kill them now."

Ben was expecting that from Anna. She hated creepies even more than the Rebels did.

"We might come back and finish the job," Ben said. "But for now, we roll on. And that is the end of the conversation."

Ben smiled as Anna muttered something under her breath. But she let the subject drop.

The convoy began the long and slow job of picking their way around the ruins of San Diego. Rebel artillery had all but destroyed the interstate loop around the city several years back and the going was very slow. To complicate matters, Ben had to wait for the westward-moving battalions behind him to start their slow turn north; to get more or less in line with his One Batt. He did not want to start the push north until everything was as ready as he could make it. And Ben knew it was going to take a good week until all the batts were lined up. When there are thousands of troops and hundreds of vehicles involved, everything becomes complicated.

"Not like the old days," Ben muttered, standing outside the wagon during a break in the by-passing of the city.

Ike had flown up to join him and the two men had been standing together quietly, content just to enjoy each other's company.

"You miss the old days, General?" a Rebel lieutenant asked.

Ike and Ben turned their heads to look at the young woman for a moment. Then the two middle-aged warriors smiled. The Rebel officer was maybe twenty-two or twenty-three years old.

How to really explain to the young how it was when this movement all started? Ben thought.

How to tell this young female warrior how it was back in the old days; back in the beginning? Ike thought.

How to explain that back in the old days I knew the name of every Rebel in my command? Ben thought.

How to explain how Ben and I first met? Ike thought.

How small groups of us talked through many a long night about a new society, a new form of government, and wondered if it would ever come to be and would it work? Ben silently pondered.

How to tell the younger generation about the hundreds of lonely graves filled with brave Rebels that dot the land from coast to coast and border to border? Ike got all lost in the misty grip of memories.

How to tell her about the few years we lived in peace and harmony in the old Tri-States of the northwest? Ben wondered.

Ike sighed, thinking: How to tell her about our rebuilding from the ashes of a society when those outside our boundaries said it would never work . . . but it did work.

"Yes, Lieutenant," Ben broke the moment of reflection. "I guess we older people do miss the old days." He smiled.

"But wasn't life so much harder, so much more difficult, back then?" the young officer asked. "I mean . . . back after the Great War, when you and General McGowan and the others were struggling to form our new society?"

"In many ways it was much simpler," Ben replied. "The Rebel army was small, we didn't have an air force, no helicopters, no sophisticated equipment. We weren't facing great armies the way we are now. We were just trying our best to educate, that is when the people would listen, and rebuilding and fighting for what we believed in."

She smiled. "It sounds like you miss that, General?"

Ben chuckled and glanced at Ike. The ex-SEAL was grinning, lost in memories. "Well, in a way I guess we both do."

The young lieutenant returned the smiles and walked on. She did not salute, for that was not done in any area outside the SUSA; every area outside the SUSA was considered to be hostile territory.

"I'll be moving my people up to highway 78 starting tomorrow," Ike said. "Dan will have a rough time of it, for he'll be taking a secondary road. It's passable, but just. But we'll all make it up to I-10." He frowned. "One way or the other."

"We'll take all the time we need, Ike. I've ordered winter

gear to be flown in. It's going to get rough for some pretty damn quick."

Ike nodded "Snowing in the mountains now. Any further word from Mike?"

"Only very short bursts. I think he's right in the thick of things and very susceptible to getting triangulated."

Ike gripped Ben's upper arm with a strong hand. "Take care of yourself, Ben."

"You do the same, Ike."

Without another word, Ike turned and walked away, quickly vanishing into the gloom of darkness.

Both men knew the assault against the massive army of Simon Border was about to kick into high gear.

The battalions in Southern California finally got lined up along what was left of highway 78 and ready for their north-ward push. Since a lot of the southern part of eastern Cali-fornia was virtually uninhabited, Ben pulled the battalions closer to each other. Now only a few miles separated the last vehicle in a column from the lead vehicle in the one following. It made for a truly awesome sight. The few peo-ple the Rebels did encounter stood by the side of the road and stared at the passing machines of war.

Ben and his 1 Batt had taken Interstate 5, which hugged the Pacific coastline. Soon that split off into 15, which Ike and his 2 Batt took north, heading toward Rancho California and then cutting slightly east up to Riverside while Ben and his 1 Batt headed for the ruins of Los Angeles.

"Jesus!" Cooper breathed, as the convoy took a break just south of the city. "I'd forgotten what a number we did on this place."

When the Rebels crushed the hundreds of gangs of punks and thugs and street slime and the Night People in L.A. a few years back, they left behind them only a shell of a city. They had pounded the city for days, and when they pulled out, the once sprawling metropolis had been reduced to rubble. The fires had burned for days afterward.

As the Rebels pulled closer, they were greeted by silence and devastation.

"What are the fly-overs telling us?" Ben asked.

"Heat-seekers are picking up some warm bodies," Corrie responded. "But damn few of them. I think we can call Los Angeles a dead city, boss."

"Scouts?"

"They have made no hostile contact."

"Have they made any contact at all, with anything?"

"No, sir. Nothing."

"That's hard to believe, Corrie."

"Yes, sir. My feelings exactly. But we've got teams of people spread out from the Pacific running east over to what used to be Garden Grove. There are a few people living among the ruins . . . existing might be a better word, but there have been no shots fired from either side."

"Incredible."

"Yes, sir."

"Bump Ike, find out what he's encountered."

Ben sat down on the curb beside the road and took a sip of water. He had expected some stiff resistance from Simon's people upon entering the city. The ruins would make a dandy place to conduct a guerrilla-type campaign, complete with long range snipers. But . . . nothing had happened. Ben smoked a cigarette and waited.

"Ike says there are a number of people living out in his area, and they're all Simon Border supporters . . . or so they say," Corrie reported. "But they are not hostile."

"Odd," Ben muttered. "It's all very odd. What do the very forward Scouts report?"

"Simon's army is still stretched out waiting for us just north of the city."

"Air recon show any buildup as far as artillery or tanks?" Ben questioned.

"No, sir. Same, same."

"The man is actually going to butt heads with us in the old-fashioned way," Ben muttered. He crushed out the butt of his smoke under the heel of his boot and stood up. "Well, let's go visit downtown L.A., gang."

"Nothing, sir," a Scout reported.

The team of Scouts had halted the column and Ben had gotten out of the big wagon to stand amid the ruin and desolation of what had once been a bustling suburb of Los Angeles.

Ben looked carefully all around him. Piles of rubble and the hulls of burned-out buildings were all that could be seen. The odor of decay hung in the air.

"No sign of creepies?"

"No sign of *anything,* sir."

"Wow!" was all Anna could manage to say as she slowly turned, looking all around her.

"We sure didn't leave much behind when we pulled out of here, did we?" Jersey said.

"We shelled this city for days," Ben said. "From all directions and with everything we had." Some of the Scouts and some of the younger members of the Rebel army now attached to Ben's One Batt had been far too young to have been a part of that campaign. "And the punks and the thugs and the street slime and the gangs died by the droves," Ben added softly.

"Ike on the horn," Corrie said.

Ben took the mic. "Go, Ike."

"Man," Ike drawled in his Mississippi accent, "this place is spooky."

"No sign of life?"

"No signs of *nothin',* partner."

Some of the younger Rebels looked pained at Ike's casual way of speaking to Ben. Ben smiled at the expressions on their faces. "Where have the creepies gone, Ike? Any ideas?"

"Personally I think they've split up into small groups and worked their way back into society, just like before the Great War. But that's just my opinion."

"I'm beginning to think along those same lines, Ike. All right, ol' buddy. I'll give you a bump if I run into anything I can't handle."

"No, you won't!" Ike said with a laugh, and then broke off.

Chuckling, Ben handed the mic to Corrie. "Well, let's go visit Los Angeles, gang. Who knows, we might be able to stir up some trouble."

But the convoy was unable to proceed much further. The roads were almost completely blocked by debris . . . and not all of it from the shelling of the Rebels years back. Southern California had experienced quite a number of earthquakes since the Rebels had waged intensive war in Los Angeles, obviously not all of them small in size. The quakes had wreaked havoc, piling debris up and blocking the streets.

Ben walked up to one of the Scouts who was kneeling down beside a pile of rubble. "What's wrong?"

"These piles were man-made, General. And I don't like it a damn bit."

"Not one sign of life has been reported here," Ben reminded him.

"They went deep underground, General. That's the only thing that makes any sense. But these piles of rubble were definitely placed here."

Ben looked behind him. The column was stretched out for several miles. He looked all around him. "Dandy place for an ambush," he muttered.

The wind picked up as the skies darkened, and with the wind came the unmistakable smell of creepies.

"Oh, shit!" Jersey said, wrinkling her nose.

"Hunt a hole, gang," Ben ordered. "I think we've just been suckered—big time!"

Seven

"Here they come!" a Rebel shouted. "They're all around us."

The Rebels moved quickly, but with no sign of panic. Cooper got his SAW (squad automatic weapon) out of the truck that always followed Ben's vehicle, and Anna and Beth grabbed two extra canisters of ammo for the weapon.

Ben did not hesitate. He picked up his old Thunder Lizard and slung a bandoleer of full magazines for the M-14 over one shoulder. Corrie grabbed a rucksack filled with grenades and Jersey grabbed another filled with full magazines for the team's CARs.

Then they all scrambled for position behind what was left of a bomb-shattered wall. Corrie pointed to a large piece of broken front window glass and Ben nodded, a smile faintly creasing his lips. The store had once housed a famous bookstore chain.

"Wonder if they sold your books here, boss?" Corrie called with a smile.

"I once did an autographing here," Ben told her, then laughed. "Nobody showed up."

"Goddamnit, get behind cover, General!" a Rebel sergeant yelled, exasperation in his voice.

"Keep your pants on," Ben said, bellying down behind the low wall.

Jersey, Beth, Corrie, and Anna all grinned at each other,

for the sergeant was considered a very handsome man among the females in the Rebel army . . . and a few of the men.

Ben caught the grins and grimaced. "Get it off your minds, ladies. Especially you, Anna," he added grimly. "You're far too young to be thinking such thoughts."

Anna smiled sweetly at her adopted father, then when Ben turned his head, made a horrible face, crossed her pale eyes, and stuck out her tongue at him.

But Ben had anticipated such a move and had not entirely averted his eyes. He hid his smile at her antics, and over the ever louder screams and wild yells of the charging creepies, said, "Now wouldn't you be a nice-looking young lady if your face froze in that position?"

Anna looked startled for a moment, wondering how Ben had seen that. Then there was no more time for conversation as Ben yelled, "Will the tanks kindly start laying down some fire on those creepie bastards? And if it isn't too much trouble, the mortar crews can drop a few down the tubes as well. It would be much appreciated."

"Will you get off your goddamn asses and go to work!" Jersey yelled at the frantically working crews behind her, in her own inimitable way.

Ben pulled his M-14 to his shoulder and snugged the butt in tight, lining up the sights on a creepie who was just getting into range. He gently squeezed the trigger and the Thunder Lizard bumped his shoulder. The creepie went down bonelessly amid the rubble and lay still.

"Chalk one up for the boss," Ben muttered.

"Ike and Dan and West are reporting they are under heavy attack," Corrie yelled, just as the tanks began cutting loose with their main guns and the mortar crews began dropping the rounds down the tubes. "Georgi and West want to know if you want them to swing around and start a push in our direction?"

"Negative," Ben said. "That just might be what the

creepies expect. Tell them to gear up for a fight. I think one is coming at them."

"They're swarming at Ike right now!" Corrie said. "Mary says it's a combination of punks and creepies and God only knows what else."

Mary was Ike's radio operator, having been with him almost from the beginning.

"Is Ike cussing?" Ben asked, smiling at Corrie.

Corrie laughed. "Mary says he's roaring like a bear with a sore paw."

Cooper opened up with his Squad Automatic Weapon, rocking and rolling, spitting the lead out. One entire line of attackers went down under the unrelenting fire.

Anna had managed to drag out her favorite weapon, a seventy-six-pound Mark 19-3 automatic grenade launcher, affectionately called a Big Thumper, and was steady slamming out the 40mm grenades. She had enlisted the help of a more-than-willing young Rebel to feed the belt. All Anna had to do was smile at a young man and he was apt to walk into trees for several days afterward.

"That bastard Simon Border made a deal with the creepies and the punks and the gangs," Ben muttered. "Has to be it. He'd leave them alone in the ruins of the cities if they'd aid him in fighting us. Shit!" Ben shouted, his one-word epithet clearly heard over the booming of fire.

"You hit, boss!" Corrie yelled.

"No. Hell no. But have all units throw up a rear guard as quickly as possible. That's why we hit no trouble in the ruins of San Diego. The creepies and punks and gangs *wanted* us to bypass them so they could launch an attack from the rear. Call in the planes and the gunships, Corrie. This is about to get dicey. That goddamn semi-sanctimonious Simon Border. That fake-assed psalm-singing fraud. If I ever get my hands on that snake-oil salesman I'm going to beat him to death."

Ben's team had nothing to say after that. Ben was pissed,

and when the boss got pissed, the best thing to do was leave him alone.

Anna had never stopped working the Big Thumper, and Cooper had been keeping up a steady ranking fire with his SAW, both of them keeping the attackers at bay. But now the attack was intensifying and some creepies and their allies were getting close to the first line of defense.

Ben was still muttering and seething with anger as he turned his attentions toward the attack. He let his M-14 help to vent his rage. The old Thunder Lizard could reach out and touch the enemy at very long range, and Ben did just that time after time that morning. Ben picked his shots carefully, and his aim was true. He made about ninety percent of his shots before the first wave of attackers broke and retreated. That gave the forward Rebels some time to catch their breath.

But several miles behind Ben's location, conditions had worsened.

"B and D companies are engaged," Corrie reported. "Coming under heavy attack."

"Move half the tanks around to back them up."

Corrie had anticipated that. "Done."

"What's the ETA for air support?"

"Thirty minutes, tops."

"Any reports of injuries during the first wave?"

"Two. Private Kovak from Company B fell out of a truck and has a slight concussion and Private Harris cut himself on the hand while fixing his bayonet."

"What the hell was he doing attaching his bayonet? Come to think of it, what the hell was he doing with a bayonet? We don't issue those."

"He got a little nervous. He was just flown in three days ago from the repple depple. It's his first time in combat. He's just seventeen, boss."

"So am I," Anna said coldly. "I think."

"Harris's world has been somewhat calmer than your world to date, dear," Ben told his adopted daughter.

"Bah!" the girl said.

Anna had never exhibited any signs of fear; indeed, she seemed to thrive on combat, the closer in the better. She was incredibly deadly with a knife and even the Scouts were in awe of her ability at silent killing.

When Ben had first adopted the girl, over the objections of Doctor Chase and others, Anna had been no more than a feral child, having been on her own since she was about six years old . . . or less. Anna did not really know exactly how old she was, but she was about seventeen—give or take a year.

Dan Gray had once called her a first cousin to a Tasmanian Devil.

Anna was a beautiful young lady, and a dangerous one.

But really, no more dangerous than most Rebels, for the Rebels were known world-wide as the undisputed experts in all types of warfare . . . especially in the down-and-dirty, hit-and-run type of guerrilla warfare.

"Ike and Dan?"

"They've beaten back the first attack with only minor injuries. Everybody is standing tall."

Lieutenant Hardin suddenly showed up in the small area that Ben and the team occupied. "Sir, I think it would be best if you moved back about a mile."

Ben looked at the young officer. "Is that right?"

"Yes, sir. I readied a CP for you. It would be much safer."

Ben's team all exchanged grins at this.

"Well, thank you, Lieutenant Hardin, but I think I'll just stay right here. I've grown rather fond of this place."

The young officer's face took on a crestfallen expression and he opened his mouth to speak.

Ben waved him silent with one hand and patted him on the shoulder, shushing him. "I know that Ike and Cecil and the others asked you to keep an eye on me, son. And I really do appreciate the effort, but I've been doing this for a long, long time. You just get on back to your people. You're doing a fine job."

"Ah, why, thank you, sir."

"Think nothing of it, son."

With a faint smile, Ben turned back to his position. But the smile was for the benefit of the young officer and no one else. There was really nothing to smile about. The Rebels were in a lousy position, boxed in, and there was no ground relief coming. Air support would help, sure, by taking off some of the strain for a time, and the tanks and mortars could keep up a barrage for days, if need be, for ammo trucks rolled with each convoy and were constantly being resupplied. But the Rebels were still in a box, and it was up to those in the box to find a way out. Ben knew it would be by one of two means: sneaky or brute force. Those were the only options open.

"West just reported in," Corrie called. "They've beaten back the first attack with only minor injuries."

"The other battalions reporting any action?"

"Negative."

"What is recon telling us about the regular troops of Simon's?"

"Still dug in tight to the north of us. No movement being detected."

"Simon wants, hopes, we'll take heavy casualties and sustain heavy losses and be so weakened when we hit his regular troops they'll be able to defeat us. The son of a bitch has another think coming."

"I would certainly hope so," Corrie said, a twinkle in her eyes.

Ben smiled at her. The morale of the Rebels was always high: the thought of defeat just never entered their minds. "Right, Corrie. Right."

* * *

The pilots of the souped-up P-51E's and the helicopter gunships could not have timed it better. Simon's allies had just begun their second attack of the day when the P-51E's came roaring in, machine gun and cannon howling out death and destruction. The second pass brought napalm and a nearly solid wall of flames leaped from ground high into the air.

"Cooked creepie," Cooper said, with no small degree of satisfaction.

"Bar-B-Qued bastards," Beth said.

"Roasted rat-asses," Jersey came through.

"Same results to the south of us," Corrie said, after speaking with companies B and D.

Only a few minutes ticked past until the familiar whack-a-whack of helicopter blades slicing the air reached the Rebels. Now that the P-51E's were long gone, the attackers were readying themselves for another attack and were caught exposed. The helicopter gunships opened up with everything they had, which was plenty, and Simon's first line of defense had no more stomach for the fight.

"They're breaking and running," Corrie reported.

"No pursuit to the south," Ben ordered. "We'll let the gunships and the planes handle that for the time being. Breakthrough—right now! Tanks spearhead. Scouts follow. I want some prisoners. Move, move!"

The Main Battle Tanks surged forward, the Scouts right behind them, a few minutes later, Ben waved the two companies defending the north sector forward. "We'll wait until companies B and D join us and bring up the drag."

That made Lieutenant Hardin very nervous. "It will be about an hour before they get here, sir," he pointed out. "You're here with only a few Rebels to protect you."

"I have my personal platoon, Lieutenant. Of which you are in charge. Don't you think you can do the job?"

"Why, ah, yes, sir! Of course, sir! I was merely pointing out that . . . ah, oh, to hell with it!" The young officer looked aghast at what he had just said to the commanding general of the entire Rebel army. His mouth dropped open and his face reddened.

Laughing, Ben once again patted the very flustered lieutenant on the shoulder. "It's all right, son. You'll get used to me in time. Set up a perimeter now. A very loose one. We have to be ready to bug out at a second's notice."

"Ah, yes, sir. I remember this maneuver from your lectures in tactics class at college."

"Very good, son," Ben said drily.

"Yes, sir. We keep the vehicles running at all times and the troops use only light weapons. That way they can move quickly without being encumbered by having to dismantle heavy machine guns."

Ben sighed. "That's the way we do it, son," he said patiently.

"A very good maneuver, sir, if I may say so."

"Thank you."

"I'll get right on it, sir."

"Please do."

Ben watched the young lieutenant trot off, yelling at his people. Lieutenant Hardin had graduated first in his class from the military academy's officer training program, and he was very thorough . . . frustratingly so.

"Companies B and D's ETA is approximately one hour, sir," Corrie said, breaking into Ben's thoughts.

"Now tell me the bad news," Ben said with a smile, knowing that Ike had been intercepting their transmissions.

"Ike is hopping mad about you splitting your command and being caught in the middle here like, as he put it, a goddamn Mississippi bullfrog 'tween a gig and a 'gator."

"Ike does have a way with words, doesn't he?"

"Yes, sir. That he does. What would you like for me to tell him?" Then Corrie realized her mistake in asking that and tensed.

"Tell him to go shit in his hat."

"Do I have the general's permission to rephrase that message somewhat?"

"Certainly."

"Thank you."

"You're welcome."

Ben sat down on the ground and took a swig of water from his canteen. Never any happy middle ground, he thought, grimacing at the taste. When the canteens were metal, the water tasted metallic, and in his opinion the heavy plastic didn't improve the taste very much. Well, hell, it was wet, highly purified and almost tasteless, thanks to the efforts of the scientists back at Base Camp One. One little pill killed practically every germ known to humankind.

Ben looked up as the whack-a-whack sounds of huge helicopter rotor blades once more ripped the air. "Now, what the hell are they doing back over here?"

"Ike sent them," Corrie said. "He said this was a damn fool thing for you to do and you needed some protection in case of a counter-attack."

"What counter-attack?" Ben griped. "I've got Rebels north, south, and east, and almost total desolation to the west of us. Plus I've got three tanks, half a dozen APC's and Bradley Fighting Vehicles, mortar crews, several Big Thumpers, an oversized platoon, my own bodyguards . . . Tell Ike he's getting to be worse than an old woman. Ask him if he looks under the bed every night . . . when we get to sleep in a bed, that is."

"I'll get right on that, boss," Corrie replied, and pretended to work at her radio.

"I'm sure you will," Ben muttered, and stretched out on the ground to rest.

Ben was the consummate combat man. He was sound asleep in two minutes.

Eight

Ben's team became highly amused at the expression on Lieutenant Hardin's face when he returned to find Ben sleeping soundly on the ground.

"How can he do that?" Hardin demanded in a soft voice. He certainly did not want to awaken the commanding general.

"Why not?" Jersey responded. "There's nothing going on."

Hardin sighed. "The enemy is all around us, Miss Jersey."

"Yeah, the boss knows that. So what? If he hears any shooting he'll wake up and shoot back."

Hardin stared at her for a moment. Then he turned and slowly walked away. He just did not understand the CG—not at all.

Ben opened his eyes and sat up when he heard the sounds of approaching tanks. The nap had refreshed him. He stood up, stretched, and looked up at the sky. The gunships were still circling slowly, about a mile away in any direction Ben chose to look.

"Tell them to return to base," Ben ordered.

"They won't pay any attention to me, boss. They're under Ike's orders."

"I'm going to have a long chat with Ike," Ben said sourly.

But everyone present knew he probably wouldn't. And even if he did, it wouldn't do any good.

"Let's roll," Ben said.

1 Batt rumbled forward and put the smoking ruins of the battleground behind them. The Rebels looked emotionlessly at the dead lying sprawled in grotesque and broken and bloody shapes. The carrion birds and various wild animals would take care of the hundreds of dead. If there were wounded among them . . . well, that was not the responsibility of the Rebels.

The Rebels were, to a person, very compassionate and caring toward civilians who wanted help, but they usually didn't give two hoots in hell about those who waged war against them. If time permitted, they would stop and patch up enemy wounded, but they would never help a creepie or a creepie ally.

"Ike on the horn," Corrie said from the second seat of the big wagon.

"What does he want?" Ben questioned.

"I didn't ask."

Ben picked up the dashboard mic and keyed it. "Go, Ike." Ben had left the speaker on, knowing Ike would detect the faint hollow sound that was just ahead of feedback and would temper his remarks.

"Dumb move back there, Ben."

"Duly noted. What else is on your mind?"

"You don't have to take these unnecessary chances, General" the clipped tones of Dan Gray sprang out of the speaker. The Englishman was highly pissed. "Those of us in command would deeply appreciate it if you would *never* do anything like that again."

"Duly noted, Dan. Anything else?"

"That stunt back yonder was a stupid-assed move, Ben," the ex-mercenary, West, fired off his verbal shots. West had never been known for his subtlety. "And you know it. That's all I'm going to say on the matter."

"All complaints noted. Is everyone lined up for the assault against Simon's people?"

"As lined up as the roads permit, Ben," Ike said. "We're going to be badly outnumbered."

"What else is new? How's your ammo?"

The Rebels were very nearly always outnumbered. They were accustomed to that.

"More than adequate," Dan said. "I calculate two days before we hit the first front. My Scouts report the airports in my sector are unusable. We'll have to be resupplied by truck and chopper."

"All major airports in this part of the state have been rendered unusable," Georgi, miles to the east, broke in. "However my people report that the runways of many of the smaller airports are still clear."

"Once we take them," Dan added.

"True," the Russian replied.

"How long are the runways?" Ben asked.

"Most are adequate for our cargo planes," Georgi said.

"Then we have no problem."

"Maybe not, maybe so," Georgi grumbled. "The roads to the runaways are terrible, and the people are most unco-operative. They are dedicated followers of that stupid potato-head."

Ike burst out laughing. "Potato-head? I got to remember that one, Bear."

"That is a good description of Simon Border," West said, chuckling over the air.

"Are the people armed?" Ben asked.

"Yes," Georgi said.

"Have they fired on our people, Georgi?"

"Yes. One of my Scouts was slightly wounded."

"Then you all know what to do. If fired upon, return the fire."

"Then we consider any Simon Border supporter the enemy?" West asked.

"I don't think we have a choice in the matter. From now on, we are in hostile territory."

"There is also that other matter concerning Simon Border," West said. "Without going into details."

"Is the rumor spreading?"

"Very fast, Ben."

"What did the prisoners tell you?"

"We didn't take any prisoners," West said.

"Nor did we," Dan said.

"Us neither," Ike drawled.

Ben's people had taken a few, but they were sullen and very uncooperative. The Rebels never took any creepie prisoners. "Let me nail it down firm. Then I'll give you the okay to tell your people. Eagle out." Ben hung the mic on the dash and stared straight ahead.

"It is nailed down firm, boss," Beth spoke from the third seat of the big wagon.

"I know, Beth," Ben said. "But I don't want our people turning deadly against every man and woman who has made the mistake of believing in the dubious gospel of Simon Border."

"Why not?" Anna asked. "They must be really stupid people to begin with."

"Not stupid people, Anna," Ben corrected. "Desperate people. Many believed that God had forsaken them. This country's been up and down like a yoyo since the Great War. Millions of people wanted very badly to believe in something. Either that, or they would lose all hope."

"Then why didn't they just embrace the Tri-States philosophy and have done with it?" the young lady asked. "I have studied other forms of government from books Beth loaned me. Socialism, communism, democracy, others. Our philosophy is by far the best. We have no hunger, full employment, no fancy-dan lawyers twisting the truth in so-called courts of law, practically no crime at all, churches for people who wish to go to church and brothels for those who wish to pay for a few moments of love . . ." She smiled. ". . . And I have been told that sometimes it is difficult to tell one from the other since many of the faces are the same. It is my opinion that anyone who doesn't embrace the Tri-States form of government is a fool. Period."

Ben joined the others in a smile. Anna would defend the Tri-States philosophy of government to the death, as would, Ben knew, ninety-nine point nine percent of those who chose to live in the SUSA. Anna, as young as she was, had seen the worst of humankind. She had seen attempts at democracy fail, and had been forced to live for years under the bloody rules of anarchy in her country. As far as she was concerned, the Tri-States philosophy was it; there was no other form of government worth fighting for.

"Liberalism ruined the United States, Anna," Ben said without turning in the seat. "You should study that philosophy and let me know what you think of it."

"I have studied it, General Ben. It does have its good points, but they are few. The rest of it sucks."

Ben chuckled. "Very aptly put, dear. I couldn't have said it better."

The next day, while Corrie was monitoring transmissions through one headphone, she said, "Scouts have a small group of prisoners about a mile ahead, boss."

"Exactly where the hell are we?" Ben asked, picking up a map. He slipped on his reading glasses. Ben's vision was fine, except for very close or detail work, then he was forced to wear glasses, and he hated them.

They were paralleling the old Santa Anna Freeway, or rather, what was left of it, picking their way through the shattered streets.

"South Whittier, I think," Beth said. "But I'm not certain of that. Everything looks the same and I haven't seen a street sign since we got here."

"I've seen old pictures of European cities during World War Two," Jersey said. "That's what this reminds me of."

"There are the Scouts," Cooper said. "On our right, just up ahead."

Cooper stopped in the middle of the littered street. There was no other place to park. The long column ground to a halt behind them.

Ben got out and walked over to the prisoners, a sad-looking bunch of men and women sitting amid the rubble. He turned to a Scout. "What's their story?"

"I don't know, sir. They said they won't talk to anyone but you. That's the leader, sort of, right there. That woman."

"Get her on her feet and bring her . . ." Ben looked around him. Spotted a one-story building with only the front wall blown out and most of the roof intact. ". . . Over there."

Seated in a camp chair from his rolling HQ, Ben stared at the woman for a moment, sitting on what was left of a wooden counter. Never see forty again, Ben guessed. Wouldn't be unattractive if she were cleaned up. He clicked on a portable tape recorder. "All right, lady, I'm Ben Raines. What's your story?"

"My name is Susan Marsh," the woman said in a hoarse voice. "Originally from Michigan. Came out here several years ago with a group of people, following the Simon Border movement. Reverend Border was different back then. He preached the gospel and had a dream . . . not unlike your dream of a better society, General Raines."

Ben grunted a noncommittal reply to that. He wasn't too sure he appreciated being compared in any way to Simon Border.

"But our dream was one of a collective society, with everyone helping out, working not for oneself, but for society as a whole. Even Reverend Border worked in the fields. I saw pictures of him hoeing in a garden."

Carefully staged for the benefit of the masses, Ben thought.

"But he's changed over the months," the woman continued with a sigh. "He's not the same man I followed west to the promised land. Or the land he said was the promised land."

"And that hasn't turned out as you hoped it would?"

"No, General. It hasn't." She tried a smile that resembled a grimace. "Which I'm sure pleases you."

"Not really, Miss Marsh. I told Simon some months back if he'd leave us alone, we would leave him alone. He agreed and all the while had no intention of keeping his word."

"Our original form of government is far superior to yours, General," the woman went on the defensive.

Ben smiled. "I doubt that you would find many people in the SUSA who would agree with that, Miss Marsh."

She shrugged. "Perhaps not. But then, General, there are many people living *outside* the SUSA who look with scorn on *both* our chosen forms of government, aren't there?"

Ben laughed at that. "Well, you have me there, Miss Marsh. You're certainly correct."

She held up a hand. "No matter, General. I didn't ask to speak with you to argue political philosophy. Reverend Border is, ah, well, he needs to be hospitalized. He's not a well man."

He needs to be shot, Ben thought. But I'll play along with you, lady. "I wasn't aware he was ill, Miss Marsh."

"I believe the strain of leadership has affected him, General." She lifted her eyes and stared at Ben directly. "Mentally, sir. I believe the Reverend needs a long rest. Away from responsibility."

That's exactly what I have in mind for him, lady. Resting in a nice comfortable hole in the ground. Ben met the woman's eyes. "Let's stop kidding each other, Miss Marsh. Simon is a pedophile. And I have information that he has always been a pedophile. He has to be stopped."

The woman's eyes became shiny with anger. Then the anger faded as quickly as it had come. She shook her head.

"But he still has hundreds of thousands of followers, General. Do you plan to kill them all?"

"I'd rather not, Miss Marsh."

"But you will if that's what it takes to get to Reverend Border?"

"Yes. So anything you could tell me about his army might help save lives."

"You know of course that he has no air force."

"Yes. I know that."

"He has very few tanks and practically no artillery except for mortars. He has plenty of those."

Ben nodded and pulled out the makings from his pocket, carefully rolling a cigarette. "These hundreds of thousands of supporters, Miss Marsh . . . they're fanatic in their loyalty?"

"Most of them. And most will fight to the death."

"Even though they are aware of Simon's sexual perversions!"

"Gods can do no wrong, sir."

"But you don't believe that Simon is a god, do you, Miss Marsh?"

She shook her head. "No, sir. I don't. Any more than I believe that you are a god. But there are many who follow you who believe you are something of a god."

"Not anymore, Miss Marsh. I've worked hard to dispel that myth."

"To your credit, sir."

"Where is Simon's headquarters?"

She shook her head. "I honestly don't know, General. If I did, I would tell you. I would tell you if for no other reason than there are thousands of good, decent people who are blindly following the dictates of Simon Border and who are going to die in this war if Simon isn't stopped."

"It might be too late." Ben's words were softly offered. "Have you given that any thought?"

"For some of his followers, it is too late, sir. I can tell

you that openly and honestly. They believe as deeply and as strongly in Simon's philosophy of government as your followers do in the Tri-States movement. They will never stop fighting."

"And anything goes; the end justifies the means?"

"Yes, sir."

"You are convinced of that?"

"Quite."

"Then we have a very long and bitter struggle ahead of us, Miss Marsh."

She met his steady gaze. "A struggle that very well might go on for years, General. For there are thousands of men and women who will follow Simon Border's doctrine to their grave. And it really makes no difference if the man himself is alive or dead."

Nine

Ben ordered Susan Marsh and her friends turned loose. He was convinced of her truthfulness when she said she and the other prisoners were through fighting and would not raise a hand against any Rebel.

"Where will you go?" Ben asked her just before the column pulled out. "What will you do?"

"I'm going back to Michigan," she replied. "Several of the others are going with me. We're going to start a small church there and try to live as Reverend Border taught us . . . before he became ill."

"I wish you well."

"Thank you, General. I believe you really mean that."

Ben nodded and the small group turned and walked away. They had a long drive ahead of them, and a dangerous one.

"They're going to take the northern route back home," Ben said. "Susan told me they wanted to pick up a few people along the way."

Cooper shook his head. "Isn't that sort of foolish on their part, boss? One of the men told me they had openly broken with their side and deserted."

"Susan told me she had faith in God."

Jersey looked very pained. "I'm sure the Christians had the same thought, just before the lions were turned loose."

"Mount up," Ben ordered. "Let's go start this war big time."

* * *

It took the column two more days to pick through the ruins of Los Angeles and suburbs and reach the northern edge of the once-sprawling city.

"There it is, General," a Scout said. "Just past that strip of desolation is Simon's army. They're stretched out all the way from Simi Valley over to San Bernardino. He's got guerrilla units in place all the way over to Twenty-nine Palms, ready to hit and run and harass our people."

"Corrie, order every piece of artillery rolling with all units along the southern edge to get into place and make ready for a sustained barrage. We'll soften up those folks for a few days and see what results that brings. Then bump Base Camp One and have the supply planes readied to fly around the clock."

"When do you want the barrage to start, boss?" Corrie asked.

"Just as soon as all the artillery is in place. Then give Mr. Border's followers a taste of everything we've got in our arsenal."

"It's gonna get noisy around here," Jersey said.

The deadly rolling thunder of an artillery barrage is demoralizing, for there is no place to run and hide, no place where you are assured of being safe.

The Rebels threw everything except their underwear and the kitchen sink at Simon's army for the next three days and nights. And while the artillery was keeping the enemy's head down, six oversized battalions of Ben's Rebels were creeping closer, ready to tangle eyeball to eyeball when the word came down. They were going in loaded down with the deadliest hand grenades ever designed and rucksacks filled with full magazines and 40mm grenades for their bloop tubes.

The cargo planes flew in and out around the clock, bringing artillery rounds, food, winter clothing, medical supplies, and replacements.

"Must be tough on those over there," Cooper said, cutting his eyes to the north.

"You've been under siege before, Coop," Jersey replied. "How did you feel?"

"I wasn't real happy about it."

Anna was sitting on the ground, sharpening a long-bladed knife. She looked up, pausing in her whetting of the razor-sharp blade. "We're going in soon."

"How do you know?" Cooper asked. "The boss tell you?"

"No. I feel it, that's all."

"Not first wave, Anna," Jersey said. "You know better than that. The boss would love to spearhead, but he knows if he did that he'd have a major revolt among his batt coms."

"There will be plenty of fighting to go around," the young woman replied. "We're outnumbered a hundred to one."

"Not after all this artillery," Beth argued.

Anna shrugged. "So we've cut it down to seventy-five to one. Big deal."

"She does have a point," Corrie said.

No one could dispute that.

Cooper pulled out his Bowie knife and a whetstone and went to work.

Jersey preferred an entrenching tool: a collapsible steel shovel. She found her whetstone and soon the air was filled with rasping.

Ben walked up, looked at the scene, and smiled. "You people getting ready for some hand-to-hand?"

"I guess it's coming, boss," Cooper replied.

"Maybe. But the first wave will take the brunt of that."

"Told you," Jersey grinned at Anna.

"They won't kill them all," Anna persisted. She sheathed her knife and walked away, pausing after only a few steps.

She turned around and stared at the team. "Something's the matter. What is it?"

Beth looked up. "Damn! The artillery barrage. It's stopped. That's what's the matter. We've grown so accustomed to it I didn't even notice."

"Get ready," Ben said. "Everybody in body armor. Button up."

The sounds of small arms fire reached the group.

"It's started," Ben said. "Now our work begins."

"Jesus H. Christ!" Jersey breathed the words.

"The fools didn't even dig bunkers," Beth said.

It was carnage any direction one chose to look. Bodies and pieces of bodies littered the ground. Smoke from fires started by incendiary rounds clung close to the earth in the early morning hours.

"Plenty of courage, but damn little military know-how," Ben summed it up.

"Intelligence with the first wave estimates about twenty thousand dead," Corrie said, after acknowledging a transmission. "Our artillery caught them flat-footed."

"I don't understand these people," Beth said, staring at a severed hand still clutching an M-16. "Are they all crazy?"

"They're digging in, preparing to make another stand in the old national forests north of the city," Corrie informed the group.

"I thought they would," Ben spoke quietly. "Well, we have to dig them out. The commanders are probably hoping we'll bypass them and leave them at our backs. They're wrong."

Corrie waited for orders to transmit.

"Get trucks and tanks with scrapers up here," Ben said. "Scoop out mass graves. This many bodies left to rot would

create somewhat of a health hazard." After Corrie had trans-
mitted the orders, Ben said, "Prisoners?"

"Being interrogated now. But there aren't that many.
Most chose death over surrender."

"Let's go see them."

A few miles to the east, Ben spoke to an intelligence
officer. "What are you getting out of them?"

"Very little, sir. And I think the reason for that is, they
don't know anything. Their commanders are deliberately
leaving them in the dark."

"That's the first smart thing Simon's people have done,"
Ben said. "How many officers did we take?"

"Only a handful. And nothing above company commanders. Their ranking officers either bugged out, or were never
on the front lines."

Ben was silent for a moment. "And what does that tell
you, Captain?"

"I, ah, don't know what you mean, sir."

"I think it means that Simon is suffering from a shortage
of experienced officers. He's got plenty of volunteers,
plenty of cannon fodder, but damn few men to lead them.
Take that tack when questioning them."

"Yes, sir."

Away from the prisoners, Ben told Corrie, "Bump Ike
and the other batt coms. See if they captured any ranking
officers. I'll wager they didn't."

That took Corrie only a few moments. "Nothing above
a captain, boss," she reported.

"That's what I figured." Ben smiled. "Simon's got himself a real problem: no leadership. We've had years to de-
velop officers, years of actual combat experience around
the world. Simon had to start from scratch and he's hurting
in that department."

"The spirit is willing but the flesh is weak," Anna stated
softly.

"Something like that, dear," Ben said. "Corrie, get me

aerial recon of the national forests. Let's see where the enemy is concentrated."

"All over the damn place," Ben muttered, after studying just-delivered photos of the national forests. He straightened up with a sigh of relief and removed his reading glasses, then rubbed his eyes, tired from hours of close work.

Simon's army was huge, that was for certain. Mike Richards had finally radioed in, confirming that Simon had reserves waiting to throw at Ben that numbered in the thousands and thousands. And since the militia people who were helping to protest Ben's eastern flank were not nearly so well equipped as the Rebels, Simon could probably bust through anywhere along that line anytime he chose to do so. The one thing Ben had on his side was winter. Up north, winter was closing in fast; up along the Canadian border, snow was already piling up, closing the roads at least temporarily.

"Our front is hundreds of miles long," Ben muttered, throwing a pencil on the tabletop. "Too damn long."

The Rebels had no more tanks and heavy artillery to send to their militia allies, who were spread thin from the Canadian border down to Kansas, and seventy-five percent of Ben's reserve had to remain back at Base Camp One. The SUSA must be protected at all costs.

And Ben also knew that the vast majority of the people living outside of the SUSA, while most had no great love for that goofball Simon Border, had even less love for Ben Raines and his Rebels and their political philosophy. Ben could count on no help from that quarter.

Except for a few thousand militia allies, Ben and his Rebels were in this fight alone.

As usual.

What else was new?

Ben picked up the other just-decoded report he had received and re-read it. The Nazi, Bruno Bottger, had succeeded in setting up dozens of cells of supporters all over what used to be known as the United States, even in Simon Border's territory, right under the man's nose . . . the thought of which brought to Ben's mind a perverted sort of amusement.

But the amusement was very fleeting.

Ben had no troops to spare to combat the growing number of Nazi supporters and he could see no way to prevent Bruno's people from spreading their hate and filth across those areas where cells were in place. At least not until he had dealt with Simon Border and his forces.

"Ike on the horn," Corrie broke into his thoughts.

Ben took the mic. "Go, Shark."

"What's the scoop on dealing with the hostiles in the woods, Ben?"

"I'm open to suggestion."

"I guess we're going to have to go in and flush them out. We lay down artillery in there and we'll have fires burning for months."

"What do your people think about it?"

"Rarin' to go, Ben."

"The others feel the same?"

"All the way."

"All right, Ike. I'll get back to you in a few hours."

Ben walked outside his mobile HQ and stood for a moment, staring toward the north. Like any commander, Ben hated to lose troops, but like any commander, he knew it was inevitable. But that didn't mean he had to like it.

If they went in those brush-overgrown forests to flush out Simon's troops, a lot of Rebels were going to be hurt and killed.

But Ben couldn't see where he had any choice in the matter.

He heard bootsteps coming up behind him. He turned. Corrie was standing there. "All right, Corrie," Ben's words were almost a whisper. "Bump all batt coms involved. We're going in."

Ten

Ben had shifted his 1 Batt west over to the Santa Ynez Mountains. Ike had pulled his 2 Batt over to Santa Barbara, Dan west to Ventura, and the rest of the battalions shifted west to fill up the gaps in the front. There had been a lot of rain during the year, and the vegetation was lush, the forests green, and the underbrush thick.

"It's gonna be a son of a bitch," Cooper muttered, looking at a map outlining the area from Santa Maria east to Palm Springs.

"It is that, Coop," Ben agreed. "And we get the Sierra Madre Mountains."

"Then let's do it," Anna said impatiently.

"Keep your pants on, kid," her adopted father told her. "Literally and figuratively," Ben muttered under his breath. He cleared his throat. "There'll be plenty of action to go around."

"Scouts reporting the heaviest troop build-ups are to the east," Corrie said.

"Crap!" Anna muttered.

"Those ranges are much more heavily wooded," Beth said, quickly consulting a well-worn and tattered tourist guide of Southern California and its mountain ranges.

"What's the word on our objective?" Ben tossed the question out.

"Very light resistance," Corrie said. "Scouts have penetrated several miles into the range and reported only scattered fighting. Nothing they couldn't handle."

"Prisoners?"

"Just a handful. The enemy keeps pulling back. They act as though they don't want to fight."

"They're trying to sucker us into something," Ben said. "Get me the latest aerial recon photos. We may have run up against a field commander with some combat experience."

But the aerial photos showed nothing out of the ordinary. Still, Ben was suspicious; something was nagging at the back of his mind. He had spent too many years in combat to be easily suckered into a trap.

"What's highway 101 look like?"

"Clear, for the most part. It's in bad shape, but Scouts report it's passable, if we take it slow."

"This town, Santa Maria, how about it?"

"About forty-five thousand before the Great War. We tore it up pretty good last time we were here. There shouldn't be much left."

"Well, then, where in the hell are Simon's settlements?" Ben asked. "We have yet to find one of any size, and damn few of those."

"Colorado, Oregon, Washington, North California, Nebraska, Western Kansas, parts of Idaho . . ."

"I get the point, Beth. Everywhere but here."

"That's about the size of it, boss."

"Well, we know for a fact the cities have creepies in them, and they've made a deal with Simon, so I can understand why no one would want to live close to those stinking, cannibalistic bastards."

"Says here that Santa Maria was good wine country," Beth read from the brochure.

That perked Cooper right up. "You don't suppose . . ."

"No, Coop," Jersey interrupted. "Sorry. We stole it all last time."

"Boss," Corrie said. "We've got to get off the main highway just up ahead. We blew all the bridges last time around, remember?"

"Oh, I remember, Corrie. And that is going to slow us down to a crawl."

"If we get any slower than we are right now, we might as well get out and walk," Cooper bitched.

"We'll be doing some of that before it's over, too, Coop," Ben said.

"Message coming in from the Scouts," Corrie said. "Hold on. She listened for a moment, then said, "Scouts say Simon's people won't stand and fight. They exchange a few shots, and then keep pulling back."

Ben was thoughtful for a moment, then his face saddened. He didn't want to do it, but felt he had no choice. "Tell the Scouts not to advance any further. They're being suckered into something. Call for artillery to get in place, anchor down, and get ready, Corrie. I hate to do it, but I won't lose people needlessly. Advise all batt coms of my decision and have them follow suit.

"Shit!" Ben said.

The Scouts cut it close, vacating the area about half an hour before the artillery opened up. But Simon's people bought the ruse and were still shooting at what they thought were Rebel positions when the artillery came crashing in.

Just before the barrage began, Ben shifted his 1 Batt west, as far as the highway would permit, over to the small town of Las Cruces, just south and somewhat east of Lompoc, right on the edge of the western boundaries of the Santa Ynez mountains. There they sat out the barrage and waited to confront any retreating members of Simon's army.

It was not a long wait.

The first group numbered an even dozen. They almost walked right into Ben and his team, freezing motionless when they realized what they had done, for they had not expected the small town to be occupied by Rebels.

"Morning, boys and girls," Ben told the mixed group of men and women. "Put your weapons on the ground, or die where you stand. The choice is yours."

A dozen rifles clattered on the street.

Grim-faced Rebels seemed to spring silently out of nowhere, completely surrounding the small band of fleeing enemy soldiers. Eight men and four women exchanged disgusted glances, those expressions quickly changing to ones of submission.

"The Lord will punish you for this, General Raines," a woman said, instantly recognizing the man clad in old French lizard camo BDUs.

"I don't think the Lord is paying much attention to this conflict, lady," Ben replied. "I think He's got better things to do."

"God is on our side," a man badly in need of a shave and a haircut popped off. "The Lord God hates a sinner."

"Pardon me," Ben said with a smile. "But I thought that read God loves the sinner but hates the sin?"

Another in the group began cursing Ben, really slinging the profanity around.

"Oh, my," Beth said mockingly. "Tsk, tsk. Now that really isn't nice."

"How un-Christian of you," Jersey said. "Just remember what Joan of Arc said before she died."

"You whore of the devil!" another prisoner shouted at the diminutive Jersey.

"What did Joan of Arc say?" yet another man asked, stepping right into Jersey's verbal trap.

"She said, 'Shit, I wish it would rain!' "

Ben could not hide his amusement at the expression on the prisoner's face as his team broke up with laughter.

"You filthy blasphemous slut!" the questioner shouted.

"How dare you allow the holy name of Joan of Arc to pass your evil lips?" a woman prisoner yelled.

"Oh, fuck you, lady!" Jersey replied.

Ben cut his eyes just as Ike's HumVee drove up and the ex-SEAL jumped out. Or rather, sort of rolled out. Ike was picking up a little weight lately; the man actually seemed to thrive on field rations.

"Have you considered switching to a large truck, Ike?" Ben asked with a smile. "Maybe put a comfortable chair in the bed? That might make it somewhat easier for you to get in and out."

"Very funny, Ben," Ike said. "Hysterical." He looked at the knot of prisoners, sitting on the road. "You get anything out of them?"

"No. Haven't tried. We've just been exchanging a few pleasantries."

"Son of the devil!" another prisoner yelled at Ben.

"Yeah, I can see how well y'all been gettin' along," Ike drawled. "I can just feel all the love flowing."

One of the prisoners suddenly jumped at Ike, knocking the burly ex-SEAL sprawling and cussing. Another leaped at Cooper and landed a lucky punch, knocking Ben's driver flat on his butt. Then everybody was mixing it up and no one dared fire a shot for fear of hitting one of their own.

One of the women jumped on Ben's back and rode him to the ground, pummeling him with hard fists. Ben tossed the woman to the ground, then just as she was getting to her knees, popped her on the jaw and returned her to the ground, stunned.

The fight had turned into a real brawl, as other Rebels joined in, fists swinging.

Jersey had squared off with the woman who had made some disparaging remarks about her and the two were exchanging blows, Jersey getting the better of the other woman.

Cooper had gotten to his boots, his mouth bloody, and

was busy giving the man who had hit him a fast and furious combination of lefts and rights. The eyes of the man on the receiving end were beginning to glaze over.

Another group of about two dozen prisoners were being led into the area just as the fight broke out. The new prisoners spotted what was happening and broke away from their guards and ran to join in the fracas. The Rebels guarding them couldn't shoot for fear of hitting other Rebels.

"Aw, shit!" one Rebel sergeant yelled, and tossed down his weapon and jumped right in the middle of the fight, landing on a man's back. They rolled on the ground, cussing and punching each other.

Anna squared off, briefly, with one stocky man. He made the mistake of calling her a whore and she kicked him between the legs, the toe of her boot connecting solidly with his nuts. He turned chalk-white, howled in pain, and hit the ground and stayed there, both hands between his legs.

Ben found himself face to face with a man with a red face and a wild glint in his eyes. "Satan himself!" the man yelled. "I'm facing the devil."

"Oh, screw you," Ben said, and popped the man on the nose with a hard right fist. The blood spurted and the man yelped, putting both hands to his busted and bleeding beak. Ben set both feet and slugged the man on the jaw. The prisoner's eyes glazed over and he hit the ground, not unconscious, but definitely out of the fight for a few minutes.

The fight ended abruptly when a Rebel officer lifted his M-16 and let go with a full magazine. He didn't hit anything but air, but he did stop the fight.

Ben had a fistful of a man's shirt and his right fist drawn back, ready to pop the brawler on the snoot with a hard left. He turned the man loose and the man sank to his knees, his mouth bloody from Ben's fists.

A dozen Rebels ran into the mob, pushing and shoving prisoners back. Lieutenant Hardin came rushing up to Ben.

He looked at Ben's face. Ben had a cut over one eye, a bruise on the side of his face, and his mouth was bloody.

"My God, General!" the young lieutenant blurted. "Are you all right, sir?"

"Just ducky," Ben said, then grinned. "Damn, but that was fun!" he shouted the words.

Lieutenant Hardin stared at Ben for a moment, then slowly shook his head in disbelief. He didn't think he would ever understand the general.

"So you people thought you could sucker us into an ambush?" Ben asked the older man, who wore the insignia of a bird colonel.

"It almost worked," the prisoner said, a very smug smile on his lips.

"It never came close to working," Ben verbally shot him down.

The smile on the man's face slowly faded and a look of discouragement and resignation took its place, He stared at Ben for a moment. Ben's face was bruised in a couple of places, but other than that, he seemed fine. As a matter of fact, the general seemed almost happy, and the prisoner really didn't understand why he should. "God is on our side, sir," he finally stated.

"Oh, bullshit, Colonel!" Ben lashed out. "All you religious fanatics spout the same line of dogma. Can't you at least come up with something more original?"

"It's the truth, sir."

"Sorry, but I don't buy it. I think God has turned away from this fight for a moment or so. And His moments just might be a couple of millennia in length. Colonel, don't you know what Simon Border is, or has turned into?"

"Rumors, sir. Just vicious lies, probably spread by your own people. I'm sure of that."

Ben sighed patiently. The counter-rumor mill was working from the other side. Well, hell, he had expected that. His people would have done the same thing if conditions had been reversed. Propaganda warfare was just a part of the game called war. He asked the man more questions, received either noncommittal grunts or cold stares for his efforts, then finally called for a guard to take the man back to the holding area.

Ben leaned back in his chair. So far, it had not been much of a war . . . which suited him just fine. The enemy had taken some hard losses, and the Rebels practically none.

But Ben had a strange feeling in the pit of his stomach that all that was about to change. Simon Border, nuts or not, was not the type of individual to keep on taking heavy losses. Besides, Ben knew only too well how fickle the gods of war could be.

He had a hunch that the Rebel advance was about to hit a snag. Whether they would merely stub their toe or break a leg was something he could not predict, but he had learned never to discount his hunches.

Corrie walked in, a grim look on her face, and Ben knew his hunch had been correct. "A Rebel patrol sent out by Georgi just got ambushed, boss. Wiped out to the last person. Georgi is roaring like an angry grizzly. It was a group of civilian women and young teenagers, boss. They suckered our people in like bees to honey."

"It had to happen," Ben replied, a sick feeling washing over him. "Simon is pulling out all the stops. Now it's going to get down and dirty. What kind of pitch did they use to pull our people in?"

"Sick kids. They begged for Rebel help. You know we've never turned down a request for medical aid from civilians."

"We're about to start, Corrie."

"This war is getting dirty, boss."

"And it's going to get dirtier. We can throw the rule book out the window now."

"What do I tell Georgi?"

"Tell him to keep his dick in his pants."

A faint smile crossed Corrie's lips.

"Or words to that effect," Ben added.

Eleven

"Scouts report the enemy has laid down mines," Corrie said to Ben. The column had just pulled out and had been on the road no more than thirty minutes before the radio transmission came in.

"What type of mine?" Ben asked.

"All types, boss. From claymores to homemade. Looks like Mike was right on the mark again."

Mike Richards had reported that Simon was mass-producing mines in factories all over his territory. And the factories were heavily guarded, with little chance of a guerrilla raid being successful. Many of them were deep in the mountains, underground, thus preventing any type of air attack.

"Simon's been planning this for a long time," Ben replied. "Perhaps even before the Great War. This is not something that was spur of the moment. I'll give the man credit for that."

"Exactly what was this nut before the Great War?" Cooper asked, stopping the big wagon in the center of the road.

Ben opened the door to step out, then paused. "At first, Coop, most people tended to dismiss him as a fanatic. But his popularity continued to grow. By the time it was discovered that he was actually a dangerous advocate of the ultra-religious right, the war came and he was soon forgotten."

Standing on the road, Ben turned to Corrie. "Bump all

battalions. Tell them to halt where they are and start checking for mines."

Seconds later, a bullet just missed Ben's head and he hit the cracked old highway and scrambled for the protection of a truck. "Ambush!" he shouted.

Ben had left his M-14 in the big wagon, not expecting any trouble. He clawed at his holster and pulled out his sidearm just as the lead began flying all around him.

He heard the whir of turrets and then the boom of the MBTs' main guns. The high embankment along the side of the road, now all grown up thick with brush, began exploding in a roar of dirt and rock for hundreds of meters along the highway as the high explosive rounds impacted. Broken bodies and various bloody body parts sailed out of the brush to land on the highway with a disgusting thudding sound. Then the heavy machine guns on the tanks opened up, raking the roadside. Ben lay under the big deuce and a half with his team, and watched and waited.

The barrage ceased and Scouts rushed forward, disappearing into the brush along the side of the road.

"No other units reporting ambushes," Corrie said, lying on her belly beside Ben.

"It's an isolated thing, then," Ben replied. "But it might be something that we can look forward to with more and more frequency."

A few minutes later a Scout yelled, "Clear!"

Ben and team crawled out from under the truck, brushing the dust from their BDUs. "Call for air, Corrie. I want the teams clearing the roadway of mines to be protected from snipers . . . as much as possible, that is."

"They were civilians, General," a Scout reported. "As near as we can tell from what's left of them, that is." The Scout hesitated.

"Say it all," Ben urged.

"Kids. Young people," the Scout said. "I'd say they were in their mid to late teens."

"Shit!" Ben cussed. "I knew it had to happen. Simon's had years to brainwash the young."

"People accuse us of doing the same thing, sir," the Scout replied. "But I don't think I was brainwashed in school."

"You weren't. And we don't brainwash kids. We just teach them facts, that's all."

Critics of the Tri-States philosophy had long accused Ben of brainwashing the young in schools, but there was no truth to it. The public schools and colleges in the SUSA were the finest in the world, staffed with the best teachers. One of the many reasons for that excellence in education is that the teachers could teach without being in fear of their lives from punks. Another reason was that discipline was strictly enforced in the classroom. Still another reason was the one Ben had stated alongside the road: schools in the SUSA taught fact, not myth and half-truths.

Hardline liberals hated that.

Simon's people could and did slow the columns, but they didn't stop the Rebel advance. And Ben knew that Simon didn't have the production capability to produce enough mines to lay on every road heading north. Two days and ten slow miles later, the mines ceased to plague the columns and the Rebels surged forward. There had been no more ambushes.

All columns reported passing through towns filled with sour-faced people, but there had been no hostile acts from Border's supporters against the columns. Just hard and un-friendly looks from men and women and children.

"They hate us," Anna remarked, as she stared back at a young woman who had just made an obscene hand gesture at Ben's vehicle. Beth returned the hand gesture two-fold.

Ben hid his smile at the reflection of the usually stoical Beth flipping the civilian two birds. "You'll get used to it Anna. Our philosophy is not well-loved outside the SUSA."

"Only proves the world is filled with very stupid and shallow-minded people," the girl replied.

"Many people don't like change," Ben told her. "They tend to cling to old beliefs even though they've been proven not to work."

"Proves my point," Anna said. Anna was not one to give up easily, and Ben had discovered that the girl usually got in the last word.

Ben sighed and dropped the subject. "How far to Santa Maria, Beth?"

"We should reach it early tomorrow morning. Scouts report it's full of Border supporters. But so far they have not made a hostile move, and don't appear to be set up for a fight."

"That means we'd better be damned careful," Ben said, without turning around in the seat. "I don't trust any of these people who embrace the philosophy of Simon Border."

"The townspeople have a lot of kids, boss. Many of them are sick."

Ben sighed again. There it was. "What kind of sickness?"

"Childhood diseases, mostly. They've never received any type of immunization. Most of the children were born long after the Great War."

"Wonderful," Ben said sarcastically. "Have they asked for our help?"

"Sort of," Corrie replied.

"Whatever that means," Ben muttered.

"They haven't come right out and asked for our help, General," a Rebel officer told Ben. "But I have a feeling they wouldn't refuse it if we offered."

The long column had stopped on the southern edge of the town of Santa Maria.

"Then we'll offer it, in a roundabout way. Have the MASH tents set up, Captain, and tell the doctors to get ready to receive patients. We'll see what happens."

Nothing at first, then, a few at a time, women began bringing their children in to see the doctors.

"There is no serious outbreak of anything," a doctor said to Ben. "Which is surprising when you consider that these kids have never been immunized against anything. Dr. Chase has ordered vaccines flown in from Base Camp One."

"Why not?" Ben questioned sarcastically. "We might as well take care of the whole goddamn world. For the rest of the world seems incapable of taking care of itself."

The doctor smiled and walked away, back to his MASH tent. The lines had grown longer, and not just women with children: grown men were beginning to gather, seeking medical aid.

"No sign of weapons, so far," Jersey commented, standing with Ben outside his mobile CP.

"Why should there be weapons?" the voice came from behind Ben and Jersey. They turned to face a clean-shaven, neatly dressed middle-aged man. "We're farmers and sheepherders and weavers, not warriors."

"Your name?"

"Charles Emerson. I'm the leader of this group of people."

"I'm surprised you would speak to the likes of me, Mr. Emerson," Ben said with a smile. "I'm the great Satan. Haven't you heard?"

"Horseshit! You're no more Satan than I am."

"How can you be sure?"

"Let's put it this way: I don't buy most of that verbal crap Simon Border spews, either."

Ben laughed. "Now I am confused."

"I was here before Simon enticed his so-called 'flock' to come here. I saw no reason to leave."

"You don't attend his church?"

"Hell, no! I wouldn't put up with that mindless drivel if you held a gun to my head."

Ben chuckled at the expression on the man's face. He waved a hand. "The rest of these people?"

"Most of them pay Simon lip service, that's all. Out of the five hundred or so people here in this community, perhaps, oh, fifty actually are followers of Simon Border. We really didn't know what sort of treatment we would receive from you people."

"We're generally pretty friendly until someone starts shooting at us," Ben said, waving the man to a camp chair. Jersey stood off to one side, the muzzle of her CAR not pointed directly at Emerson, but at the ready. "Where are those supporters of Border?"

"They ran away. To join other supporters in a couple of tiny towns to the east and south of us."

"Then they'll run smack into Ike McGowan and his 2 Batt. You're probably seen the last of them."

The man gave Ben a long stare. "What if they offer no resistance, General?"

"They'll be disarmed and left alive. We can't have armed resistance nipping at our rear, Charles."

"We have guns in this community, General. Most of us are armed. Are you going to take them from us?"

"You haven't been hostile toward us. Yet," he added.

The civilian caught the "yet," and smiled. "General, the mountain lion has made quite a comeback in the mountains, as has the bear. They don't give us much trouble, but we like to be prepared when they do."

"Can't blame you for that. How about the punks?"

"They used to give us more trouble than the puma and the bear." He laughed. "Of course, that was before they 'saw the light' so to speak, and embraced Simon Border as Lord on Earth."

"And you believe that, Charles?"

"Hell, no. I'm not saying that punks can't change; stranger things have happened, I'm sure. It's just that the gangs that used to prowl around here are totally beyond redemption."

"I totally agree with you, Charles." Ben was smiling, but in his head, every invisible alarm bell he possessed was ringing and dinging and donging out a warning. Charles Emerson was not only just too good to be true, but Ben was certain the man was lying through his teeth.

The whole community was one great big trap. While he and Charles had been talking, Ben had received several hand signals from Rebels indicating a trap and to be ready. Cutting his eyes to Jersey, Ben knew she had picked up on the silent signals and was ready.

"Well, Mr. Emerson," Ben said, careful to keep his face expressionless and his voice bland. "I'll level with you: we have absolutely no intention of disarming you or any of your people."

"I'm real glad to hear that, General. Trust is a wonderful thing, isn't it."

"It certainly is, Mr. Emerson."

"Mr. Emerson is so formal. Why don't you call me Charles."

"I'll do that, Charles. Tell me, what are your plans?"

"Why . . . to live quietly and peacefully, General. How does the old saying go? To build a house by the side of the road and be a friend to man?"

"Something like that, Charles. Although I think it reads: To live in my house . . ."

Ben didn't think this was the time or place to be correcting anyone on misquotes.

A Scout strolled up. Just a little too nonchalantly, Ben thought. He handed Ben a slip of paper. "Message from General Philpot, sir."

Ben hid his smile as he took the message. There was no

General Philpot in the Rebel army. "Thank you. Excuse me, Charles."

"Certainly, General."

Ben opened the folded paper and read: "IT'S A TRAP. WOMEN ARE CARRYING ARMS UNDER THEIR LOOSE CLOTHING. TEENAGERS ARE ARMED AS WELL. SEVERAL GROUPS OF MEN ARE SLIPPING IN, ATTEMPTING TO SURROUND THE TOWN."

Ben looked up at the Scout. "Radio General Philpot that I am well aware of the situation, son. Tell him that we are ready for any eventuality."

The Scout smiled very faintly. "Yes, sir. I told Colonel Jersey that I thought you were on top of the situation but he insisted you be reminded."

"Yes. Tell Colonel Jersey I said thanks."

"Right, sir." The Scout turned and strolled away.

"Trouble, General?" Emerson asked.

"Oh, no, Charles. Just a matter of logistics, that's all."

"Glad to hear it. Say, General, I have an idea. My wife is a real good cook. Why don't you come over to our house for some food? She'd be tickled pink to have you and she puts out quite a spread."

"What a good idea. I'm honored. Yes, indeed. Honored is the word. But I couldn't unless my team is invited. Six of us might be too many." Ben hid his grimace, thinking: *If I had written dialogue this lousy years back my editor would have sent it back for rewrite with a nasty little note.*

"Oh, not at all, General! Oh, my, no. The more the merrier, they say."

"Well, then, sure, Charles. Why don't we do that. I'm sure in the mood for a good home-cooked meal."

Charles stood up. "Come on, General. It's not far. I'll lead the way."

Ben rose to his boots, picking up his M-14. "I'll follow you, Charles."

"This way, sir."

Ben's team had been slowly gathering around, and they followed Ben. Anna's eyes were glinting with a savage light. Cooper had slipped a few more grenades into a side pocket of his field jacket. Jersey's expression was one of amusement. Beth had silently slipped her CAR off safety. And Corrie, with her back to Charles and Ben, had been whispering into her mic.

"You're sure this won't be an inconvenience, Charles?"

"Oh, no, not at all, General. My wife just loves company."

I hope she likes surprises, Ben thought. 'Cause she's damn sure about to get one . . . her last one, probably.

"Hi, Pete," Jersey spoke to a Rebel whose name was Chuck.

"Hi, Gladys," Chuck replied.

Again, Ben hid a smile. You can grab your partner and walk out onto the dance floor anytime you like, Charles, he thought. We're ready to strike up the band.

Ben passed by Lieutenant Hardin and nodded. "Everything all right?"

"Ah . . . yes, sir," Hardin replied. "Everything is a-ok. Sitting on ready."

"That's good, Lieutenant."

As they strolled along, Ben, looking around, thought: Well, it is a pretty little town. At least what I've seen of it. He sighed. Might as well get the show on the road. "Oh, Charles," he said.

"Yes, General?"

"You're a goddamned liar, Charles. But a pretty good actor. You ready to start this little war?"

Charles stopped, his back to Ben. Ben watched as his right elbow bent. Going for a pistol tucked under his shirt. "Why, I don't know what you mean, General."

A brick home was just a dozen yards away, to their right. Ben nodded his head in that direction and Jersey said, "We got it, boss. Anytime you're ready."

"Have you said your prayers, Charles?" Ben asked. "For you are standing closer to death than you have ever stood."

"What gave us away, General?"

"Call it a hunch."

Charles Emerson whirled around, a pistol in his right hand and his face dark with fury. Ben shot him in the belly, the heavy rounds from the old Thunder Lizard knocking the man off his feet and sending him sprawling on the sidewalk.

"Go!" Ben shouted, already moving toward the brick home.

The quiet town suddenly erupted in gunfire.

Twelve

Ben and team made it to the house just seconds before all hell broke loose around them. Ben kicked open the front door and was immediately confronted by a man and woman, both with guns in their hands.

"The devil!" they both shouted in unison, and lifted their guns.

Ben pulled the trigger and the old M-14 howled and bucked in his hands, the slugs knocking the couple backward against the wall. They slid down, eyes open in death, leaving a bloody smear on the wall behind them.

"So much for hospitality in this town," Ben said, then turned to the front of the house. "Cooper, you and Anna take the back. Jersey and Beth, left and right. Corrie, you and I will cover the front."

Ben wanted the radio close to him to keep in touch with the other battalions. He had a hunch this fire-fight wouldn't last long, for the Border supporters, at least in this town, were too far outnumbered for that, but it was going to be extremely intense while it did last.

"In the house!" came the shout from outside. "The Satan ran into the house after he killed Charles. We've got Ben Raines trapped!"

In the rear of the house, Cooper and Anna opened up with a few shots and screams of pain followed. Cursing drifted from the backyard.

"Not so good Christians," Ben heard Anna say when the

cursing had stopped. "They don't take their religion very seriously, I'm thinking."

"Everyone is entitled to lose it now and then," Ben called with a smile.

"Sure, General Ben," the teenager said, very sarcastically.

Half a dozen men foolishly jumped from behind cover and began running across the road, charging the front of the house. Ben and Corrie cut them down with short bursts. One flopped in the street, screaming hoarsely from the slugs in his belly.

During the few seconds' lull, Corrie bumped the others. She listened for a moment, then looked at Ben. "All battalions on both fronts coming under attack from civilians."

"Somebody planned this one pretty well," Ben admitted.

"They counted on our generosity toward sick civilians, boss," Corrie said. "Do we change our policy now?"

Ben hesitated. "I don't know."

"Heads up!" Jersey shouted from the left side of the house.

Bullets began shattering windows all around the house, the lead whining and howling around the defenders. Several men again foolishly tried a frontal attack, charging across the road. Ben and Corrie put them down in the street, to die alongside their friends.

"Stupid," Corrie muttered.

"They don't have heavy machine guns, mortars, or rifle launched grenades," Ben said, taking a sip of water from one of his two canteens. "Thank the gods of war for that much."

"But if we had waited six more months before launching our offensive . . ." Corrie let that trail off.

"Yeah," Ben agreed. "We would have been in deep shit, for sure."

On the right side of the house, Beth's CAR hammered briefly, then was silent.

"You all right, Beth?" Ben called.

"Just fine, boss. But three of Border's supporters aren't doing so well."

"Here come the tanks," Corrie said.

There was nothing subtle at all about the tanks. The sixty-odd-ton MBTs just ran right through the houses on the other side of the street, smashing anything and anybody who might be foolish enough to be inside.

"Be sure they know what house we're in," Ben said drily.

Corrie laughed. "That's the first thing I told them."

One of the lead tanks cut loose with its main gun and a house near the end of the street exploded in a mass of lumber and brick and dust. A man came stumbling out, screaming his shock and anger, and minus his left arm, the blood spurting with each heartbeat. He cursed Ben Raines and then collapsed near the street and did not move.

"Welcome to the war," Corrie said softly. "It isn't so much fun now, is it, partner?"

Corrie knew, as did all Rebels, that a great many people, civilian non-combatants mostly, had a very romanticized concept of war. Usually that perception didn't linger long; it took one confrontation with the Rebels to slap that silly notion out of them . . . permanently.

From the rear of the yard, Ben and his team heard the rumble of another tank, then the ear-splitting howl of its main gun cutting loose. The house directly behind the house where Ben and team had taken cover exploded as a HE round impacted.

"Oh, my God, my God!" a woman cried.

Corrie listened dispassionately to the pleas, no expression on her tanned face. She unwrapped a stick of gum and popped it into her mouth, chewing slowly.

The cries of the wounded woman abruptly ceased.

"The mule and the two-by-four syndrome," Ben said.

"You bet," Corrie agreed. "Sometimes you just have to get people's attention to make them listen."

"I think we succeed this day, Corrie."

"At least with these folks, boss."

Ben knew exactly what she meant: the people in the next town, and the next, and the next, and so on, would fight. It would not end here.

Front and back of the house, Rebels could be seen, clearing the surrounding homes of hostiles. They soon had a small gathering of prisoners sitting in the middle of the street, their hands clasped on the top of their heads.

"All clear," Corrie said.

Ben and his team walked out of the house to stand for a moment in the front yard. They received looks of hatred from the men and women in the street, the team ignored the hot looks. They were accustomed to the hateful glances.

"Casualties?" Ben asked.

"One dead, half a dozen wounded. None seriously."

"The other battalions?"

"It's all over up and down the line. The batt coms are asking what to do with the prisoners?"

"Carefully search the towns, confiscate all the weapons, and then turn the people loose. That's all we can do. We can't handle hundreds of prisoners."

"The wounded?"

Ben sighed. "Patch the bastards up. We wait until all battalions are through, then move out simultaneously. Corrie?"

"Boss?"

"Tell the cooks to set up the mess tents. I'm hungry."

Mike Richards radioed in the next day that the failed ambushes really set Simon Border off. It was reported to Mike by one of his people inside the Border camp that Simon flew into a rage at the failure of his people to kill Ben Raines, especially when everything seemed to be working so beautifully at first. They had Ben in a box, trapped cold, set up for the kill . . . so what happened?

Mike added that he was sure there was going to be a very drastic and immediate shake-up in Simon's top commanders.

"Bruno Bottger's people?" Ben asked.

"You got it, Ben. My people inside have reported some real arrogant bastards strutting around. They speak with a very heavy accent."

"Real old-time Prussian types, huh. Hard to believe, Mike."

"Well, hell, Ban, think about it. Bruno professes to be a very religious man, just like Simon. Bruno hates all minority groups, just like Simon. He wants an all-white society, just like Simon . . ."

"Now wait a minute, Mike. Back up here. I thought Simon welcomed all races and creeds and colors into his fold?"

"That was what everyone else was led to believe too, Ben. But I never bought it. You'll remember I told you some time back I thought that was all a scam. Oh, he's got minorities all over the place, but they're not equal to whites and never will be. And he's killed every Jew he found living in the territory he now occupies."

"Do you suppose he's been working with Bruno all along?"

"I don't have any proof of that, Ben. But it's something that's been nagging at me for some time. It certainly wouldn't come as any surprise."

"Well, if it's true, and I suspect it is, we'll cope with it. How about the supplies we dropped to you?"

"We got them all and we're ready to go."

"Good luck, Mike."

"Thanks. Mike, out."

"So Field Marshal General Grand Poobah Bottger is back in the game, huh, boss?" Corrie asked, taking the mic from Ben.

"Looks like it, Corrie. One more little hill to climb."

"You think Bottger is Stateside?"

"I don't know. If I had to guess, I'd say no. No reason for Bottger to leave the little kingdom he's set up in Africa. But he's got one of his top people running things over here, you can bet on that."

"You want me to bump the others with this news?"

"Yes. Do that. They need to know what we're going to be up against."

"No proof of it yet," she reminded Ben.

"Be sure and tell them that it's only a hunch. When you've done that, advise Cecil of it and have him bump our team in Africa. Ask them to check it out from their end."

"We're really going over there, aren't we, boss?"

"I imagine so, Corrie. Looks that way."

"And that's when we're really going to get bogged down."

Ben sighed. He agreed wholeheartedly with his longtime radio tech and friend. He frowned and shook his head. "What say we don't worry about that until the time comes?"

She laughed at the expression on Ben's face. She knew that Ben did not want to get all tied up in Africa. Few Rebels did, and that included most of the Blacks in the ranks, and she knew that Cecil was adamantly opposed to sending Rebels to Africa. But she also knew that if Ben ordered it, there would be no hesitation on anyone's part. They would go. She slowly nodded her head in agreement and watched as Ben left the mobile CP.

"And away we go," Cooper said softly, as Ben closed the door behind him.

Jersey picked up her CAR and walked to the door. "We all knew it was coming," she said, then opened the door and stepped outside.

Corrie turned to her bank of electronic equipment and made sure anything she sent and received was on scramble. She keyed the mic. "All battalions, all battalions. Heads up, boys and girls. I do have news . . ."

Thirteen

Ben and his 1 Batt left behind them a thoroughly demoralized and very pissed-off bunch of townspeople, the lucky survivors of the ill-fated ambush. They headed north on a highway that probably would be non-existent in a few more years.

"We have to stay on this one," Ben told his company commanders. "Highway 1, the coastline highway, is gone. Rock slides, cave-ins, earthquakes . . . it's just gone. Scouts are reporting a number of people living in and around the towns on the coast, but they are definitely not Border supporters, or supporters of ours, for that matter. It seems the Hippie movement of several decades past is once more flourishing." Ben smiled. "We'll have to keep that from Thermopolis, he might decide to desert if he learned of it."

"Why don't we be sure and tell Emil?" Jersey said, a hopeful note behind her words. "That might get rid of him once and for all."

Those in attendance laughed and nodded their heads in agreement, but most liked the little con artist . . . in small doses.

"From this point on," Ben continued, "we're going to be fighting every foot of the way. Our next major city is San Luis Obispo. There, we're going to meet the so-called 'born-again' punk faction of Border's army. We know they can fight, and we all know how vicious they are toward prisoners. Well, we're not going to give them much chance to take any Rebel prisoners." Ben smiled, very thinly. "As a matter of fact, we're not going to give them any chance to take prisoners, or to do anything else for that matter."

The CO's all returned Ben's smile. They knew exactly what he was going to do: reduce the shell of a city to smoking ruins by air strikes and artillery barrages.

"That's it, people," Ben concluded. "We pull out in the morning."

"Says here," Beth said, reading from one of her endless tourist brochures, "that San Luis Obispo is a lovely city, filled with Victorian homes. A creek wanders through some shopping area, and the shops are quaint."

"Quaint?" Cooper asked.

"That's what it says, Coop. Quaint."

"I think we knocked the quaintness out of the city a few years back," Ben said. "Now it's just filled with punks."

"Who all believe that Simon Border is Lord on Earth," Corrie added.

"Sure, they do," Ben replied, and lifted an old map of the city. "And everybody who believes that shout hooray and whistle Dixie."

"I can whistle Dixie," Anna said, and did so, but she was not much of a whistler and was horribly off-key.

Ben slipped into silent remembrance while the others in the big wagon grinned at Anna's attempts at whistling.

Ben recalled the time, years back, when the nation was more or less functioning in a somewhat orderly fashion, he had lectured at a writers' conference in San Luis Obispo. He had met a very lovely lady there, and they had enjoyed each other's company over that long weekend. She had driven them down a few miles south of the city and together they had walked the beautiful stretches of Pismo Beach. He recalled that the lady—he couldn't remember her name— was in the middle of a nasty divorce and shortly after that conference, she had gotten her first contract with a major publishing house. Ben wondered what had happened to her. But he didn't like to dwell on that, for he had a pretty good idea what had been her fate: millions of Americans had died during the first few hours of the Great War, some of them quite horribly during the gas attack that had silently choked parts of the nation with clouds of invisible death.

The lady had been quite an idealist, Ben recalled. Peace and love and opposed to the death penalty and believing that all punks and thugs and street crap just needed massive amounts of taxpayer money to be straightened out and they would then live peaceful and fruitful and productive lives.

"Aircraft ready to start striking the city," Corrie broke into Ben's thoughts. "Artillery will be in place and ready to go in one hour. Spec ops personnel have seized and are holding a nearby airport. It is useable and the runway is long enough to handle cargo planes for resupply."

"Begin the attack," Ben said softly.

After eighteen hours of continuous bombardment, what had been left of the small city was in burning ruins and the survivors of the barrage began staggering out in shocked and silent surrender, their hands in the air. The Rebels had not lost a single person.

Just to the east, Ike and his 2 Batt had seized and disarmed the residents of half a dozen small towns between highways 101 and 5. Dan and his 3 Batt were meeting little resistance as they drove north on Interstate 5 and West was paralleling them on highway 99, and was in the process of taking the ruins of Bakersfield.

The Rebels' relentless march north was in high gear, and most of the supporters of Simon Border had never seen anything to match the cold-blooded ruthlessness of the Rebel army.

"The devil's army!" one prisoner had told Georgi.

"Bah!" the Russian had rumbled in reply.

Ben and his team had circled around their smoking and burning objective and were bivouacked just north of the city. The winds were coming from the west, blowing the stinking odor of burning human flesh away from them.

"Bringing in about half a dozen prisoners, boss," Jersey said.

Ben looked up from a map. "Are they human, or what?"

Jersey laughed. The prisoners being marched up were covered head to foot with dirt and soot.

"Halt!" one of the guards barked, and the prisoners came to a very sloppy stop. "This bunch claims to be some of the leaders of the groups that were in the city, General. They asked to speak to you."

"Thank you." Ben cut his eyes to gaze for a moment at the sorry sight in front of him. "I'm General Raines. What do you want?"

"To tell you that we forgive you, General," one of the prisoners said. "We know the reason you attacked us was because you haven't as yet seen the light of the true Lord on Earth and accepted his gentle ways."

Cooper almost choked on his sandwich, Beth looked stunned, Jersey openly laughed, and Anna frowned. Ben smiled. "I assume by that you mean Simon 'Birdbrain' Border?"

"Insulting the great man only lowers yourself, General."

"So you boys have seen the light, eh?"

"Yes, sir. We have been borned again. Hallelujah, amen."

"Washed in the blood, so to speak?" Ben asked.

"That's right, General," another said.

"Were you sprinkled or full immersion?"

"Haw?"

Ben waved that aside and took the slip of paper a runner just handed him. "From Captain Reeder, sir."

Ben opened the folded paper and read: "FOUND ABOUT TWO DOZEN PRISONERS, ALL WOMEN,

AGES APPROXIMATELY 12 TO 40. THEY'VE BEEN HELD PRISONERS FOR A COUPLE OF WEEKS AND RAPED AND SODOMIZED REPEATEDLY BY THESE SO-CALLED CHRISTIANS."

"No reply, son," Ben said to the runner. He pointed to a nearby mess tent just set up, the cooks busy preparing the evening meal. "Get yourself a cup of coffee and relax for a moment."

"Thank you, sir."

Ben turned back to the prisoners. "Tell me, what do you do with your prisoners?"

"We try to convince them to accept the ways of the Lord on Earth, General."

"Using gentle methods, I'm sure."

"Of course, General. The Good Book says 'Do unto others as you would have them do unto you.' "

"Uh-huh," Ben muttered. He cleared his throat. Held up the communiqué. "Then perhaps you might like to tell me about these women prisoners? Their stories about treatment seem to conflict somewhat with your version."

The expression on the faces of the prisoners changed only slightly, but enough for Ben to guess that somebody screwed up; the women were probably supposed to have been killed just before surrender.

"I, uh, don't know what you mean, General," one of the punk leaders said. "We always treated prisoners well. The women you speak of must be lying."

"Sure, they are," Ben said sarcastically. "Or just maybe you boys are the ones lying?"

One of the gang leaders suddenly broke and ran. He got about five feet away from the group before a Rebel guard gave him the butt of a rifle in the gut, stopping the man abruptly and doubling him over, gagging and puking on his way to the ground.

"Very dumb move," Ben said. "Innocent people have never had anything to fear from the Rebels."

"Your mind's made up, ain't it, General?" another gang leader spoke.

"No. But it will be when these women pick you men out of a line-up as their tormentors."

"And then what are you going to do with us?" another gang leader asked, his voice shaky.

Standing off to one side, Anna laughed.

The women told of gang rape and other forms of sexual deviation at the hands of the gangs in the city. Then the women and girls picked out the men who had both ordered and taken part in the sexual torture. The men were then PSE'd and polygraphed—tests they all failed miserably. Finally one of the gang leaders broke and told the truth. He was the only one who was spared the firing squad that cool, cloudy day. The others were buried in a mass grave.

Rebel justice was thorough, but very quick.

"Enemy troops are pulling back all up and down the front," Scouts told their batt coms and the batt coms radioed the news to Ben's rolling CP.

"It appears to be a coordinated mass pull-back," another group of long-range Scouts radioed in. "Military and civilian are withdrawing."

"They're leaving everything behind and bugging out," yet another team of Scouts reported.

"What the hell is going on, Ben?" Ike radioed.

"Simon's cutting his territory down to a more manageable size, I'd guess," Ben responded "If that's really what he's doing, it's a damn smart move."

"What's Mike have to say about it?" West asked. There were five batt coms on a hook-up to Ben's CP: Ike, Dan, West, Georgi and Rebet.

"It came as a total surprise to him. He's still trying to get some intel to pass along."

"Orders, Ben?"

"We're going to push ahead, but very slowly, keeping one hell of a sharp eye out for booby-traps. Corrie's passing that word along to the rest of the batt coms now. I want every town inspected carefully; every piece of propaganda taken and studied by our intel people and filed away." Ben chuckled. "And just like back in the days of yore, folks, when we were just getting started: anything the Rebels can possibly use, take it and pack it for shipment back home."

Ben waited until the laughter had died down, both at the other batt coms CP's and in his own, before saying, "I suspect that Simon's tightening his front, people. If that is the case, it's going to be a tough nut to crack. He'll have a front miles deep and this time his supporters will defend it to the death. I'm going to try to talk to Simon, for whatever good that will do; try to talk some sense into the man. I'll tell him again, he can have his damn country, but he's going to have to pull all his people out of the other parts of North America; dismantle all the cells he and Bruno have set up."

"He'll deny even knowing the existence of Bottger," Dan opined.

"Sure, he will," Ben said. "That is, if he even bothers to speak to such as low-life as I. Just sit tight for another day, boys. I'll get back to you."

Ben turned to Corrie. "Is Simon responding to our call?"

"Not a peep, boss. And I've been sending for two days. I know he's receiving it. Or at least his communications people are."

"Keep trying, Corrie. For one more day, until we pull out. Everything you're sending is clear. There are people all over North America picking it up. No one can ever deny that we didn't attempt to communicate with Simon Border."

"If he hasn't by now, he isn't going to respond to our call, boss."

"I know, Corrie. I'm sure you're right. But I've got to try just one more time."

Ben walked over to his desk and sat down, opening a map of North America and smoothing it out. He took a pencil and carefully outlined the states of Oregon, Washington, Idaho, Montana, and Wyoming. "That's what he's going to claim," Ben muttered. "I'll bet my boots on it. Simon, I'll let you have, if you'll just agree to stop this war."

Ben leaned back in his chair. "Talk to me, Simon. Talk to me."

Corrie kept repeating her call throughout the day, urging Simon Border to respond.

But there was no response.

At 1800 hours, Ben walked into his rolling CP and looked at the radio tech who had relieved Corrie. She shook her head. "Negative, General."

"Then shut it down," Ben ordered. "Go back to scramble and advise the other batt coms we move out as planned."

"Yes, sir." The tech hesitated. She was not a part of Ben's personal team, and not as close to the general as Corrie and the others . . . but then, nobody was. "We tried, General. No one can say we didn't try."

Ben smiled at her, the smile softening his features, which had hardened and lined with age. "You're right. And we can all take some comfort in that. Thank you."

"You're welcome, sir."

A few moments later, Corrie stepped into the CP and jerked a thumb at her relief. The tech left her post and quickly exited the large room. Being around the general made her very nervous. "Susie bump all the others, boss?"

"She did. We move out in the morning. Does Susie have a medical condition or something? She seemed extremely nervous to me."

Corrie smiled. "Just anxious to get going, I suppose, boss."

"Oh. Sure. Of course. I didn't think of that."

Corrie ducked her head and pretended to check the bank of equipment in front of her. How to tell the general that most of his troops considered him to be the next thing to a god, and always had? That was a question that Ben's personal team had to deal with every day. She suspected that Ben knew how the troops felt, but didn't know quite how to deal with it.

Ben Raines was the most loved, respected, and most hated man in all of North America.

Of course, Ben knew that. Corrie smiled as she recalled Ben's usual response to his critics. "Well, fuck 'em, if they can't take a joke."

Fourteen

"Eerie," Cooper said, stopping the big wagon at the edge of town.

A Scout suddenly popped out of the brush by the side of the road and walked up to the wagon, passenger side. "A few people in the town, General. Just a handful who elected not to go with the others. They said they're tired of fighting Simon's battles and just want to go back home. And they're clean. We stripped them down to their skivvies. They have no weapons."

Ben nodded his understanding. "We'll be right over there at that old service station. Bring them to me."

"Coming right up, sir."

There were four men and four women, seven kids. The adults stood awkwardly in front of Ben. The kids were outside, eating candy bars and chewing gum . . . they had never before seen or tasted either. The medics were on the way to check them out.

"All right, people," Ben addressed the group. "What's the story?"

"We're tired of sacrificing for Simon Border," a man replied. "We just want to go back to Ohio and try to pick up where we left off."

"You have transportation?"

"Yes, sir."

"Then as soon as the kids are checked out and receive their shots, you can take off."

"Thank you, General," a woman said.

"What's Simon up to this time?" Ben asked.

"Pulling back," another man said. "The faithful packed up and followed his orders without hesitation. We have been talking about going home for months. This seemed like the right time to do it."

"Simon is going to claim the states of Oregon, Washington, Idaho, Montana, and Wyoming?"

"We don't know, General. Only our leaders knew the faithful's final destination."

Ben asked a few more questions, but received little information that he didn't already know. He believed much of what the men and women had to say, but suspected they knew more than they were admitting. He questioned them closely about where they were going, and decided they were telling the truth about that. "I'm going to radio the governor about you people. Warn him would be a better word. At the first sign of your setting up another of Simon Border's churches, I hope he boots you out. Should that happen, don't head south to the SUSA. We won't tolerate it. Understood?"

"There is such a thing as religious freedom, General," one of the women said softly.

"Not when there is a political agenda that runs counter to the beliefs of the nation, lady," Ben came right back. "Oh, those outside the SUSA might put up with it, liberals being what they are, but we damn sure won't."

There was no more to say. The group got the message Ben was putting down, very loud and clear. Ben watched them leave the makeshift CP. He had serious doubts about the bunch ever making it, for Simon's brainwashing was very thorough. But God help them if they ever came to the SUSA and tried to spread the word of Simon Border.

By the end of the day one thing stood out in Ben's mind: the followers of Simon Border lived a very spartan life, with few luxuries. Of course, most residents of a socialistic form of government did. Socialism, like communism, at least to a certain type of mentality, looked good on paper, or in theory. In practice, it never turned out quite as good as it sounded. And there were growing signs that many of the followers of Simon Border were unhappy with some aspects of Border's rule.

Back in his rolling CP, Ben sat down behind his desk and smiled. Simon's move to condense his territory just might backfire.

He looked up. Corrie was watching him, his long-time friend and radio tech knowing when Ben had something on his mind. When Ben's smile suddenly widened, she guessed accurately that he had come up with something very sneaky.

"Bump all batt coms, Corrie. New orders. Let Simon pull his people into the five state area. All battalions follow at a safe distance. Do not engage the enemy unless they force the fire-fight."

Corrie blinked. "That's it?"

"That's it."

"Boss . . . Far-Eyes are reporting that already Simon's people are working around the clock setting up a front that stretches for hundreds of miles, beginning in Southern Oregon at the Pacific Ocean and running all the way east to the Wyoming/Nebraska border and then cutting north all the way up to the Canadian border."

"That's right, Corrie."

"Then? . . ." She spread her hands.

Ben laughed. "Simon might not choose to talk to me about his new territory. But I can damn sure let him settle it; let him feel all safe and comfy within his borders." Ben leaned back, a very smug look on his face.

"And then, boss?"

"Then we go in and wreck it."

"We do?"

"We do."

"We attack his front?"

"No.

Corrie sighed, knowing Ben was playing games with her and enjoying every second of it. The rest of Ben's team sat silently for the moment, letting the two have at it.

"We don't launch an all-out assault on his front?" Beth broke the silence.

"Not really," Ben replied.

"Oh, shit!" Jersey breathed, putting it together. She knew Ben's mind better than most; knew how devious he could be, and also how the man loved to take chances.

"Something the matter, Jersey?" Ben asked innocently.

"I really hope you're not thinking what I think you're thinking," the little bodyguard said.

Ben smiled for a moment. "Corrie, have the riggers start unpacking and drying out all available chutes."

"Oh, shit!" Jersey repeated. Jumping out of airplanes was not her favorite pastime.

"Who is going to jump where?" Anna asked.

"We are," Ben replied.

"Where?" Cooper asked.

"Smack in the middle of Simon Border's new territory," Ben told them with a laugh.

"You have got to be kidding!" Beth blurted.

"Nope. It's a beautiful plan, I think."

"One that the other batt coms will shoot down as soon as you bring it up," Corrie told him. "That is, if you're thinking of going in, too."

"I wouldn't miss it for the world."

"I don't even want to be around when Ike hears of this," Cooper said.

"We'll sit on it until it's time to go . . . as much as possible," Ben warned his team.

"Come on, boss!" Corrie said. "There is too much planning involved in something like this to exclude the others until the last minute."

"Well . . . you're right, I suppose. I'll just have to listen to them bitch."

They all knew Ben was playing a game, leading them along and enjoying it. He never did anything of this magnitude without careful planning.

"Small hit and run guerilla units," Anna said, her pale eyes gleaming with anticipation. "I love it."

"You're not going," Ben told her.

She laughed at that.

"I mean it, Anna."

"I am jump-qualified," she said.

"You did so without my approval," her adopted father told her.

"Doesn't matter how I did it, I did it," the young woman stood her verbal ground. "And I've jumped into combat before."

Ben frowned. He couldn't deny that last statement. "We'll see about it."

"Uh-huh," Anna said.

"Corrie, order Base Camp One to start flying in explosives. You know what to ask for."

Corrie sighed. "Yes, sir."

"It's cold and snowy up there in the north," Cooper said mournfully.

"We have plenty of winter gear," Ben reminded him.

"You've got to inform Ike and the others," Corrie insisted.

"Later, Corrie."

"We might have to ski some of the time," Anna said brightly. "I am expert on skis."

"I'm not," Cooper said, twice as mournfully as before.

Anna snapped her fingers. "It's that easy. I will show you all. I've been skiing ever since I can remember. We had to ski sometimes to escape from the creepies back in the old country. It's fun."

"Wonderful," Jersey muttered. "I'm so looking forward to this."

"It'll never fly, boss," Beth said firmly. "General McGowan will raise so much hell you'll have to reconsider."

Ben's smiled widened. "I can hardly wait to have him try."

"You're fuckin' plannin' on us doin' fuckin' *what?* " Ike screamed over the air, his words coming out distorted over the speaker.

"Told you," Beth whispered to the others in the team.

"Not you, Ike," Ben replied. "You're much too large for jumping. I plan on placing you in charge of the troops that maintain the blockade."

"Large!" Ike screamed.

"Well . . . yes," Ben said, smiling.

"I am not large, Ben! I'm . . . I'm . . . stocky, that's all."

"You're too fat, Ike, and you know it. We'll have to double chute you." Ben had to bite his lip to keep from laughing. He could just imagine the expression on Ike's face.

"If I'm too fat then you're too fuckin' *old,* Ben!" Ike roared.

"I am in perfect physical condition for my age, Ike," Ben said calmly. "I have already been cleared by the doctors for this operation."

"Not by this doctor you haven't!" Lamar Chase came yelling over the air.

"When you left on your inspection tour, Lamar, you placed Dr. Cohen in charge, remember. He gave me a complete physical just this morning. I'm set to go."

"I know you, Raines," Lamar yelled. "You intimidated Dr. Cohen. I know you did. I've seen you work before. I absolutely, positively *forbid* you to jump, Raines. And that is a direct order from the Chief of Medicine."

"You can't issue that order until you have examined me, Lamar. And even then, if you didn't lie about it, you'd find me in perfect physical condition, capable of jumping. And you know it, Lamar."

There was a long silence from the other end. "Raines," Lamar finally spoke, "you insufferable jackass. Do you fully realize what you're planning?"

"I do indeed, Lamar. All the way."

"May I remind you that your knees are not the best in the world, Raines." Lamar softened his tone considerably.

"That makes no difference with the type of 'chute I'll be using, Lamar."

"Then I won't argue the point any further, Raines. Here's Ike."

"Ben?" Ike's voice came through the speaker. "What battalions do you plan on jumping in?"

"One, Two, and Eight."

"Two? That's my battalion . . . Why, you lousy . . . you did all that lyin' just to hear me holler!"

"That's right, Ike. I think you've got one more jump in you, don't you?"

"I damn sure do!"

"Buddy's on his way here now. So come on over for some hard skull sessions. We've got a lot of planning to do."

"On my way, Ben."

"Me, too!" Lamar hollered in the background.

Ben hooked the mic and looked around, smiling. "Told you," he said to his team.

Anna rubbed her hands together. "I can hardly wait!" she blurted.

"Shit!" Jersey muttered unhappily.

Fifteen

"We're not going to let the resistance groups in the areas know we're coming in," Ben opened the meeting. "Mike says a lot of them have been infiltrated by Simon's people so that would be suicide for us."

"Just like the militia groups before the Great War," Ike said. "The damn liberals in Washington were so frightened of them they peed their drawers every time they thought of militia or survival groups. Some of them probably looked under their beds at night."

All that was before Buddy's time. He looked at Ben. "Did the leaders in Washington ever really listen to the grievances of those who joined the various groups and do anything about them?"

"Why, hell, no, son," Ben replied. "They gave them lip service occasionally, but that was about it. Our so-called leaders in Washington always thought they knew what was best for everybody."

"And as it turned out? . . . ." Buddy asked softly.

"The senators and representatives didn't know nearly as much as they thought they did," Ben said flatly, moving to a map. "My hunch is dropping in here." He pointed to the very top of Washington State. "Buddy, you and your 8 batt boys and girls will drop in near the Vancouver/Portland area. Ike, you and your people will drop into Southern Oregon. We split up into small groups and start raising hell as soon as we hit the ground. We blow up everything that is still standing from the top of Washington down to the Oregon/California border." Ben looked at his son and his longtime friend. "We'll be doing this to demoralize Simon's civilian supporters, fuck up his factories and supply lines, and terrorize his troops . . . among other things. We're going to blow every bridge we find and tear up the newly laid railroad tracks that Simon is so proud of. Simon thinks he's going to establish trade with a few foreign countries. He's had people working on docks and ships for some time now. But he's not going to have any ships to set to sea when we're through . . ."

"You've been doing some planning on this, haven't you, Ben?" Ike asked.

"A little. All right, maps, supply points, safe houses, and some of the militia groups we know we can trust are included in your info packets. Start getting your people briefed."

"We don't have enough planes to drop us all at once, Ben," Ike pointed out. "We're talking many thousands of troops here."

"That's right. We'll be going in over a three-day period. Start raising hell just as soon as you're on the ground. I want Simon's troops spread all over the place." He smiled. "However, there will be diversions for several days beginning when the first plane of jumpers takes off . . . just to give us a little breathing room. It's all explained in your packets. I'll talk to you again on the ground up north."

Outside the CP, Buddy put a strong hand on Ike's forearm, halting him. "Why is Father doing this, Ike?"

Ike grinned. "Several reasons, Buddy: because he wants a little excitement, is one. Me and your father, we know we haven't got that many more good years in the field. That growling ol' bear, Georgi, is going to have to give it up pretty quickly himself. Probably before Ben and me. And Dan is no young rooster either. And there are other tactical reasons. But I think the main reason Ben is doing this is rather than commit all our Rebel battalion to several years' fight against one hell of a front, and lose a lot of people in the process, he figures we can shorten it considerable this way. And we can, if we do this right."

"My father wants some excitement," Buddy said softly.

"That's right, boy, and so do I. Your dad is a warrior, son. His whole life is the field. Hell, this is *his* show, all the way. Oh, he might tell you he's looking forward to the rocking chair on the porch, and so might I if I've had a few drinks, but we'd both be lyin'. We're combat people, boy. Always have been and always will be. Both of us, your dad and me, when it comes our time, we want to check out in the field, growlin' and snappin' and snarlin' as we go into that long night. You understand what I'm talkin' about, Buddy?"

The muscular young man smiled. "Yes, Ike. I understand."

Ike looked at him suspiciously. "What ever happened to Uncle Ike, boy?"

"I stopped using it. That just doesn't seem very dignified, Ike."

Ike smiled and made a silent promise to try and stop calling Buddy "boy." The young man was all grown up.

Mother Nature suddenly decided to put everything on hold, lashing the coast with heavy rains to the south and snow and ice up north, soaking Ben's plans to a soggy halt.

"Only good thing about this crappy weather," Ben groused one afternoon, staring out at the rain, "is that it's affecting Simon's plans as well."

"Suits me," Jersey murmured, too low for Ben to hear. But Beth heard her and grinned.

"Meteorologists say this is likely to continue for a week or more," Corrie said. "It's a major winter storm."

Ben grunted his irritation at the delay.

Because of the weather, hundreds of parachutes would have to be unpacked, unfolded, stretched out, and dried before repacking. More delays

"Look on the bright side, boss," Cooper said.

Ben turned. "What bright side?"

"The weather is not keeping the planes from flying. We'll have everything we need on hand by the time the weather breaks, plus months of gear for resupplying."

Ben nodded his head. He certainly couldn't argue that. "All right, Coop. There is a small bright side."

"And time for me to maybe break a leg," Jersey muttered.

Ben heard her that time and laughed at the diminutive warrior. "You know you love jumping, Jersey," he kidded her.

"Oh, yeah, boss—right."

Jersey, because of her size, was always the last one on the ground, and should a sudden updraft occur, she had been known to soar hundreds of feet back up, cussing and hollering all the way.

"You could always piggy-back with me," Cooper suggested hopefully.

Jersey gave him a very dark look.

Lamar Chase jerked open the door to the mobile CP and stepped inside. He stood in the doorway and shook off his poncho. Cooper poured the doctor a mug of coffee from the ever-present pot and Chase thanked him and sat down. The chief of medicine took a sip and grinned at Ben.

Ben scowled at him. "I suppose you find this weather amusing, right, you quack?"

Lamar laughed at Ben. "It's keeping your ass on the ground, Raines."

"And that pleases you?"

"Immensely." He took another sip and lifted the mug. "Good coffee, Cooper."

"Thank you, sir. But I didn't make it. The boss did."

Lamar frowned. "I retract that statement. It's probably poison."

"You're just PO'd 'cause you can't go along with us," Ben said. "When we go, that is," he muttered.

"I have absolutely no desire to hurl my precious body out of a perfectly good airplane, Raines," Chase countered. "If something would happen, just think of all the disappointed women I would leave behind."

Ben snorted in derision.

"Did the doctors find anything wrong with me?" Jersey asked hopefully.

"Not a thing, Jersey," Chase told her. "You're as healthy as a racehorse."

The rest of the team laughed at the crestfallen expression on Jersey's face.

"I hate to bring this up," Beth said. "But Emil wants to go along."

"He can keep on hoping," Ben said. "That's all we need to screw things up. Who told you that, Beth?"

"Thermopolis."

Ben smiled. "Tell Therm, Emil can go along only if Therm accompanies him."

Everyone in the mobile CP laughed, even Jersey, knowing that would put at end to it. The ex-hippie wouldn't jump out of an airplane under threat of death. Rosebud, his wife, would, but not Therm. Therm didn't even like to fly. "God did not give man wings for a reason," he liked to say.

Chase chatted for a few moments, then left the CP. He would stay in the area until jump-off time, going over supplies his medical people would take along on the offensive, and double and triple-checking everything.

Ben looked out the window and shook his head as the rain intensified. "It has to stop sometime. God promised He wouldn't use water to destroy the earth again."

* * *

Ben opened his eyes and glanced at the small travel clock on the nightstand attached to the side of the wall of the mobile CP. 1:30. He'd gone to sleep earlier than usual, and Ben had never needed more than a few hours' sleep a night to refresh his body.

Then he sat straight up in the single bed. Something was wrong.

He reached for his CAR, then pulled his hand back, smiling in the darkness. There was no rain drumming on the roof. The downpour had stopped.

Ben dressed quickly and made his way silently through the CP, stepping outside and looking up into the sky. Billions of stars greeted his eyes. The moon was full and bright. There was not a cloud to be seen.

"What the hell? . . ." Jersey spoke from out of the darkness.

"It stopped," Ben said. "The rain's stopped."

"The meteorologists said a couple more days of rain."

"They were wrong. Get Corrie out of the sack and have her alert the pilots to warm up their engines and stand by, then start bumping the battalions."

"We jumping in tonight?"

"We're jumping in tonight."

Minutes later, the bivouac area was pocked with light and quick-shadowed with motion as hundreds of Rebels were rolled out of the sack and made ready for the drop. At the airport, the engines of the huge planes were ticking over and pilots swigged steaming hot coffee, went over their maps, checked their instruments and controls, and thumped tires.

A half hour after Ben awakened on that clear, cold morning, he and his team were struggling into the first plane. They were so weighed down with gear their legs were slightly bowed.

"Mornin', General," the jumpmaster shouted to be heard over the roar of dozens of engine.

Ben nodded and took his seat near the door, his team lining up in seats next to him. They would be the first ones out.

The co-pilot stuck his head out of the cockpit and motioned for Ben to put on the headset hanging near him. It was Ike.

"How's it hangin', Ben?" Ike drawled.

"My dick is just fine, Ike. But my asshole is beginning to pucker up."

Ike laughed. "Yeah, mine, too. These things never get any easier with age, do they?"

"Not that I can tell."

"I am perfectly relaxed," Buddy's calm voice came on the frequency.

"That's because you're young, boy," his father popped right back. "And don't have enough sense to know what you're doing."

Jersey, sitting next to Ben and wearing a headset, gave him a very jaundiced look through her expressive eyes, but reserved comment. Ben looked at her and winked.

She rolled her eyes.

Anna laughed at her antics.

"Any glitches so far?" Ben questioned.

"Nothing major, Ben. The usual hassles is all."

"Buddy?"

"Nothing here, Father. We're ready to go."

The plane containing Ben and team lurched forward. Ben's battalion would be the first one airborne; they had the farthest to travel. The others would he staggered behind 1 Batt and would fly at reduced speed and if need be, circle until all jumpers were ready to go simultaneously.

"Good luck, you old fart," Dr. Lamar Chase's voice came into Ben's ears.

"Thank you, Lamar, but I assume you are speaking to Ike," Ben replied.

Chase laughed. "Yeah, good luck to you too, lard-butt."

"Lard-butt!" Ike shouted.

Buddy began laughing at the exchange.

"Keep your powder dry and your dick in your pants, boys," Lamar said.

"What do we keep in our pants, Doctor?" Jane Pollard, a platoon leader with Buddy's 8 batt asked.

Lamar harumped a few times and refused to reply to that question.

"You tell 'im, you mean mama," Ike said with a laugh.

Real sexual harassment was virtually unknown in the Rebel army. That had been accomplished in part by everyone knowing the next person had live ammo, too, and would not hesitate to drop the hammer on the offender. In the Rebel army, there were no special privileges offered to the female gender. In physical training they had to perform as well as their male counterparts, or they were reassigned to a less demanding non-combat job. Fuck up, and you're out, no matter the gender.

"We get all the good jobs, General Ike," Jane kidded the ex-SEAL. "General Raines knows we get the job done right the first time."

"Oh, sure, Jane," Ike kidded right back. "Right."

"We're airborne," Ben put an end to the banter. "Good luck, everybody."

"General Raines to pilot. How's the weather over the DZ?"

"Clear and starry, General."

Ben and his people would be jumping static line from fifteen hundred feet . . . but that was several hours away. For now, Ben leaned his head back, made himself as comfortable as possible, folded his arms over his reserve, and promptly went to sleep. No point in worrying about anything now. As Ben was fond of saying, "I never sweat the small shit."

Sixteen

The first teams from Ben's 1 Batt started dropping in just west of the ruins of Tacoma. Ben slept on. Jersey finally had to shake him awake.

"We'll be over the DZ in a few minutes, boss."

Ben nodded and struggled to his boots to stretch and get the kinks out of his muscles. He walked up and then back down the cavernous interior of the huge plane, smiling at his people.

The doors in the rear of the plane opened and freezing air filled the interior. "Won't be long now," Ben muttered.

The jumpmaster caught his eye and gave him a hand signal. "Stand up and check equipment!" Ben shouted.

The long lines of jumpers struggled to their boots and began checking the equipment and harness of the Rebel in front of them. Ben waddled to the rear of the plane. The red light popped on.

"Hook up!" Ben shouted, hooking his static line to the wire. He moved closer to the yawning doors. He felt the old familiar rush of adrenaline flood his system.

Jersey crowded close behind him, the rest of his team stretched out behind her.

Ben found himself humming an old polka tune: "Roll Out The Barrel." The jumpmaster was looking at him very strangely.

Ben stopped humming and smiled at the man.

The green light popped on.

"Go!" the jumpmaster yelled, slapping Ben on the leg.

Ben stepped out into the cold darkness. He felt a slight tug as his main pulled free and opened, then the opening shock as air filled the canopy and nearly jerked him to a halt midair. He looked around him: the night sky was filled with blossoming 'chutes.

The ground was also coming up fast.

Ben automatically pulled his feet together and willed his legs to relax. He released his equipment bag to the full extent of the tether rope. Then he was on the ground, landing easily. He popped the quick release to his harness and began gathering up his 'chute. He looked up, checking on the drift of the equipment 'chutes. There was no wind to speak of and the equipment 'chutes were falling right on target.

A pathfinder came running up. The pathfinder teams had jumped in hours before, to electronically 'paint' the DZ.

"You all right, sir?" the pathfinder questioned.

"I'm fine. Any trouble here?"

"No, sir. Everything's quiet."

Ben's team quickly gathered around him.

"Get the equipment unpacked," Ben ordered, as he locked a full magazine into place into the belly of his CAR and jacked in a round. "Do it quickly. Corrie, get the team leaders around me, right now!"

Ben looked into the face of one of the doctors who jumped in with them. "Anybody hurt?"

"Couple of twisted ankles. One man with a minor back injury," the doctor reported.

"How'd he hurt his back? As if I didn't know."

"Landed with his feet spread apart, General. Said he wasn't thinking."

Ben nodded in the darkness. "Your gear make it down okay?"

"Yes, sir."

"You're not assigned to me, are you? I don't remember seeing any paperwork on you. What's your name?"

"Mel Farmer. Yes, sir. I'm assigned to you. Doctor Chase's orders, and his orders came from President Jefferys. You're stuck with me, General."

"All right. Damn, boy," Ben peered through the darkness at the doctor. "You're pretty young to be a doctor, aren't you?"

The doctor grinned. "It's all due to my clean living, General."

"Well, we're all going to be filthy as hogs before this op is over. Where's your weapon?"

"I'm a doctor, General. I carry a sidearm. That's all."

"You'll be carrying a rifle before long, I can assure you of that," Ben said grimly. "And using it," he added.

"Perimeters established, boss," Corrie said. "We landed right on the money, between Interstate 5 and highway 9. All battalions are down, no serious injuries reported."

"Good deal." Ben looked around him. "Goddamnit, somebody get the team leaders to me, right now!"

The team leaders began gathering around, most of them coming on the run and panting, loaded down with equipment. This operation was a guerrilla action, the Rebels landing with only a few light machine guns, most of them SAWs, .223 Squad Automatic Weapons. But they were loaded down with plastic explosives and grenades and spare ammo. They had field rations, and not many of those; they would live off the land or they would go hungry until another supply drop.

"Forget Bellingham," Ben told the group. "It's in ruins." Then he spoke quickly to the team leaders and one by one, the men and women began vanishing into the night, running for their teams and heading out for their objectives.

"Let's go, gang," Ben said to the twenty Rebels that made up his team. "We've got some bridges to blow and other hell to raise." Ben used a penlight to quickly scan a map. He pointed. "That way. Let's do it"

They traveled over to the secondary highway that ran north and south and turned south. "What's the population of this little town just up ahead, Beth?"

"The index of my map doesn't even give it, boss. Can't be much to it."

Ben lifted his walkie-talkie and bumped the Scouts who were ranging about a mile ahead. "You reached the town yet?"

"Looking at it now, General. Not much to it. What are we going to do with it?"

"Burn as much of it as we can," Ben said grimly.

"Yes, sir," the Scout replied softly.

Ben hated to have to say that, for he disliked making any type of war on civilians. But these civilians were hardcore Simon Border supporters. Ben recalled a line he'd written in a western novel years back: You ride with outlaws, you die with outlaws.

Ben didn't know then, and he didn't know now, how original that line was, but it read well.

"Civilians just turned onto the highway from a side road!" Ben's radio crackled. "Heading your way in a pickup truck."

The team immediately took to the ditches and brush on both sides of the road. One moment they were walking down both sides of the old highway, five seconds later, they had vanished.

The pickup truck, a very old one, rattled slowly up the road and came to a stop only a few feet from where Ben and his personal team were lying hidden in the tall grass alongside the highway.

"I tell you, John," a man's voice drifted over the sounds of the laboring engine, "my wife said she looked out the window and seen the sky filled with parachutes. Keep goin', man. Why the hell did you stop for?"

"Your wife is full of it, Russell. Look around you. You can see for a mile the stars is so bright. You see any parachutes?"

"No. But that don't mean they wasn't here fifteen minutes ago."

"Then where did they go?"

Half a dozen Rebels, Ben among them, had slipped from cover and made their way silently to stand at both sides of the pickup. Ben stuck the muzzle of his CAR inside the cab and touched the cheek of the driver with the cold metal.

"Shit!" the driver hollered.

"Your friend's wife was right, partner," Ben said. "Turn off the engine."

"If I do that, it might not start again."

"Do it!"

The driver quickly cut the engine and night became quiet.

"Any military people in your town?" Ben asked.

"A few. Who are you?"

"How many is a few?"

" 'Bout twenty or so. Every town of any size has a detachment of the army. Who are you?"

"Jack Armstrong, the All-American boy."

"Huh?"

"Never mind. Get out of the truck. And keep your hands off those weapons on the seat between you."

The driver grunted in disbelief. "The dash lights been out for months. You got good eyes, mister."

"I'm half puma."

"Say *what?*"

"Forget it. Just get out of the truck."

The two neighbors exited the cab of the pickup and stood on the cracked and badly maintained old secondary road. Their eyes widened as more Rebels left cover to surround them.

"Rebels," the second man whispered. "We're being invaded, John."

John stood defiant, his voice holding no fear. "You people better get gone from here. Our army will chew you up and spit you out."

"I doubt it," Ben told him. "Where are the contingent of soldiers billeted?"

"You gonna have to find out for yourself. 'Cause I ain't tellin' you no more!"

Ben chuckled. "I won't sell you short on guts, mister. Just short on common sense for believing anything Simon Border has to say."

"Reverend Border is Lord on Earth, mister. He's a great man."

"Is that 'grate' as in the bottom of an old furnace?"

"Huh?"

"Never mind." Ben turned to a Rebel. "Get this wreck off the highway and into the brush."

"What about these two citizens?"

"We'll take them with us."

Fifteen minutes later, Ben and part of his team stood on the outskirts of the small town.

"Hell," John scoffed. "If this is all of you there is our people won't have no trouble with you. None at all."

Automatic weapons fire suddenly ripped the night, followed by several explosions. A few more shots, and all was silent.

Lights popped on throughout the town. A few men ran out into the street, carrying weapons. They were cut down. One flopped in the street, his chest and belly ripped apart. He screamed once, and then lay still.

Ben looked at John. "You were saying? . . ."

John's face was pale. He shook his head, then said, "Those first shots? . . ."

"Your army contingent being taken care of."

"What happens next?"

"Your town is destroyed."

"We ain't done nothin' to you people!"

"You're right. You, personally, have done nothing to us. But you follow the dictates of Simon Border, and he has declared war on the SUSA and joined forces with a Nazi, Bruno Bottger . . ."

The dozen or so buildings that made up the business district of the town suddenly blossomed in explosion and flames.

"Oh, my God!" Russell whispered.

"This ain't fair," John said.

"War never is," Ben responded, then turned and walked away.

A half hour later, the residents of the town were gathered at the south edge. Many of them stood in open-mouthed shock. Flames from the burning town illuminated the scene by the side of the road. Rebels had destroyed every vehicle in town, all of the businesses and many of the homes.

By this time, Ben had been recognized. A citizen standing a few feet away from him said, "Now you people are making war on civilians, right, General Raines?"

"Just like your glorious leader is doing," Ben replied.

"He is not!"

"You're badly misinformed. Now shut up."

The citizen was silent for only a moment. "It's wintertime, General. What are we to do? You've destroyed everything."

"Leave or stay here and die. It makes no difference to me."

"There are children here, General."

Ben nodded. "Yes. And I'm sorry for that. But we didn't start this war."

"We've left us nothing but a few blankets and no food."

"The children have ample food to last until relief arrives. We saw to that. If you choose to take food from them to stuff your own mouths, then that makes you shit-sorry."

"You're the hardest son of a bitch I ever saw, General."

"You're not the first to say that, and I'm sure you won't be the last." Ben motioned to Corrie. "Move out."

Ben's team destroyed one more small town and blew several bridges that morning. He called a halt an hour after daylight touched the horizon. The Rebels backtracked for several miles from their last objective and took cover in a wooded area. They made a cold camp, field rations and sips of canteen water, no hot food or coffee.

The ruse worked. Searchers drove and flew right past their hiding place and began concentrating miles south of the last blown bridge.

"Our people have been busy," Corrie reported, just before she joined the rest of the Rebels for some much-needed sleep. "Small towns and bridges have been destroyed all the way up and down the line."

"Any losses?"

"None."

Ben knew that wouldn't last. Simon's military leaders would get it together very quickly and really start putting the pressure on the small teams of guerrillas.

"Get some rest. We've got a long night ahead of us and then lots of miles to cover."

But sleep came hard for Ben that morning. He didn't like making war on civilians, but knew that in some cases it had to be done in order to break the back of the enemy. If one made life so miserable for the civilians, in most instances they would soon start calling for a halt to the hostilities. Knowing that, however, didn't make Ben feel any better about it.

He finally drifted off into a restless sleep, awakening about noon, just as the guards were being changed for their two hour shift. His team slept on, with the exception of Corrie, who had just woken up and was on the radio.

"Buddy reports Bottger's troops are all over his area,"

she said softly, so as not to wake the others. "Well-trained and thoroughly professional. He estimates about five thousand of them."

"How'd he reach that estimation?"

"His people grabbed one of Bottger's boys."

Ben nodded. He didn't have to question further, nor did he have to ask the outcome. Buddy's Spec Ops people were not the nicest nor the gentlest folks to encounter in any hostile situation. "That throws the rule book right out the window then. Simon has firmly aligned with Bottger so now the game can get just as rough as we can make it."

"Buddy gave me the coordinates for the new troops billet area."

"Planes up," Ben ordered. "I want that area to be a raging firestorm for five miles around. Hit them with everything we have at our disposal."

"I've already put them on standby."

"Good. I figured you had." He smiled. Corrie could practically read his mind. "Order Buddy and his people to get clear. It's about to get real warm in that area."

"Yes, sir."

"The drop tonight?"

"Everything is ready to go and the troops are anxious to get on the ground into action."

"We're damn sure going to see some action," Ben said, a grimness behind his words. "Maybe sooner than we expect."

Book Two

Many religious people are deeply suspicious. They seem—for purely religious purposes, of course—to know more about iniquity than the unregenerate.

—Kipling

One

Ben wanted as many of Bottger's troops to be in quarters as possible when his air attack was launched, so he ordered all his people to lie low until after the strike. There were no doubts in Ben's mind that Bottger had more troops on the way, but this strike would give the Rebels some breathing room.

"Buddy and his people are clear of the strike area," Corrie finally reported late that afternoon.

"Took him long enough," Ben groused. "What was he doing, sightseeing?"

"I didn't ask," Corrie replied with a smile.

Ben grunted in reply.

About an hour later, just after dark, just about the time Bottger's people would be sitting down for evening chow—for they were very punctual about that—Ben's planes struck the billet area. Ben knew, even though he had not ordered it, that Buddy would have observers close in enough to report damage.

"Damage report coming in now," Corrie said, as Ben's personal team crowded around close.

Ben cut his eyes to look at his adopted daughter. Short of handcuffing Anna to the nearest solid object, there had been no way he was going to keep her from going on this mission. But that didn't mean Ben had to like it. Anna was calm and her pale eyes reflected no inner emotion. Like

most Rebel women, she had cut her blond hair very short—
shorter than some men's—but only a fool would ever mistake her for a male.

She looked up, meeting Ben's eyes, and winked at him.

Ben had to smile. The young lady was gutsy, no doubt
about that. And breathtakingly beautiful. But she was far
too intense for most young men her age; she loved to read
and study and debate issues of importance . . . all of which
suited Ben just fine.

"Forward people report the billet area is blazing," Corrie
said. "The air strike was right on target. Bottger's people
were caught flat-footed. Bottger's contingent in North
America has been virtually wiped out. Their future effectiveness is nil . . . to use Buddy's words."

"Good," Ben said. "Let's pack it up and get gone." Ben
had already checked his map. "We head south and set up
some ambushes. We'll pick up the claymores from supply
drops that should be coming in just about now." He checked
his watch. "Let's go. We've got just about an hour to make
it to the DZ."

Simon's people were searching for Ben miles south of
their present location, and the DZ was just about halfway
between the point . . . having been changed several times
as Scouts kept track of and constantly reported the widening
gap between Rebels and Simon's troops.

Ben and his team headed out, paralleling the old highway
on both sides, but staying in the fields and forests. They
would see lights on in farmhouses, but kept as far away
from them as possible. The occasional dog would bark its
alarm, but no one came to investigate. Since the Great War,
the wild animal population in North America had exploded,
and the residents were accustomed to dogs barking at wild
animals.

"Winds have been coming out of the south for several
hours now," Ben said. "That means the supplies will prob-

ably be off the target and to our advantage. Bump our forward people to keep their eyes open."

Less than five minutes had passed before Corrie said, "We're almost on top of the supplies, boss. Scouts are unpacking them now. They really drifted north."

Ben looked up into the sky. There were only a few wispy clouds, but they appeared to be moving very fast from south to north. "Those winds are kicking up."

"More rain?" Cooper asked.

"I don't think so. I sure as hell don't want more snow. Too easy for us to be tracked."

The snow that had fallen was all but gone, with only pockets remaining in very low-lying areas that were shady during the day. They came up on the Scouts unpacking the boxes in the middle of a soggy field and pitched in, then hid the boxes and chutes in a wooded area.

"Roadblock about two miles up ahead," one Scout informed Ben. "Five men manning it."

"Take your people and clear it," Ben told the Scout. "We'll be getting these supplies distributed." Ben straightened up. "And if they have a couple of vehicles, bring them back. We'll ride for a few miles."

The Scout grinned in the night. "Will do, General."

There were no shots in the night, the Scouts doing their work with silent knives. The only indication the killing had taken place was a couple of prearranged clicks on Corrie's radio. By the time Ben and the others had lugged the supplies to the road, the dark shapes of three old longbed pickup trucks were visible, coming up the road, headlights off. One of the pickups was an old super-cab.

The supplies were quickly loaded into the beds of the trucks, the Rebels piled in, and the impromptu convoy headed south. Ben rode in the back of the lead truck with his personal team, Doctor Farmer, and part of the supplies. Four Rebels, counting the driver, rode in the cab, two in the front and two on the narrow seat behind the driver and passenger.

"Beats the hell out of walking," Jersey said with a sigh of contentment, leaning back against the tailgate.

"You'll get no argument from me on that," Ben agreed. "I just hope it lasts for a few miles."

So did the others, for they had not cached any of the supplies that had been dropped that night, and even spread out among Ben and his personal team, and the twenty other Rebels, the fresh supplies would make quite a load.

"What used to be a fair-sized little town is fast coming up," Beth told Ben. "There is sure to be quite a contingent of Simon's there."

The truck had no rear glass. Ben stuck his head inside the cab and said, "First side road we find, take it. We'll hide the truck and the Scouts can check out the town."

"Right, sir," the driver replied.

A few hundred yards on down the cracked old secondary road, the lead truck signaled a turn and cut off to the right onto a gravel road, the others following. A hundred yards more, and the short convoy pulled into the front yard of an old house. Before the trucks stopped moving, Rebels were out and running toward the house and outbuildings. A few minutes later, the all-clear shout was heard and the trucks parked at the rear of the house, between the house and the falling down old barn.

Ben did not have to say a word. Within seconds after parking, the Scouts had shed much of their equipment and were running down the gravel road toward the old highway, disappearing into the night.

Several of the Rebels immediately set up a perimeter. Ben and the others waited in the gloom of night, moving around as little as possible and keeping the chatter to a whispered minimum.

Ben, Anna with him, walked to the rear of the old house and Ben tried the back door. The doorknob turned under his gloved hand and the door opened with just a faint protest of old hinges. Ben and Anna stepped into the kitchen.

The very thin light from outside revealed a layer of dust over everything. Cobwebs dangled from the ceiling. A small kitchen table was in the center of the room. Stove and refrigerator had not been removed from the room.

"Places such as this make me sad," Anna whispered.

"I used to feel the same," Ben said. "I guess I've seen too many of them to be affected anymore."

"People used to sit at this table," Anna touched the dust-covered table with a gloved hand, "and talk and laugh and drink coffee and plan the day's activities. I wish I could live in a time like that. When things were . . . well, normal."

"You will, baby," Ben assured her. "Those times will come again."

"Will you live long enough to see those days, General Ben?" the young woman asked.

"No," Ben's response was quickly given. "But you will. Your children will live in a normal time, and live normal lives."

"My children?" Anna asked, and Ben could see the faint smile curve her lips. "I have not yet met the man I would even consider spending my life with."

"You will, baby. It's something that happens to the majority of people."

"Then why are you not married?"

Ben's thoughts were flung back in time, back to the many women he had known over the long years that lay behind him in time's dusty corridors. "There have been a few, Anna."

"What happened?"

"Things just didn't work out, that's all. It happens."

"Shit happens, hey?"

Ben smiled. There was no point in his admonishing the teenager for her language. She talked no worse than any other Rebel, and better than most. Hardline combat personnel often reverted to coarse language. "That's one way of putting it, I suppose."

Neither of them opened any drawers in the kitchen for fear of booby traps. Ben motioned toward the back door and they exited the house.

"Couple of skeletons in the barn," Jersey said, walking up to Ben. "They've been there for a long time. No weapons visible."

"Gender?"

"Dr. Farmer says it's a man and a woman. They're laying side by side in the loft."

"May be a suicide," Ben opined.

"That's Dr. Farmer's opinion."

Anna shook her head. "I do not understand people who would do such a thing. I can understand giving one's life for a cause, such as ours, but not suicide. Things have never looked that bad for me, and I have faced some very tough times."

"Some people just can't take it when times get too bad, Anna," Ben said. "I remember just after the Great War, hundreds, perhaps thousands of Americans took their own lives. They just couldn't face such an uncertain future. As a nation, we had it too easy for too many years. That final act of desperation was something that many of us had predicted."

"And just as many others turned to a life of crime?" Anna asked.

"Oh, yes. Probably ten times that number. Or more. And that, too, was something that many of us predicted."

"Did anybody listen to you, General Ben?" Anna asked.

"Quite a few people did, but no one that I know of in government . . . no politician paid us the slightest bit of attention. And the news media tried their best to ridicule us. Militia groups, survivalist groups, other people with the ability to see past the ends of their noses and really get a grasp on what was happening in America—they listened. And many of them survived because of what those few of us preached. I take a great deal of perverse pleasure in that knowledge."

"No reason for it to be perverse," Anna stated. "You were right and the politicians were wrong."

"From what I have been able to read about the politicians in this country," Beth said, "they seemed to be more interested in their own party's advancement and their own personal goals rather than the wishes of millions of voters . . . . and millions of people became so irritated and disgusted with the system they simply dropped out and refused to take part."

"Sad but to a large degree very true, Beth," Ben said. "The last decade before the Great War was the low point in American history . . . at least in the minds of millions of us."

"But you paid taxes, General Ben," Anna said. "Didn't you?"

Ben laughed. "I'll say we did, Anna."

"And yet you had no say in the running of the very government you were forced to support."

"That's very true."

"That is wrong," the young lady stated. "That is the glaring imperfection in that type of government, I believe."

"What was the tax burden on citizens, General?" a Rebel asked.

As usual, when Ben began speaking of the time before the Great War, the younger Rebels, who really had no knowledge of that time, listened and asked questions. Most of the younger Rebels were just children when the Great War tore the world apart.

"About fifty percent of our income," Ben replied. "That's local, county, state, and federal taxes."

"That's obscene!" the young man blurted.

Ben smiled. "Millions of us thought so too."

"And what did you receive from the government for this terrible burden?" another Rebel asked.

Ben laughed mockingly. "Well, the politicians passed laws taking away our guns, and if we didn't hand them over to the government goons we were arrested and faced large fines and heavy prison time." There was a low rumbling of anger among the Rebels gathered around. Ben smiled, thinking: I'd like to see the government, any government, try to pass and put into effect anti-gun laws among these people. The dead would litter the streets like beer cans and candy wrappers.

"No citizen was allowed to use any type of deadly force to protect his or her property from thieves. The whiny liberals, the left wing of the democratic party—we referred to them as the Take-A-Punk-To-Lunch-Bunch . . ." Ben waited until the quiet laughter had subsided. ". . . had decreed that no personal property was worth the life of a really good boy gone bad."

"What happened if you did kill someone who was trying to steal your car or TV or something, General?" the question came out of the circle of Rebels surrounding Ben.

"Oh, why the offending citizen, that law-abiding, over-burdened taxpaying person was arrested and hauled off to jail, where he or she faced all sorts of charges, and then the family of the punk could, under law, sue for damages . . . and usually win. It didn't matter if the suit could financially ruin a decent, law-abiding family and put them out in the street. That was never taken into consideration. What was taken into consideration was that the punk was hurt or killed; never mind that it happened during the commission of a crime. The liberals screwed this nation up so bad it is beyond description."

Ben looked up at the sound of a branch breaking in the deep woods around the old farmhouse. An instant later, he and his Rebels were belly down on the ground, in a defensive circle.

They all knew that it wasn't a deer or some other wild animal, for they almost never step on things that might pop and make noise. It was a human out there, and considering where they were, in all likelihood, a very unfriendly one. Or two, or a dozen. The Rebels would know soon enough.

Ben caught Corrie's eyes in the dim light. She shook her head, silently telling him that the perimeter guards were making no radio contact. That told Ben that all four sentries had either seen or heard something. So it was certainly more than one man.

It looked as though Ben and his team were surrounded, deep in hostile territory.

Two

Corrie bellied her way close to Ben. "The road guard just reported a group of men across from him," she whispered. "And the sound we heard was behind us. We have them at least front and back of the house."

Ben nodded his understanding just as voices drifted out of the woods. The Rebels relaxed just a bit, for if there were voices, those in the woods were not aware of the Rebels. Not yet, anyway. But if they spotted the old pickup trucks parked in the rear of the farmhouse, they would surely investigate.

". . . The Rebels aren't within fifty miles of here," the man's voice came to Ben and the others. "I think they cut east, not south."

"Nobody asked what you think," another man's voice drifted out of the night.

"I got a right to my opinion."

"Shut up, Johnny. You do what you're told, just like the rest of us."

"I do, Harold. But that don't mean I have to like it."

"That's blasphemous talk, Johnny. You best stop that nonsense 'fore you're reported."

"Hey!" the shout came out of the woods.

"Who said that?" Harold questioned.

Harold must be in charge of this unit, Ben thought. Or at least thinks he is.

"I think it was Rolf," another voice replied. "He was bringing up the rear."

"Rolf?" Harold shouted. "What is it?"

The Rebels knew that in all probability Rolf would never answer. Rolf had gotten too close to one of the perimeter guards and Rolf's throat had been cut. The Rebels also knew that a very intense fire-fight was very likely only seconds away. Gloved hands tightened on weapons as assholes involuntarily puckered up. That goes with the game of war known as combat.

"Rolf?" Harold shouted. "Answer me."

Only silence greeted Harold's command: a very heavy and ominous hush from the dark woods.

Are you damn people blind? Ben thought. Can't you see the outlines of the pickup trucks? What the hell is the matter with you? What kind of soldiers are you?

"Rolf's just flat disappeared, Harold," another voice was added to the growing confusion. "He ain't nowhere to be found."

"That's impossible!"

"Well, come see for yourself, then!"

"Paul!" Harold shouted. "You boys see anything?"

"There isn't a thing over here, Harold," Paul shouted from across the gravel road that ran in front of the house. "No sign of nothing."

You've probably got a Rebel not five feet from you, Ben thought, with no small degree of pride.

"Rolf, boy, you better answer me!" Harold shouted. "This is no time to be fooling around."

Silence.

"Check it out, Jeff," Harold ordered. "Take Willie with you. And you two be careful. I don't like this."

"Hey!" yet another voice was added. "What the hell is that?"

"What's what?" Harold asked.

"What are those trucks doin' back here?"

"Trucks?"

"Right there, Harold, tucked in close to the back of the house."

As if on cue, Ben's team opened up with automatic weapons fire. The night around the house and barn and from across the gravel road was pocked with sharp flashes of light as the stutter of CAR's shattered the silence.

The screaming of wounded and dying men filled the night. The Rebels were recognized worldwide as the undisputed masters of war, ranging from hit and run to stand and hold to ambush, and this night only added to their reputation.

The fire-fight was over and done with in a dozen heartbeats, with Simon's soldiers scarcely able to get off more than a few rounds that hit nothing but cold night air.

After a full moment of silence, broken only by the groaning and crying out of badly wounded men, Ben pushed himself to his knees and looked around him at the shadowy scenes of war that were all too familiar.

One more shot from the fallen troops of Simon Border cracked and a Rebel who was standing near the barn went down. Ben cursed and shouted, "Rake the area!"

The Rebels raked the area with automatic gunfire for a few seconds, each Rebel burning a full magazine.

"Who is that Rebel down by the barn?" Ben shouted.

"Secrest, sir," the shout immediately followed the question. "He's had it."

"Shit!" Ben said.

"Let me check him," Dr. Farmer said, then ran through the carnage to the barn.

Corrie was busy bumping all the perimeter guards. "No one got out, boss."

"Any wounded?"

"Negative."

"Bury Secrest in the woods. Disguise the grave carefully."

"Right, Boss.

The Rebels were always careful about burying their dead, for enemy troops had been known to dig up the bodies and either mutilate them or put them on a macabre display . . . or both.

The Rebels were both the most hated and the most feared fighting force on the face of the earth . . . and the most grudgingly respected.

Secrest now joined the hundreds of other Rebels who lay in unmarked graves all over half the world, from Alabama to Romania, Rebels who willingly gave their lives, without question, to free others . . . of all nationalities and creeds.

"Search the bodies for anything that might be of use to our intelligence people and then let's get the hell gone from here."

Ten minutes later, the Rebels were on the move, once more heading down the old highway in the pickup trucks. The Scouts had returned and reported a bypass around the town. Ben thought that over for a moment and then smiled. "Let's go raise some hell in the town. Park and hide the trucks about a half mile from the edge of town and we'll hoof it in and look things over."

"Carrying several hundred pounds of C-4, of course," Jersey said drily.

"Why, Jersey," Ben replied in mock surprise. "What a marvelous idea."

The others in the truck laughed at the expression on Jersey's face as they rolled on through the night.

Simon's home guard was sleeping in their warehouse-turned-barracks when the structure blew up and collapsed around and on top of them. In less than fifteen seconds, the town lost their entire contingent of home guard protection.

The town's gasoline storage area went up at the same time, sending a huge fireball high into the sky, after the

Rebels neutralized the two guards and dispatched them to Simon Border's concept of Heaven, a place which was free of blacks, Jews, Mexicans, Asians, Indians, and all other minorities, of course.

That done, Ben and his team drove on south through the night, the scene behind them highlighted with dancing flames.

The Rebels hit two more towns that night, destroying half a dozen buildings in each before Ben ordered a change in direction. They had pushed their luck heading south long enough. Ben cut them straight east on an old secondary road and they rode unchallenged until coming to a huge lake. There, Ben ordered a halt for the night. The vehicles were hidden in the timber after their gas tanks were topped off with gas stolen from the storage area.

"Get some rest," he told his people. "We've earned it. I think we can call this a very productive night."

Ben crawled into his sleeping bag and was asleep in five minutes.

He was up and moving long before dawn. He had spotted an old cabin the night before and checked it out while the others slept. It was free of booby traps. Ben built a small fire in the stone fireplace, using the old wood he found in the box by the side of the fireplace and some other wood that had been stacked on the falling down porch. The wood was very old and virtually smokeless. Ben made coffee; the first coffee he'd had since the morning they'd jumped in; seemed as though that had been weeks ago but in actuality it could be measured in hours.

He sat on the floor, his back to a wall, and drank coffee and smoked a cigarette, enjoying the peaceful hour or so before dawn cracked the sky.

Jersey wandered in, rubbing the sleep from her eyes, which widened when she saw the fire and the coffeepot sitting off to one side, the brew staying hot while not boiling.

"Nectar of the gods," Jersey said, squatting down and

pouring a cup. She sugared it with a packet of sweetener from her accessory pack and sat down beside Ben, taking a sip and sighing in contentment. Then Corrie came in and joined them. The three sat for a time, sipping coffee and enjoying the silence.

"At dawn," Ben said, "we use this cabin to take spit baths with water from the lake and change socks and wash out the ones we're wearing. And the same with our underwear. We're all beginning to smell just a tad gamey."

That order was met with silent nods of approval from Jersey and Corrie.

Cooper and Anna and Beth had wandered in while Ben was brewing another cup of coffee. Anna squatted down in a very unladylike position and Ben watched her gnaw on a hard biscuit from her breakfast pack, thinking: If all the rest of us got killed on this op, she would survive, for she will never be truly civilized; never entirely lose the feral side of her makeup. Even though Anna was astonishingly beautiful, and so young, she was one of the most dangerous people Ben had ever known. Ben had seen her kill, rip the hide off a rabbit, and eat it half cooked without expression, while the blood ran down her chin, her pale cold eyes glistening with pleasure while her stomach filled, her eyes darting from left to right in a protective movement.

That's how it was thousands of years ago, he thought, his coffee cup refilled and a fresh cigarette rolled and lighted. I'm looking at living proof of how humankind used to be. How in God's name could this young woman, orphaned while scarcely out of diapers, have survived? We all must have that primal streak in us. But most of us have pushed it so far back it is unretrievable—unthinkable, grossly alien to modern man and woman.

Anna wiped her mouth with the sleeve of her BDU field jacket and caught Ben looking at her. She smiled at him. "Good," she said. "A wash and then we will all feel much better."

She left the cabin and Ben and Corrie exchanged glances, Ben sensing that Corrie had been thinking the same thoughts as he.

Ben put those thoughts out of his mind and in the light from the fire, quickly studied a map of the area. "There is a small town about twenty miles to the east of our location. We'll take that tonight and work about fifty miles to the east before changing directions again."

"South?" Jersey asked.

"Maybe," Ben replied with a smile. "What I don't want to do is establish any type of movement pattern that some of the more intelligent members of Simon's army can spot. We'll see. At first light, Corrie, set up your dish and bump the others, see how they're making out and chart their locations. If you can pick out a movement pattern, so can the enemy. If that's the case, advise them to change directions. We've got to keep Simon's people off base and guessing."

"Right, Boss."

"Then bump Base Camp One and see how things are going down there. Bring Cecil up to date."

"Will do."

"For now, roust the people up and have them come in here a few at a time for hot coffee and to heat up these despicable breakfast packets. Nothing will make them taste like anything but warmed-over shit, but they're better hot than cold."

"Especially these eggs," Jersey said, frowning. "Or whatever they are."

The basics never really change, in any army, anywhere. The Roman legions surely bitched about their food, too.

"They're dehydrated eggs, Jersey," Ben said. "I think."

"From what kind of chicken?" she came right back.

Ben's detachment of Rebels spent the next two hours or so brewing coffee, washing socks and underwear, and taking very quick baths out of an old bucket. Even with nothing more than spit baths, they all managed to rid themselves of an amazing amount of dirt and felt a lot better when they started rolling east in the old pickup trucks.

The road was a gravel/dirt road, full of ruts and bumps, so they did not make very good time. The gravel road abruptly ceased, running into what had been a county highway.

"This won't do at all," Ben said, looking around him. "We're too exposed. Pull over there in those woods and we'll wait until the Scouts have checked out the town up ahead, then plan our next move."

The Rebels lounged around in the woods, moving as little as possible and waiting for the Scouts' report.

"Just about a thousand people lived there before the Great War," Beth said, consulting her copy of an old state tourist brochure. "Doesn't say anything about the town or what the people did for a living."

Corrie suddenly held up a hand. "Okay," she said. "Got it. Hang on for orders." She turned to Ben. "Scouts report that the people in that town are just about the sorriest-looking bunch they've ever seen. Nothing much in the way of weapons and not hostile-appearing at all. Just struggling to get by."

"Tell them to come on back. We'll cut south and concentrate on blowing bridges. I don't want to make conditions worse for people who have nothing to start with."

"We've been pretty lucky so far," Anna said.

"Luck has a nasty habit of running out, dear," Ben reminded her.

"Suits me," the young woman replied, picking up her CAR. "Nothing like a good fight to get the blood hot."

Three

Ben had no choice but to cut through a national forest/mountain range. Luckily, the mountain range was not that high and the old road was relatively clear. On the drive through the range, there was just one town off the road a few miles and on a whim, Ben decided to check it out. The town maybe had a population of three hundred before the Great War and as deep in the mountains as it was, Ben did not think there would be more than a few dozen residents remaining, at most.

He was wrong.

"Scouts report the town is deserted, boss," Corrie said. Ben had pulled the short impromptu convoy off the road about a mile from the tiny town. "They also say it's damned eerie."

"Eerie?"

"That's what they said."

"Let's check it out."

The Scouts halted the convoy on the edge of the village. "It's very strange, General," the team leader told Ben. "Well, you're going to have to see for yourself. I can't explain it."

"Let's go."

"Wow!" Jersey summed it up, standing on the back porch of a house and peering in through the undamaged window. "This is strange."

Ben carefully opened the back door and stepped inside.

He was standing in the kitchen. The kitchen table had been set for a meal, four plates and settings. Ben checked the pots and pans on the stove. Whatever food had been cooking had years ago burned or boiled down to an unrecognizable hardened glob on the bottom. The heat knobs were still on, in various degree settings, so the propane tanks had burned dry. Ben slowly turned the knobs to the off position.

Ben walked from the kitchen down a short hall and into the living room. The room was neat and except for a dust covering on everything, clean and well-kept. He turned and entered a bedroom. The bed was made and the blankets undisturbed. The bedding in the next two bedrooms had been turned down, so Ben guessed that had been the evening meal cooking on the stove. There were no skeletal remains to be found.

"Odd," Ben murmured. "Let's check out the house next door."

The Rebels found the same thing in the other houses on the short block.

"Let's split up," Ben said. "Two teams of ten check out the rest of the houses. I'll check out the little business district"

A grocery store, a combination hardware/sporting goods/farm supply store. A tiny post office. A general store that seemed to Ben, peering through the dust covered front show window, to stock a little bit of everything. A barber shop/beauty parlor. A service station. Two other buildings that had no name.

Ben pushed at the front door of the grocery store. It opened with a faint protest of hinges that had not been used for years. He stepped inside. The smell of rotting food wafted at Ben and his team. After all these years, cans had begun to burst and leak; the smell was not pleasant.

"The shelves are all full!" Cooper said. "It looks like nothing was looted."

"It wasn't," Ben said in a low voice. "But the rats have

been busy. And this rotting food will keep them busy for years to come. Let's get out of here."

On the sidewalk, under the awning, Corrie spoke into her mic. "Okay, I got it. Hang on." She looked at Ben. "Both teams have found like-new vehicles all over the town. Some with only a few thousand miles on the odometer."

Ben shook his head in wonder. "This town is a picture right out of the past. It is untouched by all that has happened. But where did the people go?" He sighed. "Tell the teams to pick the best of the extend-cab pickups. Go to the service station for batteries and extra tires. We might as well ride in style."

Cooper waved at them from across the street. "Hey, gang! Look. No guns were taken. The rack is filled with them.

"Incredible," Ben said, checking out a .270. He wiped the dust from it and worked the bolt. Stiff, but nothing a little oil wouldn't fix. "Take the high-powered rifles and all the ammo you can find. We're all going to have to do some long-distance shooting before this is over. Fill those backpacks over there. Check the barrels for blockage and one of you look around for scopes. We're going to be back in business, big time."

"What happened here, General Ben?" Anna asked, standing close to him and speaking in a very small voice.

"I don't know, baby. It's just one of those mysteries that happen in war. We've all seen some very strange things over the years."

"Boss," Beth called. "How about taking some of these blankets and padding the beds of the trucks."

Ben smiled. "Sure. That would make riding a lot easier on the butt, wouldn't it?"

"Teams report finding no bodies in any of the houses," Corrie said. "Dr. Farmer is checking out the local cemetery. The last headstone he can find was put up about two months before the Great War."

"And the body was buried probably several months before the stone was put in place. It's a strange situation, people. One I can't explain and won't even try. Come on, let's check out the rest of the stores."

In the tiny barber shop, Ben picked up a magazine and checked the date. A decade old. He laid it aside and carefully picked up a newspaper, crisp and brittle with age. One of the front page stories was about the civilian militia movement in the state. This reporter had his drawers all in a wad about armed men and women getting organized and about the so-called threat they posed to law and order.

"Horse shit!" Ben said, and not so carefully tossed the paper aside. Years back, when reporters started not-so-subtly taking sides instead of sticking to their job of reporting the news, Ben had quickly lost all respect for the profession.

"What the hell is Autumn Mist?" Jersey asked, staring at a poster on the wall of a model who had supposedly just received a new hairdo.

"That's the color of her hair, Jersey," Ben said, stepping through the door into the beauty parlor.

"No shit! Why doesn't she just cut that mop off and be done with it?"

Ben laughed and left the ladies looking at the fashion magazines of years back. He stepped out onto the sidewalk and sat down, rolling a smoke. Dr. Farmer strolled up and grabbed a piece of sidewalk for his butt. He looked disapprovingly at Ben's hand-rolled cigarette, but wisely kept his mouth shut about it.

"What happened here, Doctor?"

"I don't know, General. I'd be reluctant to even take a guess."

"Force yourself."

"After you, sir."

Ben chuckled. "Hell, Doc, like you, I don't have a clue. A tiny town, set deep in a mountain range, deserted and untouched for a decade. What happened to the people? I don't know. And to deepen the mystery, we'll probably never know."

"Plates had been set out for a meal, supper, I think. The cash registers of the stores are full of money. Then . . . the people just got up, walked out of their homes and businesses and disappeared. Makes no sense to me. I've never seen anything like it."

"Nor have I, not really."

"General, do you believe in, well, visitors from space? Aliens, if you will?"

"As a matter of fact, I do."

The doctor cut his surprised eyes. "You do?"

"Sure. Always have. There is no reason for us to think we're the only beings. To believe we're alone and superior is arrogant. Who knows how long a day was to God? And who knows how many times He tried to make man in His image, and failed? Hell, He just kept trying until He got it right."

"Well, I'll be damned!" Dr. Farmer blurted.

This time, Ben laughed aloud. "I wasn't always a soldier, Doc. I was a writer for years. And writers are notoriously curious people. Most of us have open minds about a great many things."

"Not that I was suggesting it was a spaceship that might have . . . well, you know what I mean."

"I know, Doc. No, I don't think that either. Maybe when the news came over the radio and TV about the missiles carrying the germ warheads hitting America, the town evaced suddenly. I don't know."

Their conversation was abruptly cut short as Rebels drove five long-bed, extend-cab trucks up the street and parked. All the trucks had camper shells on them.

Ben rose to his boots and walked across the street to inspect the vehicles. The trucks were all covered with a decade of dust, but it was easy to see that none of them had many road miles on them.

"Load them up, people. We're getting out of here. ASAP."

"Not going to spend the night here, General?" Dr. Farmer asked.

Ben shook his head. "No. I want to leave this little town just as we found it, at least as much as possible."

"I think I can understand that," the doctor said softly.

Anna strolled up in time to catch part of the conversation. She nodded her agreement. "I would not like to spend the night in this village."

"Why, Anna?" Ben asked.

She cut her eyes to stare at him for a moment before she replied. "It was left untouched for a reason. Perhaps a reason that mortals do not understand." She walked off.

"Let's pack it up and get out of here," Ben said. He did not say anything about the cold shiver that had walked up and down his spine at Anna's word.

And Doc Farmer didn't say anything about the very creepy feeling that had enveloped him, either.

Ben and team traveled on. No one said anything, but all were glad to leave the little village. The road narrowed down to a dirt road, and for a time Ben thought the highway would end. Then it started up again. By dark, the convoy had reached a major highway.

"Back up and turn around," Ben ordered. "Go back about a half a mile and pull off the highway. We'll camp there for tonight. They'll never think of looking for us this close to the highway."

Ben didn't have to worry about the troops looking for them anyplace, for they didn't.

"What the hell? . . ." he murmured.

Then it dawned on him: Simon was running a bluff. That had to be it. The man had no troops to spare; everything he had was on the battlefront.

"Corrie, get me Buddy and Ike on the horn," Ben ordered.

"Right away."

After a wait of about five minutes, during which Ben paced up and down, Ike and Ben's son came on the air.

"Where in the hell have you two been?" Ben demanded.

"Well, ah, indisposed, you might say."

"Same here," Buddy responded.

Ben laughed and shook his head. "I knew you two were full of it, but not to this degree. I won't say a word."

Both Buddy and Ike knew better than to give Ben the slightest opening. They remained silent.

"All right, listen. Have either of you run up against any of Simon's troops."

"Not me," Ike said.

"Same, same," Buddy said. "We've been wondering where they were."

"He doesn't have them."

There was a silence on the other end. Finally, Ike said, "Well, I'll just be damned!"

"You mean . . ." Buddy broke it off.

"Yes. That is exactly what I mean. All he's got left is his home guard. Everybody else is on the front."

"That's why we haven't seen anybody else," Ike commented. "He's been running a bluff."

"Exactly," Ben said. "And hoping against hope we wouldn't catch on."

"And now that we have . . ." Buddy said.

"Do either of you really want to make war against old people, babies, and women?"

"No," Ike said.

"No," Buddy said.

"Then we go in and disarm the people," Ben said. "Simon didn't think we would catch on; he thought the five thousand troops that Bottger sent in would do the trick. Must've caused the man a lot of serious sleepless nights when he discovered it didn't. All right. We work with Interstate 5 to our backs and push inland. Let's spread out and do it, people."

After Ben had hooked the mic, Corrie said, "What if you're wrong, boss?"

"Then we're fucked!"

Resistance was very light as Ben and his team drove into the first town and lined the citizens up on the main street. They had killed fourteen and suffered no casualties.

"It's over," Ben told them. "This area of the nation is now officially open to anybody who wants to live here. Get that through your heads."

It was a strange sight. Women and kids and old men and teenagers and veterans of past conflicts with missing hands and arms and legs standing sullenly staring at him.

"Anybody who wishes to see a doctor, we'll treat you." Ben, standing on the bed of a pickup truck, pointed to a large tent. "That's the MASH tent. We only have one doctor, so be patient. He'll get to you in time."

"You mean," a man with one leg said, "that you'll give us medical treatment?"

"That's right."

"No strings attached?"

"None whatever."

The man stared at Ben for a few heartbeats, then shook his head. "The Reverend Border spread the word that you people were raping our women and shooting our men after they surrendered."

"Simon Border is a liar, among other things. And I think most of you people realize that."

Again, the civilian stared at Ben for a moment. Then he slowly nodded his head. "A lot of us realize we were duped, General."

"That's good, mister. This nation doesn't need to be torn apart by a religious war."

"I agree. But a large percentage of the men and women on the front lines still swear by Reverend Border. And they won't surrender, General. They'll fight."

"I know. But if they learn of many of their own back home laying down their weapons, they might decide to join them."

"I hope so, General," the civilian said wearily. "I just want to live out the rest of my life in peace."

Ben nodded his head and watched as the man moved away on his crutches. It was a start. Now if the movement toward peace would just continue . . .

"Boss," Corrie said. "Our people in Africa just sent word that about ten thousand troops from Bottgers army are gearing up for travel to the States. And they're some of the best he has."

Ben grimaced and kicked at a can, then said some really choice words. He calmed down and took several deep breaths. "I don't know why I'm surprised. Hell, I expected him to do it. How are they coming in?"

"Ship and plane."

"Not taking any chances, is he? Hell, we don't have enough people over there to do anything."

"Boss," Corrie said softly, and Ben cut his eyes to hers. "There is more to the message."

"All bad, huh?"

"We don't have but a handful of people left over there. And they've beat it across the border. Some warlords they thought were friendly turned on them. Turned out they were working for Bottger all along. It was a slaughter. We've got five people of our original force left alive."

Ben walked off a few yards, his team moving with him. "Well, that tears it. What does Cecil say about it?"

"Nothing yet. He wants you to bump him."

"Later. I've got to give this new development some thought. Five left?"

"Unless some miracle occurred and others got out of the village, yes."

"Tell the Chaplain to pray for a miracle."

"Boss?" Cooper said, and Ben turned toward his driver. Cooper pointed to a familiar figure getting out of an old four-wheel drive vehicle. "Here's a minor miracle. That's Mike Richards."

The chief of Rebel intelligence brought Ben up to date on what he knew, then listened carefully as Ben brought him up to date on the latest from Base Camp One.

"I think we've got a handle on the situation here in the northwest, Ben. I could sense a lot of the followers of Border were becoming disillusioned with that snake-oil sales-man's babblings. But when I got word that you were jumping in to start a guerrilla action . . . well, at first I really questioned that move. Then I began to see the brilliance behind the plan. Anyway, it worked, didn't it?"

"So far, Mike. But with this latest news, we're running a good chance of getting caught between Bottger's troops and the front. And should that happen, those of us here will be caught up in one hell of a hit and run action."

Mike smiled. "Just the way you like it, isn't it, Ben?"

Ben returned the smile. "I liked it more when I was a bit younger, Mike."

"Bullshit, you old war-lover," Mike popped right back. "You love it now just as much as you ever did. Tell the young troops otherwise if you like, but don't try to spoon-feed me that peace and love crap."

Ben laughed softly. "All right, Mike. I won't try to convince you I'm some sort of peace envoy."

"Good. So do you have a plan now that you know that

Nazi asshole is sending some of the best troops he's got over here?"

"Tell the truth, I haven't had time to formulate one."

Mike nodded and sipped his coffee. Dusk was spreading her cloak over the land, warning the afternoon to prepare for night. Somewhere in the distance, out in the woods that surrounded the small town, a wolf howled. Ben lifted his head and smiled at the call.

"You and Brother Wolf, eh, Ben?" Mike questioned with a smile.

"Could be, Mike."

Mike chuckled. "Of course, Ben, to avoid the risk of getting caught between Bottger's troops and Border's troops, you could get out of here and run the operation from a safe distance. That's what Generals usually do."

"Shit!" Ben said.

The lobo wolf howled again.

Once the resistance from Border's followers began to wane, the capitulation movement spread all over the western part of Borders territory, from the Canadian border down to the California state line. As Ben and his team began moving slowly eastward, they could all see that Border had been running quite a scam. Many of the people were hungry, having settled on land that couldn't produce anything much in the way of food for human consumption. They had few doctors among them, and the kids were in rough shape. The Rebels soon were spending much more time healing than shooting. Ben called for more doctors and paramedics and medicines to be sent in from Base Camp One. Former Simon Border supporters were flocking into the aid camps by droves.

"Hearts and minds, Cec," Ben told Cecil one day.

Hundreds of miles away, the President of the SUSA

laughed. "That term certainly sounds very familiar, Ben. Where have I heard that before?"

The two men shared a laugh, then Cecil said, "Bottger's troops are definitely on the way, Ben, and his hard-core people who are spread all over North America are on the way to beef up Simon's front. It's looking pretty good out there now, but all that is going to change, very quickly."

"I know, Cec."

"And? . . ."

"I'll deal with it when the time comes."

"I know I'd be better off farting in the wind than suggesting this, but you need to get the hell out of that area, Ben."

"All in good time. Stop worrying."

"Sure, Ben." Cecil's words were laced with sarcasm. "That really eases my mind."

"I knew it would. I merely wanted to assure you I have the greatest regard for my personal safety."

Cecil called him a name and broke off.

Ben handed the mic to Corrie and looked around. "Anybody seen Mike today?"

"I think he split," Beth said. "I saw him loading his pickup with field rats and ammo this morning."

Mike's sudden departure without a good-bye did not come as a surprise. That's the way the man operated. Ben walked out of the building he was using as a temporary CP to stand for a moment and breathe the cool air. Christmas and New Year's had come and gone with few Rebels paying much attention to it. They were just too busy. The first few months of the new year had passed in a flurry of activity, with the Rebels gaining a lot of ground. Now spring was definitely in the air.

Ben's team of Rebels had crossed over into Idaho and were in a small town, seeing to the needs of former Simon Border supporters. On the long curving front east and south of Ben, Simon's loyalists had been digging in, preparing to make a last-ditch stand of it. And from all indications, when it came, it was going to be a bloody one.

Simon Border's empire was crumbling, no doubt about that, but Simon still had several hundred thousand very fanatical supporters who were ready and more than willing to lay down their lives for the man.

Intelligence believed that Bottger's people had landed on American soil several weeks back, coming ashore in very small teams, up and down the West Coast. They also believed that Simon had left caches of food and ammunition for Bottger's troops all over the Northwest.

"I think Border knew all along he didn't have a prayer of defeating us," Ike had stated at a meeting of Batt Coms a few weeks before. "I think he made the deal with Bottger just so he could go out believing there was a good chance Bottger's troops would kill you, Ben." Ike frowned and cut his eyes to Dan.

"Say it all, Ike," Ben said.

"I will," Dan said, standing up. "We've all read the intelligence reports, Ben. And we've talked at length with the people. There is only one conclusion to reach: Bottger's troops are here for one reason: You."

Ben thought about that for a second, then nodded. "You might be right. But so what? What would you have me do? And don't tell me to tuck tail and run, for you all know I won't do that."

The Batt Coms all exchanged glances, and Ben knew that was to have been their suggestion. He waved a hand. "Forget it, people. One enemy or another—civilian or soldier—has been trying to kill me for years. You all know that. I'm staying, and that's it. Let's move along."

The meeting had continued for several hours after that exchange, mapping out strategy, and the batt coms had never brought up the subject of Ben bugging out again.

But Ben felt the battalion commanders were probably correct about Bottger's troops coming in to make an attempt

on his life. The more he thought about it, the more he felt
a need to be prepared.

Several days after the meeting, Ben slipped off for a few
moments by himself and drew five days' emergency rations.
Then he managed to steal a chunk of C-4 and detonators. He
put together a ground sheet, blankets, and shelter half. A hundred rounds of ammo. A .22 caliber auto-loader with a very
good silencer and several boxes of ammo. Extra knife,
matches in a waterproof container, a hundred feet of rope.
Small camp axe. Machete. Compass. Several grenades. Socks
and a bar of regulation unscented soap. The smell of scented
soap and aftershave and cologne has cost more than one person their life in enemy territory. Water purification tablets.
A first-aid kit with a hundred five-hundred-milligram anti-
biotic capsules. He stowed the pack behind his desk in his
mobile CP, adding a few more items as he thought of them.

"Come on, you Nazi bastards, let it rip," Ben muttered,
as he patted the pack with a big hand. A slow smile curved
his lips. "If you think hunting me down will be easy, you
grossly underestimate this ol' boy."

Hell, Ben thought. That might even be fun!

Four

A squadron of headhunting gunships caught a large group of Bottger's infiltrators moving east in trucks one morning and chopped them to smoking bloody bits with machine gun and rocket fire. A team of Buddy's special operations 8 batt boys and girls caught up with another bunch of Bottger's people and sprang a classic ambush on them. Those two actions cost Bottger almost a third of his infiltrators. Another series of running fire-fights with Rebels Ike had ordered out to hunt down Bottger's people cut the odds down even more.

"Bottger's people are slowly moving east, Ben," Ike radioed one day. "To my mind, that proves our suspicions."

"I never disputed the theory," Ben replied. "I just said I wasn't running."

Several hundred miles away, Ike stomped around and cussed for a moment. Ben waited with a smile on his lips until his old friend had settled down.

"Are you through now, Ike?"

"Never, ever, have I seen a man so goddamned hardheaded as you!"

"It's one of my more endearing qualities."

"Horseshit!" Ike shouted, and broke off.

Slowly, working each town and village with care, the Rebel columns, stretching out north to south in a hundreds-of-miles-long line, moved eastward. On the L-shaped front that Simon's people had built and swore to defend to the death, thousands of Rebels waited and took no action.

Ben had Corrie try several times each day to get in touch with Simon Border, but the man refused to answer the radio calls.

"He doesn't care," Ben said. "He's willing to sacrifice thousands of his followers' lives just for a chance to get me . . . among other reasons for that stupid front he's thrown up."

"Boss, we could tear that front all to pieces just by laying back and using artillery," Cooper said.

"Sure we could, and probably will when the time comes. But even as we speak, we're closing the pinchers on Simon. We can eventually starve them out. That's a grim thought, I know. But no matter how long and hard we hammered the front with artillery, Rebels would still have to go in and finish up taking it hand to hand. When Simon's people start living on rats and bugs they'll begin giving surrender some serious thought."

Jersey shuddered at the thought of eating a rat.

"Any word on Simon's location?" Beth asked.

"Not a clue. He could have slipped through and be hiding out in Maine for all I know. I really don't expect to catch him. But I can assure you all, we haven't heard the last of Simon Border."

"What if he does surface somewhere else in America?" Anna asked. "We kill him?"

"No," Ben said, sugaring a fresh mug of coffee. "Because when, or if, he resurfaces, he'll swear he's changed his ways and seen the light. He'll wave the Bible and spout Scripture and beg our forgiveness and we'd look like a bunch of jerks if we tried to do anything to him. Then he'll start a new church somewhere and begin all over."

"And we just sit back and do nothing, allow him to do that?" Corrie asked.

"Sure. Public opinion would turn hard against us if we didn't."

"Not public opinion in the SUSA," Cooper said.

Ben smiled. "No. You're right about that. But we're realists in the SUSA, Coop. That's why our system of government works so well. Realists surrounded by what used to be called left-wing liberals. I just refer to them as a bunch of assholes and let it go at that."

"But what about all the people Simon and his followers killed?" Anna asked. "The Indians, the Blacks, the Jewish people . . . all the rest?"

"We have no proof of that," Ben countered. "And no bodies. We haven't come up on a single mass grave."

"But the people who are surrendering en masse?" Jersey asked.

Ben smiled. "Oh, they won't testify against Simon. Not against the Lord on Earth. Hell, I wouldn't trust most of those who surrendered any further than I can see them. Right now, they're enjoying the medical care and food we're providing them, but many of them will rejoin Simon as soon as possible." Ben smiled. "Of course, they don't know that we're aware of their plans, but our intel picked up on that early on."

"And we just let them rejoin Simon Border-brain and his whacky church?" Cooper asked.

"Offhand, Coop, I don't know how we could stop them."

Cooper gave that a few seconds' thought, then shrugged his shoulders. "I guess we couldn't."

Ben moved over to the wall map and studied it for a moment. "We'll be moving into some rough country in a few days. What few roads there are won't be much. We're going to wander some and see the country . . ."

His team exchanged glances. Ben wasn't fooling them a bit. He was hunting trouble and they all knew it.

"Just wander, huh?" Jersey asked, making no attempt to hide the friendly sarcasm in her voice.

"That's right, Little Bit. Sightsee. Springtime in the Rockies and all that."

"I'm sure we'll see sights we've never before seen," Corrie said.

"Oh, I'm sure we will."

"Naturally, you're going to inform President Jefferys and Ike of your plans to commune with nature?" Beth asked sweetly.

"As a matter of fact, yes, I am," Ben surprised his team by saying.

"This, I have to hear," Corrie muttered.

"I think it's a great idea, father!" Buddy Raines's voice came over the speaker.

Ben smiled.

"Oh, I do too, Ben," Ike said. "You just go right ahead and enjoy yourself."

"I think it's a marvelous idea, Ben!" Dan Gray added his voice.

"Why, thank you all," Ben said. "I just wanted to make sure I had your approval. I know how you worry about me."

"Thank you, Ben," Ike said. "Enjoy yourself in the Rockies."

"Oh, I shall, Ike. I shall."

Back at his desk, Ben turned his chair, putting his back to his team. A huge smile hung on his lips. He knew exactly why his batt coms were so enthusiastic about his planned foray through the mountains: air recon showed nothing there except a very few tiny settlements, miles and miles apart.

Ben's batt coms felt this was one way to keep him out of trouble. And, Ben leaned back in his chair, maybe they were right. But he had a hunch about those mountains, and this was the best way he knew to get away and check it out personally.

Ben had a hunch Simon Border was hiding in those mountains, and he would just dearly love to come face to face with that damned snake-oil salesman.

He rose from his chair and walked to the map. "Cooper, advise the rest of our team we'll cut off here." He pointed to a road leading through to Montana. "At this point," he hit the map, "we'll cut south, checking out these towns. We'll hook up with the lead contingent of Buddy's 8 Batt at this intersection on old Interstate 15." He smiled. "After we wander for a time in this area." Again, he thumped the map.

"Yes, sir." Cooper stared at the map for a moment. "Not much in there, boss."

"That's right, Coop. Not much at all."

Jersey and the others crowded around, joining Ben and Cooper at the wall map. "Ought to be a cake-walk, boss," the little bodyguard opined.

"Might be, Jersey. Might be."

The others smiled, with only Anna looking at her adopted father through cool, young/old and very wary eyes. General Ben was up to something, she felt. She just didn't know what. Then her eyes caught the shape of the emergency pack tucked away behind some boxes against the wall.

After Ben had left the mobile CP, Anna turned to the others in Ben's personal team. "Look here," she said, pointing to the pack.

The team crowded around while Anna opened the pack and inspected the contents.

"Keep an eye out for the boss, Coop," Jersey said, and Cooper moved to the window.

"Emergency gear," Beth said, looking at the contents of the pack. "He's getting ready for something."

"I'm with you," Corrie agreed. "I think we'd all better follow suit. But do it quietly."

"Yeah," Jersey said. "I think that, as usual, the boss knows something he's not sharing with the other batt coms."

"Especially not with Uncle Ike and President Jefferys," Anna said. "And that rings alarm bells in my head."

"Doesn't it, though?" Beth said, straightening up after helping Anna repack the emergency gear.

"I just wonder what the boss has got in the back of his mind?" Cooper questioned.

"Whatever it is, he believes a small contingent of us can handle it," Corrie said. "He likes his fun, but he wouldn't deliberately endanger the team just for some personal head-hunting."

"We'll play along with this sightseeing crap," Anna laid down the ground rules. "But we'll be ready for anything that might jump up and slap us in the face."

"Do we tell the others?" Cooper called from the window.

"It wouldn't be fair to keep them in the dark," Beth said. "I say we tell them."

They all agreed on that.

"Let's get busy," Anna said. "We've got to draw some supplies before we pull out. And knowing General Ben, we might just cut out very quickly."

But the personnel at quartermaster put it together almost from the first.

"Something's up with the general," a sergeant told another sergeant. "I don't know exactly what's going on, but the general's team is drawing some damn strange gear."

The other sergeant perked up immediately. "Oh, yeah? Like what? Tell me about it."

After listening to a list of all the gear being drawn, and all the people drawing it, the sergeant motioned to a young Rebel. "You get the word down the line to Ike, mouth to ear, no radio, that the general is about to pull something. I think he's going off headhunting on his own."

"Will do, Sarge. On my way."

Those hastening to inform Ike and Buddy had to do it by runner, for they all knew that Corrie was capable of picking up anything that squawked on the air. What Corrie didn't know about radios hadn't been invented yet, plus Corrie had a bank of scanners going all the time and could decode the conversation between two bluejays in no time flat.

Ike finally got the message about noon the next day. By that time, Ben and his team had been on the road for hours. When the roaring message from Ike nearly blew off the speakers in the big wagon, Ben smiled and said, "Ignore it, Corrie. Transmissions can get awfully garbled deep in the mountains."

"We're not deep in the mountains yet, Boss," Cooper pointed out.

Ben laughed. "Yeah. But Ike doesn't know that!"

Five

On their fourth day out, Ben looked at the passing landscape and said, "Air recon just may have been right about this area."

The team had seen no signs of human habitation since crossing over into Montana. They had passed through a dozen small towns; all had been devoid of life.

"Maybe they're deep in the mountains, boss," Jersey said. "Sitting quiet and waiting for the columns to move on east."

"I have a hunch you're right, Jersey. But how many of them?"

No one responded to that; no one among them had any way of knowing.

"So let's start cutting off the highway onto side roads and check it out," Anna suggested.

"And perhaps run into a force three or four times our size, Anna?" Ben said. "That would be very foolhardy on our part, don't you think?"

She shrugged her shoulders in silent reply. Anna loved a good fight, regardless of the odds.

Ben lifted a map and unfolded it. "Exactly where the hell are we?"

"Right in the middle of the biggest damn mountains I've ever seen," Corrie said.

"They are impressive," Ben agreed, looking out at the towering peaks that surrounded them on both sides.

They rode in silence for a few miles. The highway was

in surprisingly good shape and they were making good time as they headed deeper into the vast silent majesty of the Rockies. It was obvious that since the Great War, this highway had not seen heavy traffic.

"I can't believe that those bears we saw back a ways were just sitting in the middle of the damn road playing," Beth said. "I never saw anything like that before."

"Man hasn't made much of an appearance in this area in years, Beth," Ben told her, without looking up from the map. "This country has reverted back to the kingdom of the animals. And they were grizzlies, by the way."

"Dangerous, huh?" Anna asked.

"Very," her adopted father said. "And unpredictable, too. I don't think a grizzly has a natural enemy among the animals."

"Mountain lions around here, too, you reckon?" Cooper asked.

"I imagine they've made quite a recovery too, Coop. But they're very reclusive animals. I doubt we'll see any of them."

"Suits the hell out of me," Coop muttered. "Grizzlies are bad enough."

"I heard wolves talking to each other last night," Anna spoke. "It was so beautiful and lonely."

Ben looked up and smiled. "Yes, it was, Anna. I'm glad to see them back in such force."

"Scouts report the bridge is out a few miles up ahead," Corrie reported.

"Tell them to rejoin the column," Ben ordered. "We'll wait for them right here. Pull over, Coop. Let's stretch our legs a bit and breathe some of this fine pure air."

"We're liable to scare our lungs to death," Cooper replied, pulling over and parking, the mobile CP right behind them.

They all got out of the vehicle and walked around for a moment, getting the kinks out of their legs.

"Watch out for bears," Beth said, looking nervously around her.

Ben smiled at her expression and walked back to the mobile CP, motioning for the driver to get out. "Stretch your legs," Ben told the young Rebel. "It'll be a few minutes before the Scouts join us. Besides, we've got to figure out just where we're going to go. There aren't that many roads to choose from."

Ben stood for a moment in the middle of the road, breathing deeply of the cool, clean air.

I'd like to live up here, the thought sprang into his head. The winters are harsh, but I'd like to give it a try.

He smiled, thinking: Maybe someday I will.

Ben looked over the side of the guard railing down below. About a seventy-five-foot drop, he figured, down to the first rocky ledge. Several hundred feet or more to the bottom. He stepped into the mobile CP to get another pouch of tobacco and rolling papers. Cigarettes were still manufactured and sold by the package and carton in the SUSA (despite Dr. Chase's objections), but Ben had grown to like the hand-rolled variety. Besides, that way, he didn't smoke as much.

Ben walked over to his desk and sat down, opening a side drawer. He pulled out a bag of tobacco and papers and stuck them in the right side pocket of his jacket, securing the flap. Then he decided he'd stow some tobacco in the glove box of the big wagon and added another bag and paper to the pocket of his jacket, again securing the flap.

He pushed the chair back and started to rise when a tremendous explosion lifted the motor home off its left side tires and sent Ben sprawling to the floor as smoke filled the interior. Ben felt the motor home slam against the guard railing, and the guard railing give. At the last possible second, he reached up and jerked the mattress off the single bunk and did his best to wrap up in it as the motor home went over the side.

"Aww, shit!" Ben shouted.

Over the grind of metal scraping against rock and the dislodging and crashing sounds of objects falling inside the motor home, Ben heard the sounds of more incoming rockets exploding outside, and the yammer of small-arms fire. Then there was a sickening falling sensation, a hard slam as the motor home struck the side of the deep ravine. More bouncing. Ben was slung from side to side inside the motor home. He would have been killed or badly injured had he not had the foresight to wrap himself in the mattress.

The motor home struck something with terrific force and Ben's head smashed against the metal wall. He faded into darkness for a few seconds, then began swimming out of the gray world of unconsciousness. The falling stopped. The sounds of grinding metal ceased. Ben's pad-wrapped body ceased being flung from side to side. A groan escaped his lips from the many sore spots on his body that were just now sending pain signals to his brain.

But he was alive.

The motor home groaned in protest once and teetered sickeningly from side to side. Ben held on to one stationary leg of the bunk until the movement stopped.

"Whatever I'm hung up on isn't very permanent," he muttered.

Ben carefully and slowly slipped out of the mattress, knowing it had very probably saved his life. He glanced out of what remained of a shattered window and nearly lost the last meal he'd eaten: he could see nothing except space. He inched closer to the window and peered out. It was a very long way to the bottom.

"Oh, boy," Ben muttered. He looked up. The door was just above his head. So the motor home was lying on its side, hung up on something. A long deadly fall awaited him if whatever was holding the metal shell gave way.

For now, he was alive.

The sounds of a raging battle could be heard above him.

Ben looked around him, willing his nerves to calm down and start some rational thinking.

He spotted his CAR lying at his feet and picked it up, slinging the weapon. He picked up the pack he had put together just for something such as this. He carefully made his way, a few inches at a time, toward the cab of the motor home. On the way, he picked up a long canvas gun case, padded inside. He'd put the .270 he'd chosen back at the deserted town inside the case, along with spare ammo in two looped belts. Might need it, he thought.

The motor home lurched and groaned again and Ben spread his boots to steady himself. He could do nothing, however, to steady his stomach, which seemed to roll over a couple of times in silent protest.

The groaning and creaking of metal stopped. Ben again moved toward the cab. He could see that the windshield was gone, as was the driver's side window. If he could make the cab before the battered motor home went over the side? . . .

If not, he was death-bound toward the bottom of the ravine. He was hung up on an overhang that had prevented him from seeing the full depth of the canyon from the roadside.

One of his two full canteens pressed against his hip. It hurt, and Ben knew he had suffered deep bruises all over his body.

But he was alive.

At least for the time being.

Ben reached the cab and stuck his head out of the shattered window. His eyes rested on rocky ground a few feet away and below. He could not recall seeing anything that looked so good . . . at least not lately.

He dropped his pack. It hit the small patch of level ground and stayed put. He lowered the rifle case. The motor home lurched again and Ben grabbed the steering wheel and hung for what seemed like an eternity, but was only a few seconds. The motor home ceased its rocking. Ben heard the low hum of wind picking up; hearing that over the howl of combat some one hundred feet or so above him. If that mountain wind picked up to any sort of intensity, he was a goner, for a small gentle push was all the motor home needed to push it over the side.

A groan of pain escaped Ben's lips when he stepped up onto the side of the driver's seat. His bruised muscles were telling him to take it easy.

"No time for that," he muttered.

He eased one leg out of the window and let it dangle. Then the other leg. He dropped out of the cab, bumping his battered body against the outer shell of the motor home and sliding down the rest of the way. He grabbed for anything and burned his exposed wrist on the hot exhaust pipe. He turned that loose in a hurry.

Then his boots were on the ground and Ben's legs could hold him no more. He sank to the rocks and took several deep breaths. His gloved hands pulled his pack and rifle case close to him just as the wind picked up, and he found some small comfort clutching his meager possessions.

Seconds later, the wrecked motor home went over the side in a shriek of metal. It seemed to fall for a long time before striking the bottom. The motor home caught fire; smoke drifted up to Ben. The gas tanks did not explode. Ben knew they seldom did. That scene is more often than not reserved for the movies.

He looked up. He could not see the lip of the roadway. Rock protrusions prevented that. The sounds of combat were fainter now, and Ben had no way of knowing if the battle was winding down or the winds were blowing the sounds away from him.

But he was alive!

Far below him, the motor home was burning, sending black smoke in all directions at the whim of the wind.

Ben rested for a few moments, then began looking

around him. There was no way out to his left, no way straight down, and to climb up was out of the question. That left one way. Ben crawled to his aching legs and willed his legs to work. He struggled into the pack and adjusted the straps. He picked up the rifle case and began his trek. The only way open to him wound gently down. Fine. He'd damn sure take it.

He walked for several dozen yards, then sat down on a large rock to rest. He dug in a side pocket of the pack and took out a small bottle of aspirin. He took two, washing them down with a sip of water. He carefully capped the bottle and returned it to the side pocket of the pack.

Ben took that time to check his CAR. It was intact and had suffered no damage. He checked his side arm. Undamaged. He returned the 9mm to its flap holster and slung his CAR. Rising to his boots, he resumed his trek downward.

He reached the bottom of the ravine, or canyon, or whatever the hell it was, much quicker than he anticipated. He looked up. It was a long way to the road. The sounds of shooting were very faint, but the fight was still going on. Well, he thought, I'm sure out of this fight . . . at least for the time being.

He looked around him, seeking some sort of trail that animals might have cut out over the years, and spotted a dim path. He headed that way.

As he walked, he thought: the attack had probably been a carefully planned ambush, and he did not believe it had been carried out by Simon's home guard. That meant it was Bottger's troops. They had slipped through the lines of Rebels, and as spread out as Ben's people were, that would not have been difficult to accomplish.

And if there was one team of Bottger's troops, there could just as easily be a dozen or more.

Ben was deliberately keeping all thoughts of his team from his mind, refusing to dwell on what might have happened to them. Right now, his own survival was paramount; time for introspection would come later.

He prodded carefully on. He came to a small creek and knelt down, shrugging off his pack and laying his weapons aside only after taking a long careful look all around him. He bathed his face and hands several times, the cold water reviving him and chasing away any fog that remained to cloud his senses.

Ben had no way of knowing how many, or even if any of his team escaped the ambush. So he couldn't afford to dwell on that. He had to think of his own survival.

He felt sure that Corrie had gotten off a message, but in these mountains, whether it was received or not was a question. She would not have had time to set up her dish to bounce a signal off a satellite. Not unless she survived the ambush. If that was the case, then this area would be filled with Rebel gunships and search parties in a few hours. If not? . . . Ben was on his own. But he'd been on his own many times before; it was not a new experience.

A bullet whined off a rock very close to Ben's head and sent him scrambling for cover. He lay still amid the rocks and new vegetation and waited, only his eyes moving.

"General Raines!" the shout came from far above him.

Ben lifted only his eyes and remained silent.

"Had you not taken that last step, you would be a dead man. As it is, you have only prolonged your life an hour, at best."

Ben waited.

"My name is Hugo Runkel, General. Colonel Hugo Runkel."

"Pleased, I'm sure," Ben muttered. He pushed himself back a few inches, then a few inches more. The movement attracted no gunfire, so Ben slipped back a few feet, until he was in a small grove of trees and brush. He uncased the .270 and cartridge belts and pushed the case away from him. He would not be needing it. He slung one cartridge belt around his waist and looped the other across his chest.

"Knowing your penchant for striking out on your own, General," Hugo called, "it was a simple matter to plot your course when you entered the wilderness area. There aren't that many roads, you know."

Ben loaded up the .270 and removed the caps from the powerful scope he had picked up at the old store in the deserted town. He pulled the rifle to his shoulder, adjusted the scope magnification, and began searching the rocky area above him.

"The ambush went well, General," Hugo shouted. "We wiped out your entire team."

"Doubtful," Ben muttered. "My people aren't trained to stick around and die in a hopeless situation."

Ben spotted something out of sync with the terrain and settled the crosshairs on the object. For a few seconds it puzzled him; then he figured out what it was. Someone's knee. He calculated the range at about a hundred and seventy-five yards, uphill, which could be as tricky as shooting downhill.

Ben had sighted the rifle in at approximately a hundred and fifty yards at the deserted town. He settled into a more comfortable position and snugged the rifle into his shoulder. Just before he pulled the trigger, he thought: Be a miracle if I make this shot on the first try, and I'd better, for one shot will be all I'm going to get with this fellow.

He gently squeezed the trigger and the rifle cracked. He immediately pulled the rifle back from recoil and sighted in. The knee had turned into a man, and the man was rolling down the incline, screaming in pain. Then, as in a comedy of errors, the wounded man reached out a hand and grabbed at something. The something turned out to be another man and his momentum pulled the second man from cover. The second man held on to the wounded man, bracing against a rock.

Ben shot him in the belly.

The first man was released from a suddenly numbed hand and rolled a few more yards before coming to a stop in some scrub brush and rocks.

Smiling, Ben gathered up his gear and began crawling backward, deeper into the timber and brush. When he was sure he was reasonably safe from the eyes on the mountainside, Ben rose to his feet and began heading east, making as much time as his bruised and hurting legs could carry him.

"Come on, Colonel Runkel," he whispered. "You want to make a fight of it . . . well, me too!"

Six

Within two hours, the sky over the ambush site was filled with helicopter gunships and the terrain was crawling with Rebels. Ike had taken command and was standing grim-faced on the side of the road, looking down at the tiny twisted and charred shape of the wrecked motor home that Ben had used for his CP.

Rebels were rappelling down ropes from hovering 'copters to the canyon floor.

Ben had lost about a third of his team before the rest scattered, as they had been trained to do. The Rebels often-times adhered to the old adage: He who fights and runs away, lives to fight another day.

Anna, Jersey, Corrie, Beth, and Cooper were all bruised and scratched, but otherwise unhurt. They were all highly pissed about what had happened.

They had been checked out and over by medics and re-leased. They were standing by the side of the road, with Ike.

"But you're sure you saw Ben get into the motor home?" Ike questioned.

"Yes, sir," Beth said. "That's firm."

"And you all heard shots *after* the initial ambush was over?"

"Yes, sir. At least four shots," Jersey said. "From over the side here. The shots came long after the ambush was over."

"Motor home is empty," Ike's radio tech said. "And no bodies around it."

Ike motioned to a half dozen teams of Rebels standing by, ready to go over the side of the ravine. "Check the path of descent," he ordered. "Carefully."

Ropes were slung over the side and the teams of Rebels began scrambling down, maintaining a distance of about twenty-five feet apart. They would go over every inch of the way down to the canyon floor.

Far below, a dozen Rebels searched the interior of the motor home, pulling out everything that would jerk loose and laying it out on the ground.

"The general's CAR is not in the motor home," the tech reported. "Neither is anything resembling that pack his team told us about, or that rifle he picked up at the deserted town."

For the first time since arriving at the ambush site, Ike allowed himself a small smile. The odds of all three items being thrown from the motor home were high against. The odds that Ben had made it out alive were getting better.

Hurt, probably. But alive, yes.

"Tell the teams left and right of the wreck site to move out," Ike ordered. "Slow and easy."

"How far out do you want them to range, sir?"

"Until I tell them to stop," Ike growled.

"Pilots report no easy way up the side for several miles in either direction," the tech said.

"Thank you," Ike said gently, softening his gruff order of a few seconds past.

The tech smiled, having long ago grown accustomed to Ike's growling.

Ike walked off to be by himself. No one followed him, sensing he wished to be alone. He stopped several dozen yards off and began walking back and forth across the road.

"Dr. Chase coming in," the tech called. "ETA three minutes."

JUDGMENT IN THE ASHES 201

Ike paused, nodded his understanding, then resumed his restless pacing. He stopped, stared at Corrie. "You're sure Ben had a good radio in that emergency pack, extra batteries?"

"Yes, sir."

"All emergency frequencies being scanned since arrival," the tech said, anticipating Ike's next question.

Ike resumed his pacing.

"Dr. Chase is here," a Rebel called to Ike. "Sending a vehicle down the road to get him."

Ike nodded, then rejoined Ben's team at the guardrail.

"Scouts have picked up a lone set of boot prints leading east and south. But they didn't come from the wreckage," the tech said. "They came down the hill then cut east."

"All right!" Ike said. "Ben got out *before* the CP went over that first ledge yonder."

"Depth of prints indicate the man is limping, but not too badly."

Ike smiled. "The ol' wolf made it out. That's the hardest man to stop I ever saw in my life."

Chase joined the group and talked briefly with Ike, then stood silently by the guardrail, staring down at the wreckage.

A half hour later, the tech called, "The trackers have found signs of a fire-fight south and east of here. Brass from a .270 found at the bottom of the canyon, blood on the rocks above. Somebody got hard hit. Measuring from elbow indentation to toe marks show a man approximately six feet, four inches tall. The boot tracks lead off to the east."

"Ben," Chase said with an audible sigh of relief.

"He's being followed by a team of about ten men," the tech called.

"Ben's heading into some of the roughest country in America," Ike said.

"And doing it deliberately," Chase added.

"Yes. He damn sure is," Ike replied. He spread a map on the hood of a HumVee and studied it for a moment, Chase standing close. "There is absolutely no way to tell which direction Ben might take. He might head straight east, he might go north or south, he might circle around and come up behind Bottger's men."

"You're sure they were Bottger's people?" the chief of medicine asked.

"Yes. The bodies are stretched out over there." Ike pointed to a row of bodies laid out by the side of the road, covered with ground sheets.

"Any taken alive?"

"Two. One of them is badly hurt and won't live out the rest of the day. He's been talking some. Ben has at least a hundred men, maybe twice that number, chasing him." Ike waved a hand toward the east. "Out there in all that thousands and thousands of acres of wilderness. I did some training out there years back, Doc. Skilled trackers and experienced woodsmen have gotten lost in that wilderness. Some of them were never found."

"Were there any signs of Ben's being injured?"

"No traces of blood. Scouts say he's limping some."

"Hell, yes, he's limping. He's probably bruised from head to toe. Might have cracked a bone or two. I don't see how he survived at all."

"He's lucky, Doc. Ben is the luckiest man I've ever known."

Lamar grunted. "You know, Ike, Ben's on his own now. No decisions to make, no paperwork to wade through, no one breathing down his neck. And you know what else?"

"What?"

"He's enjoying every damn minute of it!"

Ben took the time to soak his feet in a stream, the water ice cold. He washed his socks and attached them securely

to the back of his pack to dry—slipping them through
straps—then dried his feet on his field jacket before slipping on fresh socks and lacing up his boots.

He sat for a moment, eating a vitamin-packed hi-energy
bar, then sipped some water and was off again. He did not
want to sit for any length of time, knowing his bruised
muscles would tighten up and really start giving him problems. Better to keep moving.

He found some wild berries and picked a double handful,
eating them as he moved slowly along, enjoying the semi-
sweet tartness of the wild spring berries. He also kept a
wary eye out for bears. They had not been out of hiberna-
tion long, and were extremely short-tempered this time of
the year.

Ben also knew that a .270 was not really suitable for
stopping a charging bear . . . if it ever came to that, and
he certainly hoped it wouldn't. The last thing Ben wanted
was to come nose to snout with a grizzly.

Stopped to rest on a ridge, Ben stayed low and behind
cover and uncased his binoculars, carefully studying the terrain to the west. He could not spot any of his pursuers, but
knew they were back there. He wished he had some idea
how many. He pulled his small transceiver from his pack
and knew the instant he touched the small handy-talkie it
was busted. He shook it and it rattled like a tin can filled
with marbles.

"This certainly makes it more interesting," Ben muttered.
He buried the broken radio in the ground, smoothed the
ground over, then carefully spread leaves and twigs on the
fresh dig to hide it from any experienced tracker. With a
sigh and a silent groan of protest from his aching muscles,
Ben heaved himself to his boots and continued on deeper
into the wilderness.

He looked up at the sky. Clouds moving in, dark clouds,
heavy with rain. He had to find shelter for the night, find
it soon, and sit out the storm. He also did not want to be

caught out in the open, exposed, when the lightning started, for a lightning storm in the high country is a fearsome and dangerous product of nature.

Ben came to a small blowdown in the timber, but ignored it, knowing if he were tracking an enemy, that would be the first place he'd look. He plodded on.

About thirty minutes later, he found what he was looking for. He had pushed aside some brush at the base of a rise of ground, and found a hole, just large enough for him to squeeze into. The hole enlarged to a tiny cave, long enough and wide enough for him to stretch out, and that was just about it. There were no signs that any bear or wolf had ever used the place as a den.

Ben quickly gathered some twigs and dry wood, then slowly and carefully covered his tracks leading back to the tiny cave. He was careful not to disturb the bushes covering the cave entrance, crawling in from the side and sprinkling leaves and dirt over any tracks he might have left.

Ben built a tiny fire and took a packet of dry soup mix from his pack, added water, stirred, and brought it to a boil. He glanced at his watch. Four o'clock. It would be dark in an hour. He drank his soup, munched on some crackers, and then using his canteen cup, brewed a cup of coffee and leaned back, rolling a cigarette. He drank his coffee, smoked his cigarette, and then put out the fire just as the first streaks of lightning lanced across the darkening mountain skies; thunder hammered hard, followed quickly by a driving rain. Ben took two more aspirin and stretched out on his ground sheet, pulling a blanket over him. He sighed in contentment as his aching and bruised muscles began to relax. The storm grew in intensity, but Ben was warm and dry.

The last thing Ben thought before sleep overtook him was: I hope you Nazi bastards drown out there!

When Ben awakened hours later, he was so sore he could scarcely move. There would be no traveling for him this day. But he did feel more refreshed in his mind; clearer headed. The rain had stopped, the storm having blown on past during the night.

When Ben crawled out of his blankets, he had to bite his lip to keep from crying out. It seemed to him that he did not have one inch of flesh on his body that did not hurt.

This morning he decided he would not build a fire, and used a heat tab to warm up his coffee and soup. While his soup was heating he crawled outside and relieved himself, carefully covered the spot, then it was back into the tiny cave.

A cup of soup, some crackers, and two cups of coffee later, with some aspirin, he began to feel better. He chanced one quick smoke then settled back on his blankets and promptly went to sleep.

Voices woke him: unfamiliar and very unfriendly voices. He lay still and listened to the voices talking back and forth outside his hidey-hole.

Ben could not catch all the words, but it seemed the men searching for him were very frustrated. Colonel Runkel was extremely pissed at their failure to find General Raines.

Ben smiled, thinking: Good, you Nazi dickhead, I hope your blood pressure goes right off the wall and you have a fucking stroke.

Ben heard bootsteps just outside the brush covering the entrance to his cave, but the bootsteps did not linger long. The man wearing the boots cursed Ben in two languages and then moved on.

Ben went back to sleep and slept for several hours, awakening at noon. He munched on a hi-energy bar, drank some water, took two more aspirin, and napped the rest of the afternoon away. About an hour before full dark, he crawled out of the cave to have a look around. He was alone; he could sense that. The birds were also telling him news: they were pecking for food and singing.

Ben used another heat tab to warm up some terrible-tasting glop from a dinner pack—he wasn't sure what it was—and ate the mess. It filled his stomach. But the coffee tasted wonderful and he enjoyed a smoke. Then it was back into his warm blankets and more hours of healing sleep.

The next day he was not quite so sore but he still did not feel like running any races. He lounged around the cave for a second day, eating and resting. He neither heard nor saw any sign of his pursuers.

On the morning of the third day, Ben packed up and moved on. At first he was undecided which direction to go. Runkel would not be so stupid as to throw all his men eastward. He would leave several teams behind in case Ben decided to return to the highway. So Ben plunged deeper into the wilderness, following Runkel and his men. Occasionally, a smile would crease Ben's lips.

He had a plan, of course; he'd been dreaming up and rejecting plans one after another during the long hours in the cave until, finally he had formulated a simple plan that he could accept.

Now Runkel would learn how it felt to be pursued. Ben's plan was one that guerrilla forces had been using for centuries: when outnumbered, *attack!*

"You can't be serious, man!" Dr. Lamar Chase roared at Ike.

"Sit down, Doc," Ike said patiently. "And listen to me."

Lamar sat and glared at Ike.

Ike pointed to the map pinned to the board in his tent. "By now, Ben could be anywhere out there. Thousands and thousands of acres of wilderness. We don't know where to look. It's been four days since he walked away from the ambush site. He could have covered fifty or sixty miles in any direction by now. We know he didn't come back toward the highway. Why? Because he's being chased, that's why. For reasons of his own, Ben has decided to lead the enemy *away* from us. God and Ben alone know why he's doing that. And I didn't call off the search, Lamar. I just widened it, that's all. Whoever planned this op is smart. We've got enemy hit-and-run teams attacking us all up and down our western lines, and they're keeping us plenty busy. I've got every helicopter I can spare looking for Ben."

"I can't imagine why he hasn't radioed in."

"I can. His radio's busted, that's why."

Lamar sighed with great patience. "I will never, ever, understand the mind of a dedicated combat man."

Ike laughed. "Ben likes it, Lamar. He loves the thrill of the greatest hunt of all: man against man. Winner take all."

"Never entered your mind that it's your life you're putting on the line, does it?"

Ike smiled. "What's the old saying about, 'You pays your money, you takes your chances?' "

Lamar shook his head and headed for the flap of the tent. He turned and looked at Ike. "What would men like you and Ben do if all wars were suddenly ended?"

"Be bored shitless."

Seven

Colonel Hugo Runkel looked up, a smile on his face, as the very faint sounds of two shots echoed through the cool late spring air. He could not tell what direction the shots came from. But that made little difference, for he had ordered his men not to fire unless they had a clear target, and they were superb marksmen. They would soon be checking in by radio with the good news that Ben Raines was dead.

Hugo poured another cup of coffee and waited.

Two ridges, a meadow, and a small mountain away, Ben knelt down by the first body. The .270 round had taken the man in the center of the chest, exploding the heart. The man had been dead meat before he hit the ground. Ben took the man's transceiver, two small packets of field rations, a waterproof container of matches, his grenades, and moved over a few hundred yards to the second man. Just like his partner, the man was dead.

Ben took the young man's field rations, radio, matches, and grenades, and left him in a dead bloody and grotesque sprawl on the rocky ground. Ben could not use their ammunition in any of his weapons.

Five hundred yards later, Ben squatted down and inspected the radios. The handy-talkies had pre-set frequencies, and would be no good in contacting his own people, however . . . Ben smiled, his own people would be scanning every frequency known to humankind! Perhaps he couldn't talk directly to them . . .

"Hey, you son of a bitch!" Ben's voice ripped through the speakers, and Runkel sat straight up, his fresh cup of coffee cooling and forgotten. "That's right, you, you god-damn Nazi asshole. Are you listening, Rumpelstiltskin?"

With a snarl that seemed out of place coming from a human throat, Runkel snatched up his radio. "Raines?"

"That's me, in the flesh, alive and well, you goose-stepping prick," Ben said. "I just sent two more of your Hitler look-alikes to that great Aryan resting place. I left them their to-bacco; it wasn't my brand. But I suspect where they're going they won't need a light."

Runkel cursed Ben for a moment, then managed to get his temper under control enough so he could speak without sputtering in rage. Miles away, a Rebel radio tech was tape-recording every word.

The radio tech's listening post was high on a mountain, and these were the first words he'd heard in two days. But he knew General Raines's voice.

"You are a very lucky person, General," Runkel said.

"Naw," Ben came right back. "Naw. Just a hell of a lot better man than you and these goons with you. You got all that, liverwurst?"

Runkel's eyes bugged out in rage he could no longer contain. He cursed Ben in several languages while his team stood by in shocked silence. They had never, ever, heard anyone speak to their colonel in such a manner.

Miles away, in his listening post, the radio tech laughed aloud as he kept a careful eye on the VU needle. General Raines sounded as though he was really having fun. General Ike would get a kick out of listening to this exchange.

"Hey, Bunkel!" Ben called. "Why don't you and I meet, just the two of us, and settle this mano a mano?"

"What?" Runkel screamed.

Ben sighed. "I might have known you wouldn't understand. You really are a stupid mother-fucker, aren't you, Colonel Runkel?"

Runkel screamed in an outburst of undisguised rage. He was so angry he could not form words.

"Are you still there, Funkel?" Ben asked calmly.

"You are a dead man, Raines!" Hugo screamed into the mic. "A dead man!"

"Yeah, yeah, yeah," Ben taunted him. "Tell me, puke-face, do you put yourself to sleep each night dreaming of sucking Hitler's dick?"

The Rebel radio tech was enjoying the exchange immensely.

Runkel's men were standing about, their mouths hanging open in shock.

Colonel Hugo Runkel calmed himself with a visible effort. He took several deep breaths and felt his heretofore soaring blood pressure fall to normal points. "Very good, General," Hugo spoke in a calm voice. "Very, very good. That tactic will not work with me again."

"You can't do anything again, Punkel," Ben shot right back. "Once something is done, it's done. You might do something similar, but you can't do anything again."

"What?" Runkel blurted.

"You never heard of Brother Dave? One of the great Southern philosophers of all time?"

"What the hell are you babbling about now, Raines?"

"You dumb son of a bitch," Raines said.

Runkel fought to keep his temper in check.

"Who is Brother Dave?" one of his men whispered to a comrade standing close.

The soldier shrugged his shoulders.

"I see no need to continue this conversation, Raines," Runkel said. "It's beginning to bore me."

"Me, too, Runkel," Ben didn't miss a beat. "I'd be better off conversing with a jackass."

But Ben had played this one out to its conclusion. Runkel wasn't going to bite. "Good-bye, Raines. The next time we meet, I shall kill you."

"Big words from such a little man. Good-bye, Runkel. Pleasant dreams. I'll be visiting your camp tonight."

"We'll be waiting for you, Raines! Thanks for the warning, you arrogant fool!"

Ben smiled as he turned off the radio. Of course, he had no intention of visiting the enemy camp that night. He chuckled, thinking of all the sleepy people come the morning. That's when he would strike.

"Ben's having a good time, isn't he?" Ike asked, laughing at the frown on Dr. Chase's face.

Lamar grunted his reply. "Run the damn tape again, you laughing hyena."

Ike rewound the tape and together they listened to Ben put the needle to the colonel. "What the hell is Raines up to, Ike?"

"Having fun."

"Jesus H Christ, Ike! The man is outnumbered about a hundred to one and you're talking about him having fun?"

"Ben knows what he's doing, Lamar."

"Having fun, Ike?"

"And buying us a little time by keeping the enemy busy. An enemy that is standing directly in our path. And there is something else, Lamar: You said it yourself in so many words: Ben doesn't want to be found just yet."

"I suppose you're right about that," the doctor grudgingly admitted.

"If he wanted to be found, he'd send us a signal of some sort. Amid all the horsing around with this colonel, Ben managed to give us his name so our intel people can put together a dossier."

"I've been in the military all my adult life, Ike. I can truthfully say I have never met a man quite like Ben Raines."

"Neither has this Colonel Runkel," Ike said, a grimness behind his words. "And he's about to find that out the hard way."

Ben slept well that night, despite his going to sleep with only a cold supper, no coffee, and no fire to warm him before he crawled into his blankets.

He was up long before the sun and in position about two hundreds yards from the enemy camp an hour later. If he could get lead into Colonel Runkel . . .

A slight movement to his left put an end to Ben's musing.

Well now, Ben thought. Either the man is so good I missed him coming in, or he's up to take a leak, and I suspect the latter.

"Rolf?" the softly called question came from the sentry that Ben had spotted about twenty-five yards ahead and just to his right while getting into position.

"Yes. Time to tighten our perimeters. You're the last one to come in, and you're late."

"My watch must be slow. I have eight minutes to go."

"No one has seen anything this night," Rolf said, moving closer. "We are playing a fool's game, I think."

"I certainly think so. This Raines person would not deliberately warn us of his attack plans. The colonel is overreacting, I believe."

Ben lay on the dew-damp new spring grass and smiled in the darkness. You just keep on believing that, boys. Right up to the time I put a bullet in you.

The problem is, I'm not sure what this Colonel Runkel looks like. And if he's any good at all, and he probably is very good, he will be wearing no insignia and his men will not salute. And he won't necessarily be an older man.

"No word yet on our reinforcements?"

"Nothing. They'll be here, don't worry about that. Come on, let's tighten it up before the colonel has a fit."

Ben heard soft laughter and then the whisper of boots as the sentries moved away, closer to the camp.

Reinforcements on the way, Ben silently mulled that over. But how the hell are they getting here? Ben gave that some thought.

They have to be coming in from the north, that's where our lines are the thinnest, manned only by a small force of American and Canadian militia. That is the only way a force of any size could get through. They're jumping in. HALOing, probably, in small teams. Free-falling thousands of feet and walking in. I've got to get that word to Ike . . . somehow. But I don't know how many or when. Hell, they might already be on the ground, probably are, and making their way south.

Shit!

Does this, should this, change tonight's plans? Ben thought about that. No, he concluded. If anything, I've got to make it succeed, with better results than I originally planned.

Suddenly, there was activity in the camp. Dark forms began stirring around, stretching, yawning, getting the kinks out of muscles stiff from sleeping on the ground. Ben could just imagine the soft grumbling of the men just awakened.

He stole a glance at his watch. About forty-five minutes before good light. He cut his eyes to the east. Already there were silver shards appearing, streaking the sky.

He decided to move in a few yards closer and by the time he had closed the distance fifty yards, it was light enough for some shooting. Ben uncapped the scope and sighted in. He would be shooting slightly downhill, and he compensated for that. He saw an older man that he pegged as a senior sergeant; he just had that look about him. Ben sighted him in.

A second later the man was on the ground, kicking out the last of life. Ben worked the bolt, shifted the muzzle, and drilled another man, dusting him from side to side. Two on the ground.

Ben spotted a leg sticking out from behind a tree and blew the knee into a sackful of pebbles. He could hear the man screaming from a hundred and fifty yards away.

Another man grabbed a rifle and came charging up the hill, throwing all caution and training to the wind. Ben shot him in the gut and the man folded over as if he'd been hit with a sledgehammer.

Ben quickly reloaded and shifted to a position he'd picked out while settled into his first firing post.

But there were no more targets. Runkel's men had dropped behind good cover and were not moving. But Ben had cut the odds down even more. Now it was time to get the hell gone. Ben vanished into the brush and timber.

With a soldier's intuition, Runkel sensed when Ben had left. The colonel carefully stood up and surveyed his camp. It was a grim sight that greeted his eyes. Three of his men dead or dying and one crippled. Runkel softly cursed Ben Raines, but there was grudging respect behind the vile oaths.

Hugo Runkel had been a professional soldier for thirty-five of his fifty years, having served in various armies, under various flags, all around the world. And he *knew* that he was up against a solid professional warrior.

"All right, General," he whispered. "Now we know each other well. The ground rules have been laid. No quarter, no mercy expected from either side. So be it."

Runkel looked at the aid man, working on the one man still alive. "How is Raiser?"

"He'll never walk again, Colonel. That round shattered the knee."

More wounded men, Runkel thought. Runkel knew well, as did all combat men, that a wounded man took at least two able men to care for and carry.

"Do we pursue, Colonel?" one of his men asked.

Runkel shook his head. "No. That is probably what Raines hopes we'll do. He's out there, lying in wait, to ambush any who follow." Runkel stood silent for a moment, then he waved at two men. "You two, head out to pick up his tracks. But slow and easy and with the utmost of caution. Let's try to throw a net around the general. Once we've done that, we can start closing the noose."

Runkel's men lost Ben within a half mile after leaving camp. Ben had found a rocky piece of ground at the base of a mountain and stayed with the rocks, being very careful where he placed his boots. When the rocks ended and grassy ground took over, Ben turned toward the mountain and started upward. After climbing for about a hundred yards, he turned again, onto a level space filled with scrub brush and hardy mountain vegetation, and once more stayed with the rocks for half a mile, all the while steadily but gently climbing. After an hour, he was forced to stop for a rest. He was recovering from his fall, but was still not a hundred percent, and suspected it would take several more days before he was fully back to snuff.

Nestled amid the rocks, safe from being spotted, except by aircraft—and he was reasonably sure that Runkel did not have any of those—Ben sampled some of the field rations he'd taken from the dead soldiers. They tasted the same as the rations issued to the Rebels: edible, and that was about all one could say for them. But they filled his belly. Ben had refilled his canteens from a spring that morning, and dropped in purification tablets. He washed the rations down with water and dozed as the sun rose higher in the sky, warming him and lulling him into sleep.

He awakened after about an hour and uncased his binoculars, carefully scanning the terrain below and on both sides of his location. He could see nothing. Either Runkel's men had given up, or they were following the false trail that Ben had laid out for them the day before. He smiled, hoped it was the latter, for if that was the case, unless those tracking him were highly skilled and very, very careful, they were soon going to be in a world of hurt . . . or very dead.

For Ben had booby-trapped the trail he had so carefully laid out. There were man-traps all along the trail he had made through the timber.

Ben picked up his weapons and started down the rocky slope. He headed east, not west, deeper into the wilderness. Tonight he would give Colonel Runkel a bump and bait him some more, all the while alerting his own people to the infiltrators coming in.

Ben smiled. Then he would really start making this game interesting.

Eight

Runkel looked down at the body of one of the men he'd sent out to track Raines. He was headless, having been decapitated by a grenade, set chest-level along the trail, tripped by a boot catching on a vine strung ankle-high.

What remained of his team began looking nervously around them. This Ben Raines was truly a devil.

Runkel pointed toward two men. "Find Bergman," he ordered in a low voice. "Since he's not responding to my radio calls, I can assume he's dead."

Gingerly, the men began moving up the trail.

"The rest of you bury the corporal," Runkel said, a weariness to his voice.

Runkel's team was slowly and insidiously being whittled down. But it wasn't the loss of men that bothered him so much as it was the toll Raines's actions were taking on morale.

His men were becoming sullen and tense, and worse, they were afraid. He could see the fear in their eyes, and that infuriated him. One man out there, having fired no more than ten or twelve shots all told, had done what an entire platoon had not been able to do.

But so far, Raines had not attempted to attack any of the three other teams in the wilderness. Only Runkel's. The colonel softly cursed. He lifted his walkie-talkie.

"Team two?"

"Colonel," came the almost immediate response from team two, working an area about five miles away, to the north.

"You have seen no sign of the general?"

"Nothing, sir."

"Team three?"

"Negative, Colonel," came the response from the team working the area to the south. "No sign of the man."

"Team four?"

"Nothing, Colonel," was the reply from the team working the area to the west.

"Well, where is the son of a bitch!" Runkel snarled. "If he is working his way east, *why* is he doing it? The nearest Rebel troops in that direction are hundreds of miles away. What in the hell is the man doing?"

The late spring winds sighed in reply, ruffling the newly budded leaves and gently moving the rapidly growing grass just beyond the tree line.

The beauty of Mother Nature's reply was lost on Colonel Runkel.

Runkel slowly turned, doing a three-sixty, his eyes searching all around him. "Where the hell are you, Raines?" he whispered. "And what in the hell are you up to?"

Ben had listened to the radio calls while resting in a copse of trees. So there were three more full platoon-sized teams looking for him. Say . . . a hundred men, all told. Maybe more—probably more. Standard company-sized. Not very good odds, Ben had to admit.

But the radio calls had not given him any indication of the areas the other teams were working. He would have to guess and play that loose until he could be sure. Runkel would never think, not at first, that Ben would head east, so it was easy to assume that one team was working to his west, preventing, or attempting to prevent, Ben from returning to his own lines in that direction.

So that left two teams working north and south of his location. It was an educated guess on Ben's part, but he had no way of knowing just how accurate his guessing was.

Not yet, anyway.

Assuming, and that was a lousy word for a soldier to use, his guessing was correct, what to do about it?

Well, first thing was to warn Ike of the infiltrators, and then to lead Runkel and his men deeper into the wilderness. If he could somehow convey his plans to Ike while putting the needle to Runkel, and if Ike caught on, he would then drop teams behind the infiltrators and catch them from the rear.

If. Biggest little word in the dictionary, Ben's father used to say.

"Hey, gooberlips!" Ben's voice startled the radio tech. "You, Runkel-Funkel, whatever your name is. Are you listening?"

With only a slight narrowing of his eyes and his suddenly stiff back expressing his true inner feelings, Colonel Hugo Runkel picked up the mic. "I'm here, Raines."

"Resting on your ass savoring past glories, Colonel? That's about all you've got left, isn't it. Since you started pushing me east, you've struck out every time we've met."

Miles away, Ike's listening posts had begun both taping the conversations and taking notes.

"I am not driving you east, Raines."

"Well, I sure as hell can't go west, now, can I," Ben responded. "I'd run smack into more of your people. That would be rather stupid on my part, wouldn't it?"

"You're doing all the talking, Raines. Are you getting lonesome out there all by yourself?"

Ben laughed. "Not at all. I'm having too much fun killing more of your men each day. Oh, by the way, Sunkel, my people have captured or killed most of those infiltrators that were coming down from Canada to link up with you."

"You lie, Raines. I spoke with . . ." Then Runkel realized what Ben was doing and bit back his words The son of a bitch had tricked him.

Runkel knew then that Raines's people had set up listening posts around the area and were monitoring everything he said.

"Good-bye, Raines," the colonel said. "We shall speak no more."

Ben clicked off the radio to conserve the batteries. Runkel had finally caught on. Well, it had gone on longer than Ben had felt it would when he began. He only hoped that the Rebels manning Ike's listening posts—that's if they were even set up and operating—had taped it all. If they had, Ike could act immediately and the infiltrators would be in a fight for their lives . . . which they would lose.

But for now, Ben shifted positions and searched until he found a suitable place to spend the night. He brewed his coffee while he ate some rations, and then smoked a cigarette and went to bed. He wanted to whittle down the odds a bit more come the morning.

Ike listened to the tape and smiled. A minute later, he ordered every helicopter gunship and fixed-wing aircraft that could fly up and searching for the infiltrators.

"All that is very good, but Ben gave us no indication where he is," Dr. Chase bitched.

"He feels he can do more good out in the field, Lamar. Obviously, he's taking a toll on the enemy troops out there."

"He'll run out of rations before long. If he hasn't already."

Ike couldn't argue with that. But he had a hunch that Ben was taking field rations from the enemy soldiers he killed. Still, he wished he could think of a way to get Ben resupplied. The techs at the listening posts were triangling each signal, and Ike had a pretty good idea where Ben was . . . in a rough sort of way. But any air drop would give away Ben's position.

"When he gets hungry, he'll let us know, Lamar. Ben's not going to miss many meals."

"It wouldn't hurt you to miss a few," Chase popped right back.

Ike sighed.

Chase held up a hand. "All right, all right, Ike. I'll get out of your hair. But I'll leave you with this: When is Ben going to get it through his head that he is the commander of a huge army, not a one-man wrecking crew?"

"Age will take care of that, Lamar. All in good time."

"Providing he lives that long," Chase came right back, then walked out.

The soldier's foot stepped into the punji pit, the stakes ripped into his calf, and Ben was out of cover and on him like a hungry puma, stilling the man's panicked cries of pain before they could get out of his mouth. Ben wiped the bloody blade of his knife on the dead man's shirt and quickly fanned the body, taking the man's grenades and field rations: food for another day. But Ben knew that, sooner or later, Runkel would catch on to what he was doing and start sending his people out with no rations.

Ben left the body where it was and slipped away, moving silently as a puma through the brush . . . Ben smiled at that thought. Well, an older puma, at least.

But this test of Ben's endurance and effectiveness in the field was proving one thing: Ben still had what it took to survive in the field. And he doubted Ike or Chase or anyone else would argue that point with much enthusiasm.

Ben squatted down at the edge of a meadow, staying well inside the timber and surveyed the terrain. He could see nothing out of the ordinary, but knew that meant nothing. He also knew that he had been awfully lucky so far. One misstep on his part and he would be dead, cooling meat, and that was not something he relished.

He decided not to try the meadow and slipped back into the timber and brush. Since the Great War, there had been a virtual explosion of growth in the nation's wilderness areas, and natural cover was abundant . . . if one knew how to use it effectively, and Ben certainly did.

Ben checked his watch—almost noon, and his stomach was telling him to put something in it. He crawled into a thick stand of brush and made himself comfortable. He peeled the wrapper off a hi-energy bar and slowly ate it, washing it down with sips of water. On a hunch, he slipped the earplug into one ear and turned on the radio, letting it scan. He was both surprised and pleased to hear Ike's voice fill his head.

"Colonel Runkel, I repeat, this is General Ike McGowan. We have stopped your infiltrators and to continue this fight will be pointless on your part. If you surrender, I give you my word you will be treated in accordance with the rules of the Geneva convention and shipped back home. Please respond to this message, Colonel."

"This is Colonel Runkel, General. I'm listening."

"You can't win this fight, Colonel. Give it up."

"I may well die out here, General. But the odds of my taking your General Raines with me are slowly swinging over to my side. And I think you are well aware of that."

So Ike got my message and chopped up the incoming reinforcements, Ben thought. Well, my people probably got many of them, but I bet a few got through.

"Ben is an ol' curly wolf, Colonel. Don't ever sell him short."

"Oh, I realize that he is a formidable foe, General. He has more than proven that. But time is on my side. Since we know he is using one of our radios, he cannot give you his location. We would be there long before you arrived. I have people monitoring all frequencies, General McGowan, so there will be no more clever messages from or to General Raines. And this will be the last communication between us. Good-bye, General McGowan."

After a few seconds' pause, Ike said, "If you're listening, Ben, give 'em hell!"

Ben smiled and turned off the radio. "I plan on doing just that, Ike. Count on it."

Just as next dawn was streaking the sky, Ben climbed up a good thousand feet above the terrain and settled in amid the rocks, uncasing his binoculars. He began carefully scanning the area all around him. One of his radios, with fresh batteries in it, was on, with the volume turned down low and the radio on scan. If Runkel had spoken to one of the infiltrator teams, as he had told Ike, they should be arriving anytime.

Ben wanted to know how many more he was facing.

Then he stiffened as he spotted movement far below him. He shifted the lenses. More movement to his left and to his right. All right, then, so Runkel had called in at least one of his other platoons, maybe all of them, and they were trying to flush him out, guessing at his location.

Too late for Ben to look for a new location now. He would just have to sweat this out.

"Hell, it had to come, sooner or later," he muttered.

He took a long drink of water, then stretched out on his belly. His tiger-stripe BDUs were filthy, caked with grass stains and dirt, so he blended right in with his surroundings. Ben watched and waited.

The noose began to tighten. Ben had plenty of ammo, so he knew he could take plenty of them before they ever reached his location. And with the .270, he could do some long-distance killing before they came into range of his

CAR. He had four grenades in the rucksack he had taken
from the body of one of Runkel's men.

"If it comes down to Raines's last stand, boys," Ben muttered. "I will take a hell of lot of you with me before I go
into that long good-night."

Several of the men stopped at the base of the mountain
and looked up. Ben did not move, although he knew damn
well the searchers could not see him from where they stood.
Then three of the men started climbing up.

"And away we go," Ben whispered, remembering the line
from an old TV program.

One of the men waved at the other group, and two men
broke off and started climbing up the gentle slope.

Closer they came, until they had closed the distance to
less than two hundred yards. Looking through the scope,
Ben could tell the men were talking, but the distance was
still too great to make out any of the words.

Ben lifted the .270, sighted a man in the crosshairs, then
hesitated, lowering the rifle. The men seemed to be arguing
and reluctant to climb any further up the grade, for the
going was becoming more difficult.

From down below, near the base of the mountain, someone
shouted. The men paused and looked back. They were now
about a hundred yards from Ben's position and Ben had lined
up what appeared to be a noncom in the crosshairs.

The noncom waved toward the mountain, then shrugged
and lifted his arms in a gesture of "I do not understand."

Ben was using the earplug to the radio and orders suddenly crackled in his ear. Runkel's voice. "You're wasting
your time up there. Raines would not put himself in such
a position. There is no way out for him."

The noncom waved his understanding and shouted at the
others. They paused in their climbing, turned, and then
started down the slope.

"Lucked out again, Raines," Ben muttered.

Ben waited amid the rocks until the searchers had faded

into tiny dots in the distance. Then he began working his way down the mountain. The men were heading for deep timber. From intense study of a detailed map, Ben knew that timber extended for miles and miles in all directions.

"Dandy," he said. "I love it. Now, Runkel, I'll show you some tricks, you asshole."

Too far away for Ben to see, Colonel Hugo Runkel paused and looked back toward the mountain. Then he scowled and shook his head.

"Something, Colonel?" a sergeant asked of him.

Runkel cut his eyes to the man, then shook his head. "No, I guess not. Damn that Raines!"

"He is good, Colonel. We cannot take that from him."

"He's very good, Sergeant. But this time I think we just might have him in a box. At the very least, we're pushing him, putting him on the run."

"He is proving to be a very elusive prey, Colonel."

"I think he is in the timber just ahead, Sergeant. Pass the word to the men to be very, very careful. Look before taking each step. We have lots of time. Our own people and those aligned with us are attacking at spots all up and down Raines's eastern lines. General McGowan will be too busy there to worry much about us. I want Raines dead."

"Yes, sir."

"I am confident that this time we have him."

"I'm sure you're right, sir.

Runkel stared at the senior sergeant, mulling over whether the man's words held any note of condescension. He decided they had not. "Move the men forward, Sergeant. Have them maintain a twenty-five-yard interval."

"Yes, sir."

Some distance away, Ben had circled wide, jogging for several hundred yards, then walking for a few minutes, then repeating the drill, covering a lot of ground that way. He paused, taking a tiny sip of water and checking his compass. Then he was up and moving.

He cut to the north a few points, heading for the timber at an angle. He wanted to come in behind Runkel and his men, but did not want to come in directly in the middle of the wide line of searchers. He wanted to give himself some running room, either left or right.

He was in the timber, and it was deep, dank in spots, and dim. Runkel's men were making no effort to hide their tracks. The foliage in most areas remained damp all the time, and their trail was easy to follow.

Ben had slung the .270 tight behind his back, at an angle. He wished he did not have the added encumbrance, but he did not want to abandon the weapon. He might never come this way again. Ben paused, squatting down in the deep brush and silently screwed the long silencer onto the threaded end of the muzzle of the old Colt Woodsman. He slid a full magazine into the butt. It clicked into place. Ben chambered a round.

The little .22 did not have much of a punch, it certainly wouldn't knock a man down, so any shot he made would have to be a head shot, because Runkel's men were all wearing body armor. But the sound suppressor was the best his lab boys and girls could manufacture, and was constructed to last for a lot of rounds. Many silencers lose their effectiveness after a few rounds, but not this one.

Ben knew that, because he had personally tested the suppressor before allowing it to go into production, and he had used one just like it many times before in combat, when the situation called for silent killing.

He squatted there, mulling over whether to leave his pack and long rifle. He finally shook his head in rejection. He couldn't afford to lose his equipment. He would have to take it all with him, as cumbersome as it was.

Ben heard the faint pop of someone stepping on a dead branch, then silence. He could just imagine the soldier silently cursing himself for his carelessness.

Ben waited.

The soldier came into view. Too far off for Ben to chance a shot. The man stepped closer, moving slowly, slowly. Ben lifted the .22 and sighted in. The man took one more step and Ben shot him in the head, the bullet entering through the temple. The man sank silently to his knees, then softly fell forward, making so little noise the sound would not carry more than a few yards.

Ben eased over to the dead man and relieved him of his grenades and rations packs. Three days of rations and a full pack. Runkel was going all out this time. Ben faded back into the timber and waited. A couple more kills and he'd be set for food.

"Come on, boys," he muttered. "Ben's hungry."

Nine

Ben stayed where he was, not wishing to be spotted moving away.

"Herman?" the man working to what had been Herman's left called. "Where are you?"

Herman softly broke wind in death as gasses escaped him.

"Herman?"

Ben waited.

The second soldier came into view, dim in the thick timber and brush, his outline too obscure for Ben to chance a shot. The man again softly called out Herman's name and moved closer.

"What is it, Hans?" Another voice was added, this one coming from Ben's right.

Shit! Ben thought.

"Herman has vanished, Nils. He is not responding to my calls."

"Be careful, Hans."

Hans did not reply. He took two more steps and Ben shot him between the eyes. The man died with a very strange expression on his face. He slipped to the ground almost noiselessly. Ben turned just as Nils was making his way through the brush, almost on top of Ben's position. Ben shot him twice in the face and caught the body before it could hit the ground.

Ben shoved the .22 autoloader behind his web belt and

quickly fanned Nils's body, taking matches in a waterproof container, grenades, and field rations. He did the same with the other dead men. Now his rucksack was more than half full. He had nine days' rations and nearly twenty grenades.

Ben fell back about a hundred yards, then cut straight north. He had gone about half a mile before he heard the first shout. He smiled and kept on making his way through the timber. He hadn't done as much damage as he had hoped to do this day, but he had certainly given Runkel and his men something to think about.

He kept moving north for a time before cutting straight east. Come get me boys, he thought. I'll be waiting.

Colonel Runkel stood over the bodies of his men, now wrapped in ground sheets in preparation for burial, and cursed Ben Raines. He had slapped one of his men for referring to Raines as a ghost, and a moment later had apologized to the man for striking him.

Runkel had inspected the bodies, peering closely at the tiny bullet holes. Raines had to have shot them at very close range, using a silenced small caliber pistol. No doubt about it, Raines could move as silently as a ghost. Runkel vowed to keep better control on his temper.

Runkel checked his map. This forest range continued for miles, and Runkel concluded, so must they.

"Bury the men," he ordered gently. "Then we'll move out."

"Which direction, sir?" a sergeant asked.

"East," Runkel said wearily. "East."

Several miles away, Ben built a small fire from dead, dry wood that would be practically smokeless, and brewed a cup of coffee and heated some rations. He leaned back against a boulder and savored his coffee; the brand that Runkel's men carried in their accessory packs was better than what the Rebels carried. He'd have to check that out . . . if he ever took a prisoner alive, that is.

Ben tried to plan his next move, but that was difficult because he did not know which direction Runkel planned to move. He made a silent bet it would be east.

From his position in the rocks, several hundred feet high, Ben had a clear view of the beginnings of the vast forest range. How quickly nature reclaims her own when there is no interference from man, Ben mused. This area should remain nature's own, he decided, just as it is. Another place for the animals to run free and wild, just as God intended them to do. He'd see about that when this little private war was over.

Ben smiled. If I survive it, that is, he added.

Ben always liked to put a disclaimer on self-certainty, lest he become over-confident. Too much of that can very easily cause a man to become careless and make a misstep. And that could earn a man a very narrow place in the ground, very quickly.

Ben buried his food wrappers and carefully extinguished the small smokeless fire. He drank the last of his coffee and rolled a cigarette. Then he set about rearranging his gear so he could carry it more comfortably and move more swiftly.

That done, he strapped on and shouldered his gear and moved out. He stayed on the south side of the vast range of timber and covered a lot of ground before deciding to call it a day and begin searching for a place to make camp.

Ben felt sure he was at least several miles ahead of Runkel and his teams, for they would be moving very cautiously in the deep timber, placing each step carefully, wary of another ambush.

Ben found a tiny creek and after looking all around, decided to bathe and wash his BDUs, putting on his only spare set. He carefully shaved in the icy water, and then sat for a time, soaking his feet in the creek. As he wriggled his toes in the cold water, he became slightly amused at how such simple pleasures could fill a man with content- ment. No TV, no radio, none of the amenities that he had long grown accustomed to.

We are not that far from the caves, Ben thought, turning philosophical. For the most part, we are still hunter/gather- ers. The man who is the best hunter will claim the most attractive woman and the best and most secure cave, and he will have followers. The man who couldn't hit a dinosaur in the ass with a spear would be relegated to living in a hollow tree, surrounded by losers of his own ilk, most with- out the comforts of a help-mate; or at the best, a female companion who whined and complained constantly and who physically resembled the first cousin to an ape, and who had the intelligence to match.

Ben carefully dried his feet and sprinkled on some foot powder before pulling on fresh dry socks. He felt at least a hundred percent better. He had inspected the many bruises on his body—those that he could see—and was pleased to find they were changing colors, healing rapidly.

He packed up and moved a mile or so away from the creek, making his night camp well away from the tiny stream. He spread leaves thick on the ground to soften his bed before he spread his ground sheet. He was camped under a low and thick overhang of leafy branches, and judg- ing from the sky, there was no chance of rain.

Someday I'll write a journal about all this, Ben thought. Or perhaps allow some skilled interviewer to tell the story about how I played a small part in pulling this nation out of the ashes of defeat and despair. I could explain in depth and detail what has become universally known as the Tri- States philosophy of government. Might be fun to do that someday, he concluded. But I'd have to pick the interviewer carefully.

Ben stretched his frame out, sighed in contentment, and snuggled into his covering. Just before sleep took him, he smiled at his use of the word "someday." If he wasn't real careful and if luck didn't stay with him, there was a good chance his somedays could end in a matter of a few hours.

So don't get too cocky, Raines, were his last thoughts just as he settled into sleep.

Ben slept deeply, far too deeply, but he was very tired, and his body still had not fully recovered from the battering it had taken in the fall off the roadway in the motor home.

When he awakened, it was already grey light and someone was watching him—standing, or sitting, very close to him.

"You don't have to pretend you're asleep, General," the female voice said, coming from behind him. "I know you're awake. Your breathing changed. Relax. If I was an enemy, you'd already be dead."

Ben turned and stared. The woman was kneeling down about three feet from him. "Good morning," Ben said, struggling out of his coverings and reaching for his boots.

"Mornin', General. You have been leadin' those people chasin' you on a merry chase, now, haven't you?"

"I have certainly been trying."

The woman laughed softly. "You've been doin' more than tryin,' General. I've been listenin' on the radio and sometimes watchin.' You're damn good in the woods."

"Thank you."   .

"I'm better," she stated matter-of-factly. "But I was raised in these parts." She leaned over and stuck out a hand. "Jenny Marlowe."

Ben took the hand. It was as hard as his own. "Ben Raines. What in the world are you doing out here alone in the wilderness, Jenny?"

"It isn't wilderness to me, General. Told you, I was raised not too far from here. My pa used to run cattle just south of here. You want me to start a fire for coffee? I could use a cup."

"If you have some dry wood."

She smiled. "I reckon I know that much, General."

"Sorry."

"That's all right. Why don't you go take a leak and wash your face and hands and I'll get things going here."

Ben chuckled. "I'll just do that, Jenny. The rations are in my pack."

"Don't need 'em, General. I got bacon and eggs and potatoes. How does that suit you?"

Ben's mouth started watering at just the thought. "It sounds wonderful!"

Jenny reached behind her and pulled a pack closer. She pulled out a battered skillet and coffeepot and then started gathering up wood from the small pile Ben had put together and covered the night before.

By the time Ben had finished his morning business, Jenny had built a small fire, sliced the bacon, and it was sizzling in the pan. The aroma was absolutely delicious.

She tossed Ben a couple of potatoes and without question, he pulled out a knife and began peeling and slicing. Jenny filled the battered pot with water and set it on the inner edge of the crude circle of stones that kept the fire from spreading.

Ben stole several looks at the woman as the light got better. He guessed her to be about forty. Not beautiful, but, well, very attractive in an outdoorsy way.

She moved the fresh-sliced bacon over to one side of the skillet and dumped in the potatoes. Then she looked square at Ben. She had beautiful grey eyes. Her hair was light brown, and cut very short. "Alone, you said awhile ago? Good guess. Yeah, I'm alone. Me and my horses and a few pigs and chickens and cattle I got hid out. You're lookin' at what I guess is the last livin' member of what used to be known as the Montana Mountain Militia."

"I'm familiar with it. Quite a group before the Great War."

"That it was, General. That it was. Blacks and whites

and Indians and Orientals and Hispanics all mixed up and workin' together without nary a hitch. Then the Great War fell on us."

She stirred the potatoes and turned the thick-sliced bacon. Four eggs were sitting off to one side, ready to be cracked and dropped into the hot grease.

"And? . . ." Ben prompted.

"Oh, those of us that made it through the first few days held together for several years. Then one by one we grew smaller and smaller. Ambush, gangs, illness. Then it was just me and my husband and two sons, and my oldest son's wife. One day my husband went out hunting and never came back. His horse came back late that day, blood all over the saddle. I never did find his body. Then my youngest got all tangled up with a grizzly one day. It wasn't anybody's fault. David should have known better than to get as close as he did, especially when that grizzly had cubs with her. He lived for five days afterward. It was a hard death. Then came Simon Border and his religious nuts, followed shortly thereafter by Colonel Runkel and his bunch."

That startled Ben. "Runkel's been in here that long?"

"Not in this area, but he's been with Border for over a year. Maybe a lot longer than that. I'm not sure. Runkel's men killed my oldest boy and took his wife, Betsy, prisoner. They had their way with her, until they tired of her. Then they killed her when she was trying to escape. One of them told me all this, after I used the hot end of a runnin' iron on him a time or two."

Ben smiled. This was one woman to, as he used to write in his Westerns, ride the river with.

Jenny caught his smile and blushed. Ben had seen very few women blush since the age of so-called female liberation. Being somewhat of an old-fashioned sort of man, Ben rather liked it.

"I got a little carried away with that runnin' iron," Jenny admitted.

"Perfectly understandable."

She speared out the bacon, scraped out the potatoes, and then cracked and dropped in the eggs. "Scrambled or over easy?" she asked.

"Either way is fine."

Ben could not recall when a breakfast tasted so good. He took his time, chewing slowly, savoring each bite. Then they both leaned back, coffee mugs full. Ben rolled a smoke and offered the makin's to Jenny. She hesitated and then took the bag and papers.

"I ran out of smokes some months back. Never did smoke much. But I alway's enjoyed one after a meal. Thanks."

She rolled her cigarette slim and tight and quick. Then the man and woman spent a couple of moments just staring at each other.

Ben broke the silence. "Do you live far from here?"

" 'Bout ten miles. I got me a cabin in a little valley. It was me and my husband's getaway place. No roads, no electricity, no runnin' water 'cept what you pump up yourself, wood-burning stove, no indoor plumbin.' But you got to be right up on it before you can spot it. Not far from the cabin is a little hidden meadow. That's where I keep the horses and a few head of cattle. The hogs is sort of on their own and they're 'bout half wild now. You got to hunt 'em."

"So you've been following me?"

"Yeah. In a way. I was curious as to who it was takin' on Runkel and his men. I couldn't believe it was you at first. Then I thought you might be about half-nuts when I heard you stickin' the needle to Runkel the way you did. Then I finally realized you were tellin' your people you were all right and about Runkel's reinforcements comin' in. Smart." She took a sip of coffee and a drag. "But you don't have to be doin' this, General Raines . . ."

"Call me Ben, please."

"Okay, Ben it is. So I figure you're 'bout half curly wolf,

the other half puma, and you're not goin' to let anybody push you around. Then I remembered all your books. My husband had them all. I still got most of them up at the cabin. I hauled them out and read a couple. You got in trouble with the government over a couple of series of books, didn't you?"

Ben chuckled. "I sure did. I was visited more than once by federal agents from various departments, agencies, and bureaus."

"Well, screw 'em if they can't take a joke. I never did have much use for big government. And I can't hardly tolerate these cry-baby liberals."

"I think we're going to get along, Jenny."

She fixed those grey eyes on him. "I 'spect we will, Ben."

Ben helped with the cooking and eating utensils and then rolled his bed and packed up while Jenny carefully put out the tiny fire and covered it.

"That's a hell of a load you got there, Ben. Let's share it. Let me have the rifle and the rucksack. It's a long walk to my cabin. We might not even make it this day. Rain comin' in. Gonna be a storm."

Ben looked up at the sky. Clear and blue.

She smiled at him. "I can smell it."

"I'll take your word for it, Jenny. It's your country."

"Was," she corrected. "And will be again, soon'as we kill all those Nazi bastards and run Simon Border and his fruitcakes out. You ready?"

"I'm ready."

As Ben followed the woman away from the camp, he couldn't help but observing: Nice view from the rear, too.

Ten

About noon, the sky darkened and the rains came. Ben and Jenny spent the rest of the afternoon and evening warm and dry sitting under a nature's-hollowed-out overhang overlooking a meadow. They were about five hundred feet above the meadow and hidden from eyes below by brush.

"You know most of the little hidey-holes in this country, Jenny?"

She smiled. "Don't nobody know everything 'bout this country, Ben. There are caves and little hidden places that have never had a human eye put on them. At least not to my knowledge. A lot of this country is as wild as the day God made it. Any number of people have come into this country and never come out . . . or been found, for that matter."

"I can believe it."

"I find human skeletons from time to time. First one really jarred me. I was just a kid. Used to come up here with my daddy. I was ridin' around one day and 'boom.' There it was, a bony hand stickin' out of the sand along a creek. I rode quick back for my daddy and we dug him up. Found an old six-shooter and the metal parts of an old re-peatin' rifle. Daddy said the man was probably a wanderer; been dead for about a hundred years, he reckoned. Horse might have throwed him, Injuns might have got him. Who knows? We reburied him along the creek bank. One time I found several skeletons in a cave. Had metal breast-plates and helmets and old-timey muskets alongside 'em. Spanish explorers, I suppose. I just left them be to rest in peace. Before the Great War, there were tiny bands of Injuns livin' out here. People from a number of tribes: Cheyennes whose ancestors refused to surrender a hundred years or more ago, various descendants of Sioux, all kinds of Injuns, but not that many of them. They pretty much stayed to themselves, but Daddy would help them when he could: get medicines for sick kids and so forth."

"Where are they now?"

She cut her eyes. "Some are still around. They been watchin' you, too. Wonderin' 'bout you. They know where we are right now. Bet on it. But they're not savages, Ben. Many are well-educated. We share what we have from time to time."

"Would they help us, Jenny. I mean, join us in the fight against Runkel and his men?"

She smiled at him. "Why the hell should they help the white man, Ben?"

"Good point. But there was right and wrong on both sides, Jenny. The Indians broke just as many treaties as the white man."

"Oh, I know that, Ben. But I still think they got a dirty deal."

Ben smiled. "So do I."

Jenny looked out at the thick falling rain. She shivered. "It's goin' to be cool tonight."

"Yeah. Must be a front moving through."

"Fire's goin' out."

"You want me to add more wood?"

"No."

"You plan to just lay there and shiver?"

"You have something else on your mind?"

"Well . . ."

"Move over."

* * *

They were a little awkward with each other come the dawn, but that did not last long. After the third time of bumping into each other and then looking at one another in silence, both Ben and Jenny began laughing at their antics. That broke whatever tension was left between them.

"You want to know how many men I've been with in my life, Ben?"

"Only if you want to tell me."

"You're number two. My husband was the first."

Ben looked at her over the rim of his coffee-mug, then slowly nodded his head. Even though Jenny had come of age during that time just before the turn of the century, when sex was viewed by so many as no more important than two rabbits humping, still there had been women, and men too, Ben supposed, who placed a great deal of value on that most important sharing between a man and woman.

They chatted for a time over breakfast, bacon and fried potatoes, then packed up and headed out. The rain had ceased during the night and it was much colder than the day before, with a strong wind out of the north.

"We're about four miles from the cabin, Ben," she said. "Right up here we'll take an old Indian trail that leads off to the right; come up to the cabin that way."

They had not gone another mile before Jenny held up a hand and dug in her pack, pulling out battered old binoculars. She adjusted the magnification for the range and sighed.

"What's the matter?" Ben asked.

"My horses," she said, casing the binoculars. "They got loose. Two of them grazing over there."

"They do that often?"

"No. Probably a puma or a bear got close and they broke out. They'll come home."

"We weren't going to do any riding anyway, were we?" Ben asked.

She looked at him and smiled. "No. What we've got to do is best done on foot."

"That's a relief," Ben muttered. Ben could ride, did ride as a kid, but in later years felt the same way about horses as Jersey did about jumping out of airplanes.

Jenny laughed at the expression on his face. "Not much of a cowboy huh?"

"Not much, Jenny."

"Well, we all have faults," she kidded him in a gentle way.

The cabin had been very cleverly built, set up in front of a cliff, on a slope, amid a stand of timber the builder had wisely left alone. If one was not looking specifically for the cabin, odds were it would not be seen.

"That took someone with some engineering knowledge to build," Ben remarked.

"Yes, it did. My father had a degree in engineering and architecture. But he could never get ranching out of his system. He lived for a time in Chicago where he worked for a big firm. But he wasn't happy. He came back home and met my mother and got married, returned to the ranch, and never left it. Come on in and take a load off, Ben."

The cabin was snugly built, out of stone and logs: two big rooms. Living and cooking and dining area, and a bedroom.

"The bathhouse is out back," Jenny said. "Daddy built it sort of like a sauna, where you can heat the rocks and bathe comfortably even in the coldest of days. There is a natural tunnel leading to the meadow behind the cliff front. The horses broke out of the rear, though. They always do."

"Want to check back there?"

She shook his head. "Later. No point in it now. Let them graze on new grass. We won't be needing them."

"One thing puzzles me."

"What?"

"The bacon you brought. It wasn't overly salted, so how do you keep it from spoiling?"

She laughed. "Come on, let me show you something. I guarantee you've never seen anything like it. My father planned well before he built this cabin. He must have ridden over thousands of acres before he chose this land. Then he bought a ninety-nine-year lease on it. Not that it makes any difference now. Come on."

He followed her out the back into the tunnel that led to the meadow. Then she just disappeared. Took Ben a minute or so to find her. And then because she giggled. He crouched over and stepped into a wonderland.

Ben had never been thrilled about caves. A spelunker he was not. But this cave amazed him. It was an ice cave. He'd heard and read about them, but never seen one.

"You want to keep things just cold, you store them closer to the surface. To freeze them, you go down here about a hundred feet, and store them. Nature's deep freeze."

"Well, I'll just be damned!"

"Neat, hey?"

"I'll say so."

"The entrance was not nature made. Daddy hacked it out after some Indians told him about the legend of the ice cave. He just took a chance and it proved out."

Ben looked around him. "Quite a refrigerator."

Jenny had put up vegetables from a large garden she tended, quick frozen fresh, and there were two sides of beef hanging.

"Steak for supper tonight, Ben, with corn and beans."

"Sounds great to me."

"Then we'll start hunting at first light."

"For the horses?"

"No. For Runkel and his Nazis."

With a place now to stow his gear, Ben could move faster, and he had to move to keep up with Jenny. She went over and through the rocks like a mountain goat, following trails that Ben was certain had been made by mountain goats. But within two hours, she paused and pointed to a thin sliver of smoke rising from the timber.

"Runkel's camp. Now you take over."

"It would make me very happy if you just stayed out of it, Jenny."

"Forget it, Ben. I have more of a score to settle with those bastards than you. I'm in it all the way."

Ben nodded. He didn't have to ask if Jenny was a good shot. He could tell by the way she handled her old bolt action 30.06 she knew what she was doing. "All right, Jenny. First, we determine how many men are in this particular camp and what our odds will be of getting away alive. Then we decide where we'll link up after it's over. Then we split up and start some long-distance shooting." Ben pointed. "You're on that ridge over there, I'm over there."

She studied the ridge he had assigned her for a moment. "Suits me."

"What's the longest shot you ever made?"

"Oh . . . 'bout five hundred yards, I reckon."

"Let's go check this out."

They worked their way close and together studied the camp through long lenses.

"Be like shootin' sittin' ducks," Jenny remarked.

"You ready?"

"See you in awhile, Ben. Good shootin'." Then she was gone, fading into the brush, moving silently. She would circle the camp wide, then give him two clicks on a pre-arranged frequency when she was ready.

Ben moved into position and waited. They both would be shooting from a good vantage point, and the distance would be long, but within the accurate range of both weapons.

Ben took a sip of water and made himself comfortable in a prone position. He scooped up a mound of dirt in front of him to rest the rifle on, patted it firm, and waited, the earplug to the radio stuck in one ear.

He heard two clicks and pulled the plug out and stowed the radio. They would not use the radios again.

He pulled his rifle to his shoulder, snugged it up, and sighted in. He and Jenny were about a half a mile apart, on opposite ridges, looking down at a meandering little creek, Runkel and his men camped close to the stream.

One of Runkel's men took a canvas bucket and walked to the creek, preparing to fill it. Ben chose him. The man by the creek would be out of Jenny's line of sight due to the trees to his left. The man knelt down, offering a full view of his back to Ben and began washing his face and hands in the cold water.

"Nothing like going to hell with clean hands," Ben muttered.

He heard the boom of Jenny's 30.06 but did not take the crosshairs off the man's back. The man straightened up his back, still in a crouch, and turned his head. He waited a half second too long to react.

Ben squeezed the trigger and when he had pulled the rifle down to sight in again, the man was facedown in the creek and not moving.

The camp exploded in frantic activity. Ben had spotted Runkel moments before, but when he swept the camp through the scope, the colonel was nowhere to be seen. Runkel was an old hand, and had reacted instinctively, seeking cover from the unseen shooters.

Ben sighted in on a man who had taken very dubious cover behind a tree that was just not adequate cover for him. He squeezed off another round and the bullet slammed into the man's shoulder, knocking him backward, his mouth open in shock and pain.

Ben shifted the rifle a few inches just as Jenny's rifle sang its deadly song, the boom echoing across the little valley. Another of Runkel's men went down in a lifeless sprawl. She was as good a shot as Ben had thought she'd be, and as she had said, this was personal to her.

Ben set the crosshairs on a very iffy target and missed by a few inches. But the man then made the mistake of attempting to move in the wrong direction. If he had chosen the other way, he would have been in the brush and safe. Ben shot him in the hip just as he was scrambling on his hands and knees. The round flattened him out on the rocky ground, both hands to his bloody hip.

Jenny fired once more and another man went down. Ben glanced at his watch. Their pre-arranged time was up. Ben began backing away, hoping that Jenny had checked her watch and was doing the same.

But in the heat of combat, time was a fickle thing. It would seem to drag for some, and speed by for others. Ben made his way carefully through the brush and rocks, staying low, very much aware that Runkel would have snipers among his personnel . . . if they hadn't already been taken out by the long-distance shooting.

Ben checked his surroundings, visually checking the landmark Jenny had pointed out before they split up. He was almost dead on. He shifted a couple of compass points and picked up the pace.

Runkel's men would be very wary about moving out too soon, with no way of knowing if the snipers were pulling a muse, holding their fire deliberately. Ben and Jenny would have a good five or ten minutes to put some distance behind them.

Ben stopped to rest twice, taking very small sips of water, then he was at the base of the landmark and changed directions, heading toward the south. He found the lightning-blazed tree and squatted down. The minutes ticked past; there was no more shooting.

"Over here, Ben," Jenny's voice reached him, and he cut his eyes. She was standing at the edge of a small growth of timber about fifty feet away.

She could move as silently as any skilled guerrilla fighter Ben had ever worked with. He moved over to her.

"Runkel has reinforcements coming in from the north at a dead run," she said. "We'd better hunt a hidey-hole and do it real quick. They're platoon-size."

"Then we'd better make like the shepherd and get the flock out of here."

Jenny grimaced at the old joke.

Ben laughed at the expression on her face. "It's your country. Lead out."

She hesitated. "You want to try for the cabin and den up?"

He gave her his lewdest look and it was her turn to laugh. "I'd love to, Jenny. But, no. Maybe we'll get a chance to lay some more hurt on Runkel's people. I wouldn't want to miss that opportunity."

"Me neither. Okay. Follow me."

But they had taken all the toll they were going to take for that day. Finally, during a rest break, Ben made the comment that Runkel must have buried his dead, picked up his wounded, and then pulled back and dug in somewhere in the timber. And he was not chancing any fires.

Jenny glanced at him. "You don't know what Runkel does with his badly wounded, Ben?"

"No. Do you?"

"Yes. He shoots them."

Eleven

Colonel Hugo Runkel knelt down beside the body of his forward recon. The man was lying on his back, his eyes wide open, as if staring at the blue of the mountain sky. They stared in death, seeing nothing. What was left of Runkel's men, and the new people who had just arrived from the north, were gathered around. They were all fixated on one thing: the arrow sticking out of the man's chest.

The morning had dawned bright and cool, and Runkel had been filled with anticipation for the upcoming hunt. With the addition of the reinforcements, he felt sure this time he would be successful in hunting down and killing Ben Raines and whoever the hell that was with him.

But Runkel certainly hadn't counted on running up against any wild red Indians.

Runkel suddenly felt old beyond his years, and with this new development, any joy he might have been experiencing about the day's hunt was gone.

Standing a few feet away, one of the new men suddenly grunted, and sank to his knees, a strange look on his face. Then he screamed and fell forward. There was an arrow sticking out of his back, the head of the mini-spear imbedded in the man's spine.

"Down!" Runkel yelled.

That was a rather useless command, for his men were already on the ground, behind whatever cover they could find, which was not very much.

But no more arrows came whizzing out of the timber as the minutes ticked past. The ranking officer who had arrived with the reinforcements crawled over to where Runkel lay and stared at the man for a moment.

"What, Captain?" Runkel asked.

"We are getting our asses kicked all up and down the eastern front, Colonel. I told you the latest reports. We are blocked from retreating to the west or the south by Rebels. Those damn Canadians are rushing in to beef up their lines in the north."

"So?"

"We are trapped, Colonel. We have no place left to run. Now the red Indians have obviously declared war on us. What happens next: do we get our scalps lifted while sleeping?"

"Don't be ridiculous!" Runkel snapped.

"It was not my intention to sound ridiculous, Colonel. I was merely pointing out that we have run out of all but one option."

"You are talking surrender, Captain?"

"What else is left, Colonel?"

Runkel sighed, knowing the captain was not yet finished. He waited.

"We will run out of supplies by midsummer, or sooner. Probably the latter. The red Indians have been systematically looting the caches left us by Border's people. Obviously they've known all along where the caches were. There will be no more supplies for us. Then what?"

Runkel did not lose his temper, for the captain was only speaking the truth. "I have never surrendered, Captain," he stated quietly.

"Nor have I, Colonel," the captain said. "Personally I find the prospect repugnant and degrading. But Raines is a fair man, and General McGowan has extended that option to us. We would be treated well."

"Marlowe," Runkel suddenly whispered. "That's who is with General Raines."

"Sir?"

"Jennifer Marlowe. The mother-in-law of the young woman we captured some time back. She was killed trying to escape."

"That has some bearing on our situation?"

"Oh, yes, Captain. Indeed it does. My men entertained themselves quite enthusiastically with the young woman. In various ways and using all orifices . . ."

"I have never been involved in rape or torture, Colonel," the captain said stiffly.

"Well, you haven't been a soldier for that long either, Captain."

"One has nothing to do with the other," the captain countered.

Runkel's only reply was a noncommittal grunt, but his face reflected his growing contempt for the captain who espoused such high ideals.

Both men cut their eyes as a grizzled sergeant crawled over and joined them. "The men are grumbling, Colonel."

"So? Soldiers always grumble. It's when they stop grumbling that leaders should worry."

"Not this time, Colonel," the sergeant who came in with the reinforcements said. "You have a growing mutiny on your hands, sir."

"I will shoot any man who attempts to desert!"

"They are armed as well, Colonel," the sergeant pointed out, his tone very dry.

"My men are not talking desertion," Runkel said.

"That is correct, Colonel," the sergeant agreed. "The few you have left will stand by you and die needlessly in this Godforsaken wilderness."

"You're out of line, Sergeant!" Runkel snapped.

"Sue me," the sergeant responded, and crawled away, back to his men.

"Impudent bastard!" Runkel said. "You have obviously failed to maintain discipline among your people, Captain."

"We are soldiers, Colonel," the captain replied. "Not brigands or rapists."

"You have killed niggers all over Africa, Captain," Runkel pointed out.

"Only those who resisted us, Colonel."

"Aren't you the noble one, though?" Runkel sneered at him.

"Not noble, Colonel. Just soldiers." The captain suddenly stood up, holding his weapon high in the air, as far over his head as he could. Most of his men stood up, doing the same with their weapons. The captain looked down at Runkel. "Good-bye, Colonel. We are through. If we can make it to Rebel lines, we shall surrender."

"Go to hell!" Runkel told him.

"In due time, Colonel. All in due time." The captain took a white handkerchief out of his pocket and tied it to the barrel of his rifle, near the muzzle. The others followed suit. They began walking single file away from the others.

Runkel watched them leave. For a moment, he entertained the thought of shooting them, then changed his mind. That would be a waste of ammunition, and the captain had been correct about the supplies. Once their existing supplies were exhausted, they had but one cache left, but it was not far from where they lay, and Runkel knew it was undisturbed, for he had buried it himself, and it had been intact only a few days ago.

Runkel stood up and the men who elected to remain with him did the same. Twenty men, including himself. "Will there be any talk of surrender from any of you?"

He was met with cold stares. These men left had been with him for a long time, or had served with him before. They were hard professional soldiers, dedicated to the ideals of Nazi Germany of decades past. There was no surrender in them, for they knew if any civilian survivors of this mountain campaign had talked, telling Rebels of their months of rape and torture, the Rebels would not hesitate in hanging them. To a man, they knew all about Rebel justice.

"Let's go," Runkel ordered. "We'll stock up with supplies from a cache I personally buried and then head for cover and keep down until this campaign is over. It is my belief that General Raines will not waste a lot of time and effort looking for so small a group, and the brave captain and those cowards with him will be sure to tell his captors how few of us were willing to fight on." He turned and walked away, the others falling in a single file behind him.

Miles away, Ben and Jenny were unaware of the events of that morning. They were still in the sack, wrapped up in each other. Forming a closer bond, one might say.

Those Indians who had elected to fight against Runkel and his men watched the new soldiers leave, while waving gestures of surrender tied on their rifles. They let them go. They had taken no part in the awfulness that Runkel and his men had wrought upon the people who lived in the small towns in and around this area. No point in making war on them. And now that Jenny Marlowe—who had been a friend to them all—had taken up with General Raines, they really did not need to look after her any longer . . . if indeed they ever had had to.

Runkel had only a few men left, and together, Ben Raines and Jenny Marlowe would take care of them.

The Indians went back to their own people, to live out their lives in peace. Maybe.

"Well, now," Jenny said, lowering her binoculars for a moment. "Would you just take a look at that."

Ben lifted his binoculars and viewed the scene on the

valley floor far below them. About fifty uniformed men, all marching along, with white handkerchiefs or rags tied to the muzzle of their rifles.

"I bet that's most of the new bunch," Ben said. "They're packing it in, marching toward Ike's western lines."

"That'll leave Runkel with about thirty men," Jenny said, a smile on her lips.

Ben cut his eyes and returned the smile. "Wanna go pay the good colonel and his men a visit?"

"You sure you've got the strength left?" she asked, a very mischievous look dancing around in her grey eyes.

"Since I seem to have misplaced my walker, you might have to cut me a crutch."

She leaned close, whispered a very suggestive few words, and then jumped up and darted away before Ben could grab her.

Five minutes later, they were on the trail, heading east.

Runkel lifted a hand and then motioned for his men to take cover. Something had alerted him, but he was not at all sure what it was.

He looked out across the long narrow valley that lay in front of them and cussed. "Damn!" he muttered. He had led his men first down a box canyon, then back-tracked and into this obscenity, with high rocky cliffs on both sides. What a perfect place for an ambush. Just the place Ben Raines would pick—that son of a bitch!

"Two at a time, at the run to that clump of trees," Runkel said, pointing. "And don't stop. If you stumble and fall, stay down and crawl for a few meters before getting up. And should that happen, when you do rise, don't hesitate. Get up running. Move out."

The first four men to attempt the dash to the safety of the trees made it. The lead off man for the next two got halfway across and stumbled, falling to his knees and staying in that position.

"Get down, you fool!" Runkel shouted.

But his warning came too late. Jenny's old rifle cracked, the bullet dusting the man, going in one side and blowing out the other.

Runkel cussed as his man disappeared from view. He glanced up at the sun. Far too early in the day to wait until dark to cross the valley. Raines and that bitch Marlowe could stay up in the rocks and kill a half dozen more simply by shooting randomly in their general direction, for the cover was not great. He looked back at his men. "Go!" he ordered the next two men.

Both of them made it. Runkel lifted his walkie-talkie. "When the next two start their run, two of you in the trees take off. We'll double our chances of making it that way." He motioned for two more to make the run then keyed the radio. "Go!"

No shots echoed from the rocks, and that puzzled Runkel. "What the hell are you up to now, Raines?" he muttered.

Using a series of clicks on their walkie-talkies, Ben and Jenny had moved, staying in the rocks along the steep sides of the cliffs, heading down the valley. The next good cover was at least a good two-hundred-yard-run from the clump of trees. And the men would be forced to jump a small creek that ran through the valley. Ben and Jenny stationed themselves on either side of the creek and waited.

Runkel and the first three pairs in the clump of timber to try to long run across the creek made it to the trees and caught their breath. Ben and Jenny let them go.

The next two men failed in their jump across the creek and both rifles cracked. Ben's shot struck his target in the center of the chest, killing him instantly. Jenny's shot went low and took the man in the stomach, leaving him lying by the creek, screaming hideously.

"Goddamn this country," Runkel cussed. "Goddamn Ben Raines and that bitch with him."

"And goddamn Bottger for sending us on this fool's mission," a senior sergeant added, not giving a damn whether the colonel liked his comment or not.

Runkel thought about that for a moment before nodding his head in agreement. "Yes. We should have stayed home. That fool Border was sure to fail anyway."

Seventeen of us left, Runkel thought. How pathetic. We came in here strong and proud and sure we could not be defeated. And look at us now. Being slowly cut to pieces by one man and one woman.

"We can't stay here in this tiny clump of trees," Runkel said, looking around him. "If we do that, those two in the rocks will just start shooting randomly in here and take us out that way. Has anyone spotted their positions?"

"They've moved about a hundred or so meters down the valley," a man said. "They're about twenty-five meters on either side of the creek. That's as close as I can tell."

"We could lay down covering fire as each team makes their run," it was suggested.

"A waste of precious ammunition," Runkel replied. "And we can't spare it. Set all weapons on single fire."

Ben and Jenny missed their next two shots, both of them taking a chance on nailing running targets. It was close, but close only counts in hand grenades and horseshoes.

Ben glanced up: the sky was rapidly filling with ominous-looking clouds, hanging low, filled with moisture.

His radio crackled. "Let's get out of here, Ben," Jenny's voice came through the tiny speaker. "This storm has all the makin's of a bad one."

"I'm with you," Ben radioed. "Meet you at the head of the valley."

The valley widened from that point on, until it was over a mile wide at the head. Ben and Jenny met in the center of the valley floor just as a light drizzle was beginning to fall. Lightning was licking around the high ridges, the thunder rumbling in the distance.

"I know a cave about a mile and a half from here," Jenny said. "Well, it's sort of a cave. But it's large enough for the two of us. Come on. This storm is gonna be a piss-cutter, baby."

Ben grinned at her language. "Lead on . . . baby."

She winked at him and took off at a trot, Ben right behind her.

They just made the tiny cave before the heavens opened up and obscured the land with a deluge of water. They had both picked up bits and pieces of dry wood along the way; each carried an armful. It would be enough for a tiny fire that day and part of the night, if they were careful.

"Runkel and his men will be sure to take advantage of this storm and get clear of us," Ben said.

"We'll find them," Jenny said, raising her voice to be heard over the hammering and howling of the mountain storm. "We cut them down a little bit this day."

"And we'll cut them down a little bit more tomorrow," Ben said. "I'd like to take Runkel alive, if possible."

"Why?"

"So I can watch the son of a bitch hang."

"I'd like to see that myself," Jenny said, adding water to the tiny, two-cup coffeepot and setting it carefully on the rocks around the fire.

"But I'll settle for seeing him shot dead."

"Yeah. If we get a chance, give me the shot, Ben. Okay?"

"You got it."

The storm grew in intensity and Ben and Jenny spent the rest of the afternoon talking . . . when the roar of the storm would permit normal conversation. The lashing at the earth slacked off a bit, but showed no sign of reaching its zenith any time soon.

Warm and dry, Ben and Jenny dozed in each other's arms. Two miles away, Runkel and his men marched through the torrent, knowing they were reasonably safe as long as the storm continued its ripping at the land. Once, during a rest break, one of his men asked, "If we do make it out of these mountains, Colonel, where do we go to find our way back to our Homeland?"

Runkel did not immediately reply. He finally sighed and shook his head. "I don't know, Skyler. I doubt any of us will ever again see the new Homeland. I imagine we shall have to remain here, in this torn-apart land, and try to fit in somehow."

"I despise this place," Skyler said, water dripping off his face.

The others in the group nodded in silent agreement. They were all soaked to the skin and cold and uncomfortable. They could not risk a fire even if they had the dry wood to start one or a place out of the elements.

"At least no one is shooting at us," another of Runkel's men added a positive note.

"Yet," another added glumly.

Twelve

The point man looked around him, alert eyes sweeping his surroundings. The morning had dawned bright and clear and Runkel and his group had pushed on. The point man was working about a hundred yards ahead of the small single-file column. He turned his head and lifted his right arm to give the "come on" signal when a crushing blow struck him in the chest. He sat down hard on the ground. In the minute he had before dying, he cursed Ben Raines soundly before toppling over, facedown on the wet grass.

The bullet had nicked his heart before passing on through his body and blowing out his back. The man died without ever asking God to forgive him.

"Damn!" Runkel muttered from his hiding place in the tall meadow grass. "How in the hell did they find us so quickly?"

The gentle wind sighed its mysterious reply.

Another of Runkel's men broke under the strain. He jumped up and began screaming and cursing and firing his weapon in all directions.

"Get down, you idiot!" Runkel yelled.

Jenny's rifle cracked and Runkel watched as the soldier sank to his knees, then toppled over, his weapon dropping from lifeless hands. He fell over on his side, his unblinking eyes staring straight at Runkel.

For the first time in his professional soldier's life, Colonel Hugo Runkel knew he was going to die. There was no doubt in his mind. For years he had been hearing about Ben Raines, the man, the legend, the myth. He had been certain .99 percent had been lies. Now he knew better.

Ben Raines was everything people had insisted he was: lucky, a man's man, a solid solider, relentless, ruthless.

"And a dyed-in-the-wool son of a bitch," Runkel added, muttering softly.

"Sir?" his one remaining ranking sergeant asked, lying a few feet away.

"Nothing, Sergeant," Runkel told him. "Just cursing our luck."

"I think it's run out, Colonel."

"As much as I hate to admit it, Sergeant, and as a commander it's something I should never do, but I think you just might be right in that assumption."

"I have pinpointed the location of one of them, sir!" one of Runkel's men called, not taking the binoculars from his eyes. "It's the woman, and she's moving away, heading out toward the east. Now she's disappeared from view."

"Thank you, Thomas," Runkel replied, cutting his eyes to his sergeant, who was scanning the other side of the meadow with his own binoculars. "See anything, Sergeant?"

"I did catch a flash of something, Colonel. Moving toward the east. I think it was General Raines."

Runkel smiled grimly. "In twenty-four hours, those two have cut our strength by twenty-five percent. Perhaps they're taking a rest break."

"Do we bury the men, sir?" another called.

"No, Aaron, we do not. Sergeant, start the men working toward that ravine to our left. That will give us some protection from the sniper fire. We'll follow it until it peters out. Stay on your bellies, people. To rise up means death."

"Move them out now, sir?"

"Move them out now, Sergeant."

An hour later, there had been no more deadly fire from

either side of the meadow, and Runkel and his men were huddled together in the ravine. The protective ravine had run its course, and it was a hundred yard dash to the timber. There was no cover between the ravine and the timber's edge. The men were eye-balling the timber through nervous eyes.

Runkel was entertaining thoughts of suggesting the men split up once they reached the dubious safety of the timber. He crawled over to his sergeant and broached the idea to him.

The sergeant shook his head. "I had the same thoughts, sir. One or two of us might make it that way; probably would make it. But the men? . . ." He shook his head. "I don't think they'll go for it. They're scared, sir. A few have reached the point of falling apart. Put them on their own, in pairs, and they're dead men for sure."

"We're dead men any way you slice the cake, Brodrick," Runkel said in a whisper.

"I know, Colonel. I know. Which is why I believe . . ." The sergeant hesitated.

"Go on, Brodrick. This is no time to stand on rank. Speak your mind."

"Attack, sir. The next time they start sniping at us, we determine one of their positions, and attack. We might well all die doing it, but it's better than dying this way, and, who knows, we might get lucky."

Runkel thought about that for a moment, then slowly nodded his head in agreement. "All right, Brodrick. You've discussed this with the men?"

"No, sir. But I have heard them talking. It's what they want. They want to die as soldiers."

And die we will, Runkel thought, but he did not put that thought into words. "Collect and then divvy up the ammunition and grenades. When that is done, we'll move out."

"Yes, sir."

The decision seemed to lift the pall that had been settling

over the men like a stinking shroud. They were soldiers again, not just sheep waiting around to be led off one by one to the slaughter.

Runkel started again to count the men left, then stopped himself with a grimace. He knew exactly how many men he had left: fifteen, counting himself.

He looked over at his sergeant and the man nodded. "Ready, sir."

Runkel stood up. "Let's go find General Raines and his whore."

Ben and Jenny were two miles ahead of the colonel, lying in wait on a ridge, looking down at a flowering meadow filled with blossoms, waving gently in the warm breeze. The rain that had passed on east during the night had brought out nature's beauty in full bloom.

This time they were both on the same ridge, about fifty yards apart, relaxing in the sun, waiting for Runkel to show. It was the only way the colonel could go, for there were towering mountains in front and behind the pass, and a swift running stream gurgling down the center. Once Runkel and his men entered the pass, they could either retreat or die. Neither Ben nor Jenny had given any thought to Runkel mounting an attack.

And that mistake came close to costing them both their lives.

Thirteen

The first warning that something just might be wrong came when Ben, searching the terrain through binoculars, caught very furtive motion at the far end of the meadow. He studied the area for a moment, trying to get another glimpse, and was just about to pass it all off as his imagination, when another darting shape flitted through the long lenses for just a second and then was gone. The men were behaving . . . well, in a peculiar manner.

Jenny had moved closer, and was now about twenty-five yards away, relaxing under the warm sun. Ben called to her and she was instantly alert.

"What's up, Ben? And keep it clean, will you?"

Ben smiled at that and motioned to the meadow below. "Company, Jenny. But I get the impression they're taking the offensive this time around."

"The offensive?"

"Yeah," Ben called, the binoculars still held to his eyes. "There's another. They're working our way and keeping close to our side, staying in the rocks." Ben lowered the binoculars. "I think Runkel has decided to start behaving like a soldier."

Jenny hesitated a moment before asking, "Why now, Ben?"

"That slight hesitation tells me you already know the answer, Jenny."

Again, she hesitated. "Are we getting ready for a last stand, Ben?"

"Both sides are, Jenny."

"Then this fight might prove to be very interesting."

"I think you're safe in saying that," Ben's reply was very drily offered.

"Any orders, boss-man?"

"Take a good drink of water and then start laying out grenades and extra ammo within easy reach, but safely away from any stray bullets. We've got a good spot to defend, but we're limited in movement. Once it starts, Jenny, we're stuck right here. We have to either win it, or die."

"But we've got the high ground."

"That's about the only thing we've got going for us. Runkel's got fifteen/eighteen men. And that just isn't very good odds for us. They'll be fighting as desperate men with nothing to lose, so we've got to maintain a cold, clear head."

"All right, Ben."

"The grenades have a five-to-six-second fuse on them. Remember that. It's going to be up to you to decide when to lay aside that .30-06 and start using that automatic weapon we took from Runkel's man. You've got six thirty-round spare magazines and one full one in place. That gives you two hundred and ten rounds to blow through that short-barreled bastard. I can but assume that as a former militia member you've fired weapons on full auto?"

"You'd be safe in saying that, Ben," her reply was tinged with sarcasm.

"That's what I figured."

She smiled sweetly at him. "I thought you were always in favor of citizen militias?"

"I was and am. Why?"

"Just wondering, Big Boy."

Ben looked at her and shook his head in mock exasperation. "Women!" he said.

"Men!" she said.

Then they laughed at each other and began settling down, laying out grenades and spare ammo. That done, Ben munched on a cracker and Jenny ate a handful of wild berries she had picked that morning and kept in a tin. They waited.

"Jenny?"

"What?"

"We could always haul our butts out of here, you know. It doesn't have to turn into a last stand for us."

"Is that what you want to do?"

"Not really. Might as well settle it now, I suppose."

"I'm with you on that. No point in talking about them is there?"

"I guess not."

Both of them began scanning the area with binoculars. Ben broke the silence by saying, "When this is over, I want to take a sauna in that place of yours. And several hot baths."

"Do the latter first," she replied with a smile. "You're getting a little gamey."

"You ain't no rose yourself, lady."

She laughed, knowing the truth in both remarks. Their clothing was filthy, and their hair needed a good washing . . . several times. When you reach the point where you can smell yourself, you need a bath.

"Heads up!" Ben said. "They're getting a little bolder now. I don't believe they know for sure we're here."

"Then they're stupid. Past this point, the way opens up and is clear for miles."

"But they don't know that, Jenny. As a matter of fact, neither did I."

"I wish you hadn't brought up a hot bath, Ben. I'm beginning to itch."

"Wouldn't surprise me if both of us had fleas."

She grimaced at that thought.

"I wish I knew just what was happening along our fronts," Ben said.

"We'll either know the whole story in a few hours, or we won't know anything at all until we stand before God."

"What a cheerful thought!"

"You ever think about God, Ben?"

He lowered his binoculars to see if she was serious. She was. "From time to time, yes."

"Then you believe in Heaven and Hell?"

"Yes, I do. At least I believe in some form of Hereafter."

"Me, too. You go to church, Ben?"

"No. But I do attend the chaplain's field services occasionally."

"But I bet you were raised in the church."

"Sure. You?"

"Oh, yes. You probably passed right through the little town where I went to school and attended church. But if you blinked your eyes twice you missed it."

"Any brothers and sisters?"

"They're all dead. You?"

"They're all dead. Killed in the germ attack during the Great War. Except for one brother."

"What happened to him?"

"I killed him years ago. He came up into the old Tri-States to kill me. Damn near succeeded, too."

"How awful! But why would he do such a thing?"

"He was a Nazi, Jenny; a member of some sort of minority-hating group. We never were close and I didn't realize he had changed so over the years. He grew to hate me and everything the Tri-States stood for."

Jenny said nothing in reply, and Ben suspected it was because she didn't quite know what to say. Then he cut his eyes to the woman and she was silently crying, the tears spilling down her tanned cheeks. After a moment, she pulled a bandanna from a hip pocket and wiped her eyes and blew her nose.

"If you're all through blubbering, we've got a battle to fight," Ben said.

"Screw you, Raines!" She honked into the handkerchief again and then wiped her nose on her sleeve as a child would do. She looked like a little girl who has just lost her favorite doll.

Ben chuckled at her.

"What's so damn funny?"

"You."

"When we get back to the cabin, you can take a damn sauna by yourself, you insensitive jackass!"

Ben's chuckling turned into open laughter.

"Asshole!" Jenny muttered. Then she hiccupped and Ben roared with laughter.

Luckily, Runkel and his men were still hundreds of yards away. But they were closing the distance rapidly.

"About three more minutes, Jenny," Ben said, sobering quickly as he lowered his binoculars.

Jenny wiped her eyes one more time, stuck the soggy handkerchief in her back pocket, and lifted her long lenses. She studied the situation for a moment, then laid the binoculars aside and picked up her rifle. "I'm ready." She cut her eyes toward Ben. "Why do men think it's unmanly to cry, Ben?"

"I don't think that way at all, Jenny. I just don't cry very often. I guess a lot of men do their grieving differently. I did my grieving for my brother a long time ago. Do I wish things could have been different? Sure, I do. But I can't change what happened." Ben lifted his glasses. "Well, hell, Jenny, they've stopped. I guess they're talking things over."

"Gettin' suspicious, I reckon. It's been easy for them so far this day."

"A couple of hundred more yards and we can start the dance."

"You like to dance, Ben?"

The question startled him. Then he smiled, knowing they

were talking to relieve the growing tension that always comes before a hard battle. "I used to dance. Used to like to dance, I guess."

"You *guess?*"

"It's been so long I don't remember. I don't do any of the dances that were popular a decade or so before the Great War."

"I don't either. Never called all that jumpin' around like a bunch of wild monkeys dancin.' But I did used to love to square dance."

"Yeah," Ben said wistfully. "I remember square dancing when I was a kid. Couple of times each month, on a Saturday night, families would gather at the VFW hall for supper and dancing. I'd forgotten all about that. It was a long time ago," he added softly.

"Don't families still do that in the SUSA, Ben?"

"Why . . . I imagine they do, Jenny. But the SUSA is a very large nation, and commanding generals and presidents of countries just don't get invited, I suppose."

"Would you go if someone did invite you?"

"Probably. I like to have fun just as much as the next fellow."

"Maybe someday you and me can go to a dance."

"I'd like that, Jenny. I really would."

"I still have a few dresses. But Lord, I haven't had a dress on in so long . . ." She was quiet for a few heartbeats. "You have a civilian suit, Ben?"

He had to think about that. "You know, Jenny, I don't believe I do."

"Well, we'll have to do something about that."

"Yes. I guess we will."

"I'm not goin' to get all prettied up just to have you wearin' combat boots, steppin' on my toes."

"I seem to recall I was pretty good at stepping on my partner's toes."

"Two left feet."

"Something like that."

Jenny had lifted her binoculars. She lowered them midway and said. "They're movin' again. Won't be long now."

"No. We'll be through by midafternoon."

"Should be."

"How far back to the cabin?"

"Too far to make it in one afternoon. But I know a place a couple of miles from here. It's an old cabin built long before my daddy arrived. Settlers, I reckon. The fireplace is still standin' and the roof is intact. Least it was the last time I looked."

"Sounds good to me."

"I wish those Nazi bastards would come on and get this over with."

"The point man's in range. Let's wait until the man behind him gets closer. I'll take the point man, you take the second one."

"Will do, Ben."

They waited. Ben lifted his rifle and sighted in, Jenny following suit.

"You ready?" Ben asked.

"Any time, baby."

"Now!"

The high-powered rifles cracked together and two men went down, both of them chest shot.

"I make it fifteen to go, Ben," Jenny called.

"I think it's thirteen. But either way, we're getting there."

"What's next?"

"Maybe a rush, coming in from our left, with them staying in the rocks."

Jenny turned her head and inspected the area to her left. "That wouldn't be good for us."

"No. It damn sure wouldn't. But that would be a logical move on Runkel's part."

Jenny suddenly jerked her rifle up and snapped off a shot.

"Damn. I missed. Time to get rid of this scope. They're so close now we won't need them."

"I'm switching to my CAR. No front sight on this rifle."

"Think I'll switch to this squirter myself."

"They've split up, Jenny!" Ben said, urgency in his voice. "One group is staying on the meadow, near the rocks below us, the other group has begun climbing up and will be coming at us from our left. You're going to be on your own."

"I've been there before, Ben."

"There won't be much time for talking until it's over. Good luck, honey."

"Okay, Baby. Same to you. And, Ben? . . ."

"Yes?"

"I . . . ah, I'm looking forward to spending some time with you once this is over."

Ben cut his eyes and smiled at her. "Well, I'll just have to do my best to stay alive, won't I?"

"I'm going to be awfully irritated if you don't."

Then Runkel and his men came in a rush, and there was no more time for talking.

Fourteen

Jenny sprayed the first man to come into range with automatic weapons fire, knocking him backward, to sprawl dead among the rocks.

Ben put another down with fire from his CAR.

The others kept coming in a snarling, shouting, hate-filled rush, closing the distance alarmingly fast.

Jenny chunked a grenade and two more of Runkel's men went down, dead or dying, their bodies torn with shrapnel.

Ben tossed a fire-frag and the screaming of the wounded halted the charge. Two more of Runkel's men were out of the game. The entire wild rush had not lasted more than a minute, but both Ben and Jenny were sweating when it finally broke.

The sun slowly inched higher. One man lay badly wounded among the rocks, moaning softly. Finally, he gasped in pain and then was quiet.

Ben guessed that Runkel had either eight or ten men left. He wasn't sure, but that was close enough. He and Jenny were still far from being out of danger.

"You have proven to be quite a formidable foe, General," Runkel's voice came out of the rocks. "I congratulate you on your skill."

Ben offered nothing in reply.

"It's been a most interesting chase," Runkel said.

Ben waited. Runkel was just below him, well concealed

in the rocks. Ben figured he was maybe twenty-five yards away, no more than thirty.

Was Runkel using this time to send a couple of men around in a flanking movement? Probably, Ben thought. Two to the left, two to the right, and the remainder of them would charge right up the middle.

Ben hissed softly at Jenny until she cut her eyes. He pulled the pin on a grenade and held the spoon down, then pulled his Beretta 9mm from leather, motioning for her to do the same. Her eyes widened, but she did as he silently instructed.

"You want to surrender, Runkel?" Ben broke the silence of the late spring day.

Runkel laughed at that. "Oh, my, General, you do have quite a sense of humor. I think not. Dying by a hangman's noose has never appealed to me."

"It would buy you a little more time here on earth, Colonel."

"But not quality time, General. No, I think I shall take my chances here on this miserable slope. Who knows? I just might get lucky and kill you and your whore."

A stone rattled off to Jenny's left and Ben could see her tense. He smiled grimly. She suspected she was being flanked and was ready.

Movement caught Ben's eyes off to his right. Part of a man's leg, from the knee down, was exposed. Ben triggered off two fast shots with his pistol and the man screamed as his knee was shattered. He reared up on his one good leg and Ben shot him in the chest. One more down.

"Careless of Aaron," Runkel spoke calmly. "I thought he was better than that."

Jenny suddenly tossed the grenade and her aim was true. The grenade landed behind a boulder and blew. One man rolled down the hill, his lifeless and bloody form tumbling loosely. The second man stood up, dazed and bloody, his face torn and unrecognizable. Jenny shot him with her pistol.

Two more down.

Jenny pulled the pin on another grenade, holding the spoon down. She waited patiently.

"Then there were five, Colonel," Ben called.

Runkel softly cursed, then said, "You keep very good count, General. Yes, I suspect the game is rapidly coming to a conclusion."

Ben had listened carefully and was impressed to sense that Runkel had moved closer. The man was very good; as good as Ben had ever encountered.

Ben tossed the fire-frag and hit the dirt just as Sergeant Brodrick came in a rush at Jenny. She shot him three times, holding the pistol in a one-handed grip, twice in the chest, once in the throat as the pistol bucked upward.

The fire-frag exploded.

When the dust had settled, a voice rose from the rocks. "That is all, General. We yield. It is over."

"Stand up," Ben ordered. "Hands empty."

Two men stood up.

"Where is the third man?" Ben called.

"Lying beside Colonel Runkel. Neither man is moving. I believe them both to be dead."

"Your grenade landed close to the colonel's head, General. He is decapitated. I hate this goddamn country. I wish we had never left our homeland."

"Europe or Africa?" Ben called.

"Either one, General."

"Walk down to the meadow. When you clear the rocks, stand very still, your hands in the air. If you move, I'll kill you."

"We believe you, General," the other man said.

"Watch them, Jenny," Ben called. "Don't hesitate to shoot if they move."

"You can count on that, Ben."

Ben inspected the bodies, keeping count. They were all

accounted for. Runkel was headless, blood and brains splattered all over the rocks where he'd been hiding.

Ben walked over to the two prisoners. He took their sidearms, leaving them with only a knife and canteen. "Start walking," he told them. "Toward the east. You might make it to our eastern front. If you do, fine. If you don't, that's fine. But if I ever seen either of you again, I'll kill you without hesitation. Is that understood?"

"Yes, sir," both men said.

Ben smashed all the weapons, rendering them useless, then turned to the prisoners.

"Move!"

They moved.

The hunt was over. Ben and Jenny watched amid the rocks until the two men had disappeared into the timber at the far end of the valley.

"They won't make it," Jenny said, no emotion in her voice. "The further east you go, the wilder this country gets."

"Suits me," Ben replied. He looked at her and smiled. "You mentioned something about an old cabin a few hours from here?"

"I sure did." She waved her hand at the bloody carnage sprawled silently around them. "What about the bodies?"

"You terribly concerned about them?"

"Hell, no!"

Ben smiled and together they turned away from the bloody ridge and walked westward. Neither of them looked back.

They camped that night at the old cabin Jenny knew of and were up and moving the next day before dawn, reaching Jenny's a few hours later. Ben built a big fire just behind the sauna house and Jenny showed him how to heat the rocks for the sauna hut. While they both were sweating out days of tension and strain and bloodshed, Jenny had water heating on the stoves, one inside and one outside. Then they both took long, hot, soapy baths . . . Jenny first while Ben heated more water in every container he could find. Then Ben helped her wash their stinking clothes, and they hung them out to dry. Jenny's late husband had been a tall man, and his clothes fit Ben pretty well. Dressed in jeans and flannel shirt, he felt clean and comfortable for the first time in days. They had steaks and potatoes for supper and then sat out on the porch and watched the sun slip over the mountains.

"What happens now, Ben?" Jenny broke a long silence.

"I go back to my troops. You're coming along, aren't you?"

She hesitated, then shook her head. "I don't think so, Ben. I think it's over, here in the mountains, and I want to stay home and live in peace. It's been so long since I didn't have to wake up afraid every morning it'll be a unique experience."

"I'll miss you."

"And I'll miss you."

They both sat in silence while dusk spread shadows all about them. In the dark timber, an owl hooted. Far away, a wolf began singing his song to the heavens; the call was answered.

"Every night I'll sit out here and think of you when the wolves talk, Ben."

Ben took a sip of fresh brewed coffee and smiled. "Is that what I remind you of, Jenny?"

"In a way, yes. An ol' lobo wolf who doesn't like to run with the pack."

"Well . . . I have a soft spot in my heart for wolves, Jenny. Always have. I'm surprised a rancher's daughter would feel the same way."

"Not all ranchers hated the wolf, Ben. My daddy used to say they were God's creatures and should be respected.

I enjoy listening to them sing. I've never lost a single head of cattle to the wolves. No reason I should. There is plenty of game for them to hunt and eat out there." She waved a hand. "Now," she added.

"Humankind sure as hell screwed things up, didn't we?"

"We sure as hell did. And I like the way you've set aside all that land in the SUSA for wildlife."

"You'll have to come for a visit, Jenny."

"I just might do that." She cut her eyes and smiled. "When you decide to settle down and stay in one spot for a time, that is."

Ben chuckled softly. "Got to know me pretty well in a short time, didn't you?"

"Better than you think, Ben."

Ben reached over and took her hand in his. "Anything you'd like me to do before I go?"

She squeezed his hand. "Well . . . as a matter of fact, there is."

They rose as one and walked into the cabin. In the distance, the wolves sang their lonely songs.

The next morning, Ben worked out map coordinates and then went outside, a walkie-talkie in his hand. He keyed the mic and said, "This is General Raines." He gave his location. "Colonel Runkel is dead, and so are the men who elected to stay with him. The war is over in here. Send a chopper in here to pick me up. Along with that chopper, I want additional choppers carrying a team of doctors and medics and several tons of supplies: food, clothing, blankets, first-aid kits. If I forgot anything, you can go back and get it. By now you should have rigged something to transmit on this frequency. Give me a bump."

Within seconds, Ike's voice came through the tiny speaker. "Ben? You receiving this?"

"Five by five, Ike."

"I gather by this list you are not alone in there."

"I found some friends and want to leave them well-supplied and checked out by our medical people, ten-four?"

"We're on our way, Ben."

An hour later, Ike stepped out of the lead helicopter and walked over to Ben and Jenny. He grinned at Ben and shook his hand, then briefly took Jenny's hand in his and squeezed gently. "Well, you both look okay. Neither of you took any hits?"

"We're fine, Ike. Good to see you."

"Chase is on the eastern front with our people. I bumped him and told him about your transmission. He's hopping mad because he can't be here."

"I'll be back by the time you get the choppers unloaded, Ben," Jenny said. Then she turned and walked off to where a saddled horse was waiting. She rode off.

Ben smiled at the expression on Ike's face. "Come on up to the cabin, Ike. I'll fill you in. How is my team?"

"Fine. All of them took minor wounds and suffered a lot of bumps and bruises in the ambush, but nothing serious. They're waiting for you back at our western lines."

"How about some coffee while we wait?"

"Sounds good, Ben. Damn, but it's good to see you."

"Come on. The coffee's hot and I'm anxious for a briefing."

There were several Indian doctors among the various small bands who lived in the wilderness. They met with the teams of Rebel doctors and then boarded choppers to take the doctors and the supplies back to their camps.

The supplies for Jenny were quickly off-loaded and stored. They included a couple of cases of good bourbon, for she had told Ben she enjoyed a drink in the late afternoon and Ike had taken a chance and included the bourbon . . . just in case.

After Ben had brought his old friend up to date, Ike shook his head and sighed. "You lucked out again, ol' buddy."

"Once again, age and skill have excelled over youth and enthusiasm," Ben said with a smile.

"We found you a new motor home to use as a rolling CP, Ben. Started work on it within an hour after you first coded in. It's a damn nice one. Bigger than your old one. Plush," Chase said. "Fit for a king," he added.

"I can just hear the sarcastic old bastard."

Back from her ride, Jenny walked toward the two men, a big smile on her face.

"Jenny's not going back with us?" Ike asked.

"No. She wants to stay out here. This is her home."

"I sure can't blame her for that. It's beautiful and peaceful."

"But I might decide to come to the SUSA for a visit now and then," Jenny said. She poured herself a mug of coffee, and then sat down.

"You'd sure be welcome, Miss Jenny," Ike said, falling back on his Mississippi drawl and upbringing. "Anytime." He cut his eyes to Ben as the sounds of the medical choppers returning reached his ears. "We got to be pushin' on soon, Ben. There's a storm brewin' and if we don't get out soon, we're here for awhile."

"All right, Ike. I'll get my gear together."

Ben gone from the porch, Ike stood up. "I'll leave you two alone for a time, Miss Jenny."

"Sit down, Ike," she told him. "Finish your coffee. We said our good-byes last night."

"Yes, ma'am." Ike sat. He glanced at the woman. "I can tell that Ben sure took quite a shine to you."

Jenny smiled at his language. "The feelin' is mutual, Ike.

But it's too soon for both of us. Ben's got some ramblin' to do yet."

"I know, Jenny. I know."

Ben stepped out onto the porch, his gear packed up. "You ready, Ike?"

"Ready." Ike left the porch, leaving the man and woman alone.

"I'll see you, Jenny," Ben said. "And that's a promise."

"One I will hold you to, Ben."

He bent his head and kissed her, then walked down the steps and strode over to a chopper and boarded. Seconds later, the chopper had lifted off.

Ben slipped on a headset so he and Ike could talk over the roar.

"That's a fine lady there, Ben."

"Yes, she is."

"You ought to think of holdin' on to her."

"I have. And I will, someday."

"But for right now? . . ."

"Wars to fight, Ike. You located Simon Border?"

"We know approximately where he is."

"Then let's go get him." Ben took off his headset, leaned his head back, and said no more. The tiny figure of Jenny Marlowe, standing in the front yard waving at the chopper, faded from view.

Ben knew it was not possible, but he would always swear he heard the sounds of wolves singing as the chopper flew over the wilderness that day.

Fifteen

Ben was amazed to learn that the Rebels' western front was now a hundred miles east of the ruins of Great Falls.

"We haven't been standin' still," Ike told him.

"I can see that."

Ben's team was waiting at the small airport just off highway 87 at Lewistown. After lots of hellos, hugs and handshakes, Ben inspected his new wagon and rolling CP.

"Scouts found the wagon in a barn," Ike told him. "All covered with a tarp and then covered with a mound of hay. They almost missed it. And your new mobile CP is plush, man."

It was all of that, and more. Ben nodded in satisfaction and appreciation and stepped back outside.

"Simon Border's whole organization is falling apart," Ike told him. "We've got them in a hard squeeze and the front-line troops can't get supplied. Their morale is down to nothin' and they're givin' up by the droves."

"What are you doing with the prisoners, Ike?"

"Disarmin' them and turnin' them loose. Hell, we don't have anyplace to keep them under guard, even if we wanted to."

Ben nodded his approval. "How are they reacting to that?"

"Confused, mostly. Border filled their heads with so much crap about what we were goin' to do, it was pitiful. He had his people convinced that we would rape all the women and torture the men and so forth. Ben, it was almost as though he had them on dope."

"He did, in a way, Ike. Verbal dope. Crap from the mouth. Hell, we know now he's had years to brainwash them. A few more years of it, and we would have had to fight them to the last person."

"Boss," Corrie called. "Dr. Chase's chopper just touched down. ETA this location ten minutes."

"I'm gone," Ike said.

"Chicken!" Ben told him.

"You got that right. See you, Ben. I'm back to my battalion. Have fun."

A few minutes later, Lamar Chase hopped out of the HumVee, very nimble for a man his age, and stalked up to Ben. Without even shaking hands or giving a greeting, he said, "You should be in the hospital, Ben. Why aren't you?"

"Because I feel fine, Lamar. Besides, I've got a war to run. How have you been in my absence?"

"Don't change the subject. A war? Hell, this is a pitiful excuse for a war, Raines. A bunch of half-starved, brainwashed, disillusioned wretches. I feel sorry for many of them. And the kids are in really bad shape."

"Do what you can, Lamar."

"I don't need you to tell me that, Raines!" he snapped. "You run the army, I'll take care of the medical business. What's this about you hooking up with a woman and then leaving her out in the wilderness to fend for herself?"

Ben chuckled. "More than likely she saved my life, Lamar. And I didn't desert her. She didn't want to come back with us. It's a long story. I'll tell you about it sometime."

"I'm really not interested in your wild tales of debauchery, Raines. You didn't leave her pregnant, did you?"

Ben laughed out loud, knowing that Lamar was having his fun. "I don't think so, Lamar. She told me she had her plumbing worked on just before the Great War."

"Uh-huh. Well, are you going to invite me into that rolling palace of yours for coffee?"

"Come on, Lamar." Ben put a big hand on the doctor's shoulder. "Let's go get this over with. You're never going to be satisfied until I tell you the whole story. And then you can go back and gossip with the rest of your quacks."

"Gossip!" Lamar roared. "Quacks! Why you long, tall drink of swamp water! I ought to slap you in the hospital and call in a team of proctologists to look you over. You go off alone in the Goddamned wilderness to fight some personal battle and don't give a whit about those of us behind who worry about you. You are the most inconsiderate, stubborn . . ."

Ben walked away, a smile on his lips, Lamar right behind him, yelling at him and waving his arms, his speech liberally sprinkled with profanity.

"Things are back to normal," Cooper remarked, standing with the team, a safe distance away.

"Yep," Jersey agreed. "Everything is A-Okay again."

The Rebel columns moved slowly eastward, covering fifty or more miles a day, toward the now mostly collapsing eastern front of Border's army. The northern and southern fronts had caved in and Border's people were surrendering by the hundreds. The Rebels could do little except take their weapons, give them a hot meal, then turn them loose.

Simon Border's empire was falling down like a house of cards in a stiff wind. The troops that Bottger had sent over had fled like rats from a doomed ship as soon as they realized the Rebels were not going to be stopped. Most tossed their weapons aside, changed into civilian clothing, and did their best to blend in with the civilian population.

For all intents and purposes, the war with Simon Border and his fanatics was over. All that remained was digging out the many small pockets of resisters that remained, determined to fight to the death for a lost cause.

And Simon Border had again slipped through the net and disappeared.

"Not a trace of him," Mike Richards reported, showing up one day, seemingly appearing out of thin air, as was his custom. "My people think he went to Michigan, but they're not sure. Hell, the nut could be anywhere." Mike smiled at Ben. "Enjoy your stay in the wilderness, Ben?"

"It was interesting. You done with this part of the country for a while?"

"Like you, Ben, I found a woman who can put up with me. When I get tired of following you around, I'll probably come back and settle down."

"I think we're heading to Africa next, Mike."

"Shit!" Mike said. "We'll be bogged down there for the next fifty years. Our grandchildren will be fighting long after we're dead and gone."

"I don't think so, Mike. Our objective is Bottger. Once he's dealt with, we're out of there."

"You promise?"

Ben laughed at the expression on the man's face. "Yes. I have no interest in getting involved in tribal disputes that have been going on for centuries. If they can't get along, then they can damn well kill each other off. I don't care."

"That's a relief to hear. Of course, the newly reorganized United Nations will probably piss and moan and try to convince you to turn us all into peacekeepers."

"They know better than to even try. Put that out of your mind, Mike. Any one who points a gun at us or comes after a Rebel with a machete or a spear is going to get suddenly very dead. The troops will know all that going in."

"Well, then it might turn out to be a very interesting tour of duty."

Ben nodded. "Now let's go deal with Simon Border."

The Rebel columns pushed eastward, slowly, slowly. They

accepted the surrender of ten times their own number of Simon's troops and still more came in, their hands in the air. They were half-starved and many were sick.

"He had the people," Ben mused aloud one day. "And they had the will to fight and die for him. But he made one big mistake: he couldn't feed them."

"Scurvy," Chase said. "My people are actually treating cases of scurvy. That is incredible."

"What else, Lamar?"

"You name it. Dysentery and gangrene, to name two. And my people had hit a couple of infections that aren't responding to anything we've got. And as you well know, we've got the best."

"What are you doing with those people?"

"Isolating them from other patients."

"And when we leave an area?"

Lamar spread his hands in a gesture of helplessness.

"Then these people will die?"

"Well, not necessarily. Sometimes, occasionally, fresh air, good hygiene, and a proper diet will bring them around. For others we have to amputate and hope for the best."

"Jesus!"

"He's about the only one who could help some of these patients," Lamar said softly.

The columns moved eastward, out of Montana. The war with Simon Border ended not with a bang, but with barely a whimper. But it was over. The Rebels had collected thousands of weapons and huge stockpiles of ammunition. They left behind them a sick and starving and beaten people, many of whom refused any and all help from the Rebels.

When the Rebels could do no more, they pushed on. There was no point in trying to help those who would not help themselves.

Ben's team never asked him about the days he spent in the wilderness, and he never volunteered much. But they all knew, from Rebel gossip, that he had met a woman whose memory he could not shake.

"He's in love," Cooper said one evening, while Ben was going over maps in the mobile CP.

The team was sitting away from the mobile CP, drinking coffee and talking.

"Well, it's about time," Beth opined. "It's taken him a long time to get over Jerre."

"Once you've loved someone, you always will," Corrie said. "He will always carry a part of Jerre with him. Right up and into the grave."

"That must be awful," Cooper said with a grimace.

Anna looked at the driver. "You have never been in love, Cooper?"

Cooper smiled. "Sure. About five hundred times."

Jersey snorted. "Cooper, you stay in heat, that's all. But when you do fall in love, it's going to be a sight to behold. I hope I'm around to see it."

"Well now, I have very fond feelings for you, my little Apache desert flower."

"Screw you, Cooper!"

"I try," Cooper said mournfully. "Lord knows, how I try."

In military units of the past, banter such as that would have sent women running to their commanding officers, screaming sexual harassment. In the Rebel army, women just came right back at the man, and if the man didn't like it, he could go to hell.

When the laughter had died down, Cooper asked. "You, Anna?"

"Love?" She shook her head. "No. I think not. I have experienced very deep friendship, but love? . . . No."

"All in good time, Anna," Beth said. "I promise you that."

"I don't think soldiers have any business falling in love,"

another Rebel who had walked up said, after listening for a time.

"Yeah?" Jersey challenged. "How do you propose to block a human emotion that is as natural as grass growing or birds flying, Nat?"

The Rebel smiled. "I didn't say it wouldn't happen, Jersey," Nat replied. "I just said I thought it wasn't fair. To either person."

"I agree with Nat," Beth stepped in. "Who the hell knows where we'll be in a month or a year?"

"We'll be in Africa," the Rebel standing with Nat said. "That's the scuttlebutt going around."

"If so, when that's settled, we'll be in South America, then what used to be called Russia, or maybe China," Corrie said. "But we'll always be in the field. We chose this way of life, and if we didn't like it, we wouldn't be doing it."

"So we are going to Africa?" Nat questioned the group of Rebels closest to General Raines.

"None of us knows, Nat," Beth replied. "The boss is playing this one close to the vest. I don't even think the batt coms have been informed. It's anybody's guess."

"We'll know after the boss has dealt with Simon Border," Corrie said. "Not before."

"Hell, that might take months," Nat said.

"No, it won't," Cooper replied. "I think the boss has got a pretty good fix on that nut. This campaign will be wrapped up in a week or ten days. Bet on it."

"How much?" Nat asked.

"Ten bucks," Cooper told him.

"You got it!"

"I'll take ten myself," the Rebel standing beside Nat jumped in.

"Suckers," Anna told them.

"Easy bet," Cooper said.

"So when are we going to know?" Nat asked.

"Soon," Corrie told him. She looked around her. "What damn state are we in anyway?"

"North Dakota," Beth said with a smile. "It does get confusing, doesn't it?"

All the Rebels standing around laughed at that, for sometimes the Rebel columns did move so fast it was difficult to know exactly where they were. And state maps were a rare thing. No maps had been produced, except by Rebels, for over a decade. The days of stopping at a gas station for a bag of chips, a Coke, and a road map were long gone.

"Dealing with Bruno Bottger is not going to be as easy as dealing with Simon Border's people," Nat observed. Most Rebels still had vivid memories of tangling with Bottger's people in Europe.

The door to the mobile CP opened and Ben stepped out. He spotted the knot of Rebels and walked over to them, a mug of coffee in one hand. A folding camp chair appeared almost as if by magic and Ben sat down and looked at the group.

"Anything of great importance being discussed here?" Ben asked with a smile.

"Africa, sir," one of the Rebels said.

"Huge place," Ben replied, and took a sip of coffee. "Beth probably knows all the stats on the continent."

"I haven't figured them out yet, boss."

"You're slipping, Beth." Ben rolled a smoke and lit up. Drained his coffee mug. "Yeah, people. We're going after Bruno Bottger. Better there than here. This campaign will be all wrapped up in a week or ten days."

Nat and his friend groaned. Cooper smiled and said, "Easy money."

"We have Simon Border pinpointed, General Ben?" Anna asked.

"Yes. I just got that word. Buddy and his team have dropped in and thrown up a circle around him. We'll be moving out in the morning."

"Is he in Michigan as the intel people thought?" Cooper asked.

"They were close. He's in Wisconsin, holed up with several thousand of his fanatical faithful."

Jersey looked up. "We're not going to jump in, are we?"

Ben and the others laughed at the expression on her face. "No, Jersey. We're not jumping in."

"That's a relief," she said.

"A target date set for shoving off for Africa?" Cooper asked.

"As soon as possible after dealing with Simon."

The Rebels all knew what that meant: very soon. The Rebel army could move very quickly.

"Well, I joined the Army to travel," Nat said drily.

"Regrets?" Ben asked the soldier.

Nat shook his head. "Not a one, sir. At least not yet."

"Good. All of you get some sleep. We're flying over in the morning. Let's get this over with. We've got places to go and things to do."

Sixteen

Ben's plane touched down on the just-cleaned runway outside a town in the northeastern part of the state, about fifty miles from the Michigan state line. Before the Great War it had been a town of about ten thousand souls. Now less than a thousand people called it home.

Buddy met his father's plane and father and son shook hands. "You're looking well considering your time in the wilderness, Father."

"I had some help in there, Son."

"Yes. So I heard."

"I just bet you did. Simon is in the town?"

"No, sir. North of town in an old park. He's got several thousand of his faithful surrounding him and they say they are fully prepared to die for the kook."

"They say, Son? Well, come morning, we'll see."

"What happens then?"

"Helicopter gunships and P-51E's are going to knock a hole in Border's lines about four miles wide and then we're going to pour across just like ants to honey."

Buddy smiled. "Going to take the subtle approach, hey, Father?"

"That's me, Son."

"You still want Border alive?"

"If at all possible."

Buddy hesitated. "If we do take him alive, Father, what are your plans?"

Ben shook his head. "I don't know. Kill him and we make a martyr out of the flaky bastard. If he remains alive and loose, he'll always be something of a threat. But . . . he may be certifiably insane. Our latest intel reported a team of doctors with him around the clock."

"And if he is insane?"

Ben shrugged. "We lock him up in a hospital, in a padded room, and throw away the key."

Ben nodded his agreement. "And you have already ordered the loading of ships for the trip to Africa." It was not posed as a question and was stated with a smile.

"I've forgotten how far and fast scuttlebutt can travel. But in answer to your question, yes."

"I'm rather looking forward to it, Father."

"You're about the only one," Ben said, not able to keep the sarcasm from his voice.

"The troops have read too many old newspaper accounts of the United States's disastrous forays onto the continent. We are not going in as peacekeepers."

"You damn sure got that straight."

Buddy smiled. "Where will we land?"

"I don't know yet. The captains of the ships are studying satellite passovers as we speak. But for sure we'll cover the continent from top to bottom."

Buddy's radio tech called, "The commander of Border's forces on the horn, sir."

Ben walked over and took the mic. "This is General Raines. Go ahead."

"Leave us alone, General," the man's voice sprang from the speaker. "The war is over. We are harming no one."

"It will be over with your unconditional surrender," Ben bluntly informed the man. "And I must talk with Simon Border face to face."

"Impossible!"

"Why it is impossible?"

"The Most Reverend Simon Border is very ill. He is

seeing no one. He poses no further of your imagined threats to anyone, General. Leave us alone."

"Can't do that. I've told you my terms."

"Then proceed at your own risk, General. If you attack us, many of your troops will die."

"You pays your money, you takes your chances, pal."

"What?"

Ben smiled and lifted the mic, but the man had broken off. "Strange," Ben muttered, handing the mic to the tech.

"What?"

"I don't know, Buddy. I've just got a very weird feeling about all this. I get the impression that guy," he pointed to the radio, "really doesn't want a brawl with us. Something's wrong here."

"Is the attack still on for tomorrow morning?"

Ben shook his head. "I'm going to have to think about it. I don't want needless deaths when they could have been prevented. Where's the mess tent? I could use some coffee."

Ben pondered all afternoon over the strange conversation he'd had with the commander of Simon's remaining forces. Late that afternoon he called off the air attack scheduled for the next morning.

"Tell our people to hold their positions and keep on middle alert," Ben ordered.

"Middle alert?" his son questioned.

"That's what I said. Middle alert."

Buddy looked at his father's face for a long moment, but Ben's face was unreadable. "Yes, sir."

Just as dawn was silently ripping away the dark the next morning, Ben was standing about five hundred yards from Border's front lines, studying the situation through heavy long lenses. He turned to Corrie. "Get the commander on the horn, please."

"Colonel Morrison here, General."

"Colonel, what if I gave you my word that no harm will

come to Simon Border? All I want to do is see the man in person."

"I'd . . . have to think about that, General Raines."

"Give it some thought then, Colonel. And get back to me ASAP. Colonel, I don't want needless deaths any more than you do. But you have eyes that can see. I can fill the skies with gunships within the hour and I will overrun your position. You're a soldier. You know that. You're right when you say the war is over. We can end it violently, and it will take most of the morning, or we can end it without a drop of blood being spilled. It's up to you. Get back to me as quickly as possible."

Within the hour, a white flag was fluttering over Border's south front.

"It might be a trap," Buddy warned.

"Could be, son. But somehow I rather doubt it. Send your Scouts in to check it out."

Only a few minutes passed before Buddy's Scouts radioed back. "It's legit, General. Border's troops have stacked their weapons."

"Move your battalion forward, son, and secure the position," Ben said quietly.

Ten minutes later, Ben stepped out of a HumVee and came face to face with Colonel Morrison. The man looked very tired. Ben stuck out his right hand and the colonel shook it.

"Do you have wounded who need medical care, Colonel?"

"Yes, we do, General. We're out of medicines."

Ben waved his medical people forward. He looked around at the gaunt faces of Border's troops. "From the looks of things, Colonel, you all could use a good hot meal."

"Yes, sir, we could."

"We'll get you all fixed up. Then we can go about bringing peace to this torn-up nation."

"Sounds good to me, General."

"Simon Border?"

"He's being prepared to meet you now, sir."

"Prepared?"

"You'll see what I mean very soon, General. You, ah, wouldn't have a smoke on you, would you?"

Ben smiled and handed the man bag and papers. The colonel deftly rolled a tight cigarette, licked it closed, and held out the bag. "Keep it, Colonel."

"Thank you, sir."

Trucks began rolling in and mess tents were quickly set up. Moments later, the wonderful aroma of hot food was wafting through the air.

"Line your people, up, Colonel," Ben said. "Breakfast is now being served."

Simon Border's last front collapsed with not a shot being fired.

After breakfast, Colonel Morrison walked over to an old home Ben was using for a CP and was waved to a chair. Ben poured them both coffee and set out the sugar and milk.

Colonel Morrison sipped and smiled. "It's been a long time since I tasted real coffee, General."

"The pot is full. Help yourself. Tell me about Simon Border, Colonel."

"He's insane, General. A few of us saw the signs months ago. But we couldn't convince others that it was actually happening. Now he's . . . well, completely around the bend."

"Did you know about his sexual appetites, Colonel?"

"No. I was never a part of the inner circle. Probably no more than twenty-five or so people ever knew of his tastes for . . ." The colonel grimaced. ". . . young boys and girls. Had that ever been widely circulated, his followers would have deserted him very quickly. I learned of it only a few weeks ago, and then by accident."

"The people who did know of it? What happened to them?"

"They fled like frightened rabbits when the army began collapsing." The colonel sighed. "It all sounded so good in the beginning."

"Most socialistic programs do, Colonel. They all look good on paper, in theory. In practice, they quickly begin to stink like three-day-old fish."

"First the medicines ran out, then the food was rationed. Except for the leaders, that is."

"That's the way it always works. What will you do now that it's over, Colonel?"

"I'm going back to farming."

"Around here?"

"Oh, no. I'm from Indiana originally. I'll go back to the home place and have a go at it there."

"Have you thought about the SUSA?"

The colonel laughed. "As a matter of fact, I have, General. If it doesn't work out back at the homeplace, I just might be asking for residency there."

"Come on. We've got plenty of room. So you weren't always a soldier?"

"Oh, no. Farmer first, soldier second."

An aide stuck his head inside the door. "Simon is ready now, Colonel."

"Fine. Thanks, Bernie. As soon as I finish my coffee we'll be along." He lifted his eyes to Ben. "This is not going to be pretty. I want to warn you of that. Sometimes he's quite lucid, but most of the time, not."

"He has to be cleaned up by others?"

"Several times a day. And he's getting worse. You have a place for him in the SUSA?"

"Oh, yes. We have institutions there." Ben pushed back his chair and stood up. "You ready, Colonel?"

"I guess so. Might as well get this over with. The quicker we do, the quicker we can start picking up our lives."

"Nobody ever said it was going to be easy, did they, Colonel?"

"They damn sure didn't, General. And it damn sure hasn't been."

Seventeen

Ben could hear the ranting and chanting and wild raving all mixed in with profanity as he was getting out of the HumVee in front of the house. He looked at Colonel Morrison. "Simon Border?"

"Yes."

A man who looked to be on the point of exhaustion was sitting on the porch. He did not make any attempt to rise at Ben's approach. Ben felt it was not disrespect on the man's part: he was just tired.

"What happened, Doctor?" Colonel Morrison asked.

"Who knows?" the medical man answered wearily. "He was fine twenty minutes ago. That's when I sent word over to you. Bathed, shaved, all dressed up, lucid. Now he's a raving mad man again." He looked at General Raines. "You're General Raines. I've seen your picture. And this gentleman? . . ." He cut his eyes to the third man to get out of the HumVee.

"Dr. Goldsmith," Ben said. "Major Goldsmith of the Rebel Army."

"Well, Doctor" the seated man said. "I hope you're a shrink and can tell me what's happened to Simon Border. I was OB/GYN before I foolishly joined the flock of Simon Border." He smiled. "By the way, I'm Dr. Schnider. Call me Tom."

"I'm Josh," Dr. Goldsmith said with a smile, extending his hand. "But I'm no shrink."

"Pity," Tom said, shaking hands with all the men. "I guess I'll never know what happened to the Lord of All Living Things, the Pouty Pedophile, his Majesty the Fruitcake in there." He jerked a thumb.

A chuckle slipped past Ben's lips. "Aren't you one of the faithful, Tom?"

"Hell, no, General! I am a very unwilling conscript. And personally, I hope the pecker on that lunatic son of a bitch in there rots off."

Ben cut his eyes to Colonel Morrison. Even the colonel could not contain the twinkle in his eyes. "We need doctors in the SUSA, Tom. Lots of babies being born down there."

Dr. Schnider slowly, wearily, got to his feet. "Where do I sign up?"

"Just be ready to go sometime today. Hell, take a nap, man. We'll wake you."

"Thank you, General. But who can sleep with all that howling?" Again, he jerked a thumb toward the house. "I'll just wait out here for you. That's my duffle bag sitting just inside the front door."

"Were you planning to slip away regardless, Dr. Schnider?" Colonel Morrison asked.

"Damn right, I was. The very first chance I got."

Ben stepped up to the front door and pushed it open, Doctor Goldsmith behind him. The stench hit them first. A foulness that permeated the closed room.

"I am the Lord Jesus Christ on Earth!" Simon shrieked.

Ben and Dr. Goldsmith exchanged glances.

"Fuck you all!" Simon shouted.

A man appeared in a hallway and motioned to the men. "This way, gentlemen. We've had to put Reverend Border in a straitjacket for his own protection."

"I want some pussy!" Simon shouted.

Dr. Goldsmith arched one eyebrow.

"Somebody come suck your God's wangdoodle!"

"Was that the cue to bring the bastard a young boy or girl?" Ben asked the guard, his voice filled with sarcasm.

"I knew nothing about that side of him, sir. I was assigned to Reverend Border two weeks ago. After I got out of the hospital."

Ben gave the guard a very hard look; hard enough to back the man up a few steps. "If you ever again refer to that perverted son of a bitch as 'reverend' in my presence, I will personally shoot you stone dead."

"Yes, sir. Just a habit, sir."

"Break it."

"Yes, sir. Consider it done, sir."

"Glory, gory, hallelujah!" sang Simon. "Mine eyes have seen the beauty of a tender young twat! . . ."

Ben pushed open the door to Simon's room and stood for a moment, staring at the man.

"Ben Raines!" Simon screamed. "The anti-Christ in person. Somebody kill the son of a bitch. Take his head. Dismember the heathen. That is an order."

"Screw you, Simon," Ben replied.

Simon stank of his own excrement. Slobber leaked from his lips. Snot dripped from his nostrils. He had pissed in his trousers. He lunged and flung himself about on the mattress covered floor. He howled like a rabid animal. He snapped his teeth together so hard Ben did not know what prevented them from breaking.

"Tell my driver to bring that small suitcase in here," Ben told the guard.

"Yes, sir. Right now, General."

"I'm a turd burgler, I'm a turd burgler!" Simon sang. "Got my religion at my mammy's knee."

"What's in the case, General?" Colonel Morrison asked.

"A tranquilizer gun. I felt that might be the safest way to knock him out."

"I wish we had access to one," Morrison said. "He's bitten a dozen people."

"I shall rise from the ruins and be proclaimed King of the Gentiles. Fuck all Jews and niggers!" Simon shouted. "Run 'em all off. Send them over the cliffs of salvation to their deaths on the rocks below. So saith the Lord of All Living Beings. His Majesty Simon Border! All praise the pussy hound!"

"I think he's slipped from grace somewhat," Dr. Goldsmith said.

"It would certainly appear that way," Ben replied.

"I know you, Ben Raines!" Simon screamed. "You are the devil and I am the light of truth and beauty."

"No kidding?" Ben said.

"My way leads to the gates of Heaven," Simon howled. "To follow you leads to the fiery pits of hell and damnation."

"War is hell, isn't it, Simon?" Ben replied.

"You think you're such a know-it-all smarty-pants, don't you, Raines!" Simon slobbered. "You nigger-lovin', Jew-humpin' fuckface!"

"Is he genuinely nuts, Josh?" Ben asked. "Or just a damn good actor?"

"I don't know, General. My guess would be a little of both."

"Onward Christian Soldiers, marching off to war!" Simon sang, decidedly off-key. Then he fell over on the stinking mattresses and began howling and kicking.

"Has the van to transport this screwball to the airport arrived yet?" Ben asked Colonel Morrison.

"Not yet, sir. But it's on the way." The colonel took off his sidearm and offered it to Ben.

"Keep it," Ben told him. "You might need it. Probably will need it."

"Shoot the infidel!" Simon squalled. "KillhimKillhim-Killhim. I order you to kill him!"

"Oh, blow it out your bunghole," Colonel Morrison muttered.

"I heard that!" Simon screamed. "I shall have my faithful draw and quarter you, you traitor!"

"I'm going back to Indiana, General," Morrison announced. "Do you need me here?"

"No. Good luck, Colonel."

Morrison shook hands with Ben and Josh and walked out of the house.

"Come back here, you farthead!" Simon yelled.

Without turning around, Morrison flipped Simon the rigid digit and kept on walking.

Ben looked up as a Rebel came walking swiftly down the hall. "General, Scouts have found a house filled with dead kids. It's about twenty miles west of this location. They took one adult prisoner and threatened to hang him on the spot if he didn't talk. He talked. The kids were Simon's private, ah, harem, so to speak. Those few who remained loyal to Simon wanted to get rid of all the evidence. The kids ranged in age from about eight to twelve. They were all machine-gunned. All dead."

"Good God!" Dr. Goldsmith blurted.

Ben nodded. "I expected something like this. Well," he sighed. "Here's the trank gun. Do your stuff, Josh."

"Where do you want me to shoot him, General?"

"I don't care if you shoot the son of a bitch in the head," Ben replied. "Just knock him out and get him gone. Before I decide to end it permanently."

"Doesn't anybody want to see my weewee?" Simon asked. "Then take a good look at this!" He crawled to his hands and knees, showed his butt to Ben and the others, and farted.

The newly arrived Rebel put a hand on the butt of his sidearm. Ben stopped it there. "I do understand your feelings, Sergeant. And sympathize with them. But, no."

"The van is here, General," a Rebel called from the porch.

"Good," Ben said. "Pop him, doctor."

Goldsmith lifted the trank gun and fired. The dart hit Simon in one cheek of his ass, burying to the hilt, and the man howled and jerked.

"How long before the juice takes effect?"

"Not long, General. A few minutes max."

"I'll be outside."

Ben sat down on the edge of the porch, leaving the steps clear, and watched as the medics took a stretcher out of the van and entered the house.

"If you wait until they're eight it's too late!" Simon yelled.

Ben frowned. In the SUSA, pedophiles had a very short public trial and were promptly hanged.

Ben rolled a smoke and waited.

Moments later, Buddy drove up and got out, walking up to the porch. "Is it over, Father?"

"Just about, son."

". . . Where is my crown?" Simon called, his voice much weaker as the knock-out drug took effect. "Why are you doing this to me? You can't treat me in such a manner. I am the King of the Gentiles."

"Are you all right, Father?" Buddy asked. "You don't look well."

"My stomach is a little queasy, Son. Other than that, I'm all right."

"I forbid this!" Simon yelped.

"Idiot," Buddy muttered.

"You sure have that right, son." Ben stood up and brushed the dirt off the seat of his BDUs. "I'm heading back to the SUSA, boy. This campaign is all over."

"Going to be on the same plane with Simon, Father?"

Ben looked closely at his son. There was a definite twinkle in the young man's eyes. "You've been hanging around Ike too long. You ought to watch that. You're likely to catch a bad case of the smart ass."

"I wouldn't dream of doing that."

"Ummm," Ben said.

"Tell Uncle Cecil hello for me."

"I'll sure do that, boy."

Cecil Jefferys was the President of the Southern United States of America. The first black man in America ever to be elected to such a high office.

"We should be through here in a couple of weeks," Buddy said. "Then three weeks to get back to Base Camp One. And I imagine we'll be sailing shortly after that."

"If all goes well, yes. I plan on giving everyone ten days leave to see family."

"After we've set sail, any stops planned along the way?"

"No. At least not at this time."

"Straight through?"

"Straight through."

"Are we taking everyone?"

"At least ten battalions. Maybe more. I don't know for sure yet. It'll all be worked out by the time all the battalions are back home."

"See you back at Base Camp One, Father."

Buddy walked away from his father and got in his Hum-Vee. As he drove away, he lifted his hand in a salute. Ben smiled and waved a hand in acknowledgment. He turned as the screen door banged open. Ben watched as the now unconscious Simon Border was carried out to the van and loaded inside. Dr. Goldsmith climbed in and the van pulled away.

"Strange way to end a war, General," the Rebel who had driven Ben over said.

"Yes, it is," Ben agreed.

"But it really wasn't much of a war, was it, General?"

"Those who died fighting it might not agree with you."

"No, sir, I guess they wouldn't. Never looked at it quite that way."

"Which way did the Colonel go?"

The young Rebel pointed. "That way, sir. He said he was

going to find him the nearest creek and take off his boots and soak his feet for a time, then he was going back home."

"You ready to go back home for a few days and see friends and family?"

"No family, sir. And my friends are all right here in 8 Batt."

"I see. Well, I do know that feeling. A soldier's life is not an easy one, is it?"

"Oh, I don't know, sir. I lied about my age and joined up when I was fifteen. The army is the only real home I've ever known."

"How old are you?"

"Twenty-two, sir."

"So you've been fighting for seven years."

"I've been fighting since I was old enough to remember, General. Lost my folks when I was about six, I think it was. Bused around until I was about ten, livin' on scraps of food and so forth. I looked up one day and this big Rebel was lookin' at me. He said, 'I do believe that under all that dirt, there just might be a little boy.' " The young man laughed. "He picked me up and toted me down to a creek and scrubbed me until I was pink. I rode in the back of a truck for a long time after that, until he could arrange to send me down to Base Camp One. The placement folks found a foster home for me and they were real nice people. We lived up on the northern border of what is now the SUSA. They treated me just like I was really their own. Punks slipped over the border and killed them when I was fourteen."

"And you joined the army right after that?"

"After I tracked those bastards who killed my adopted parents all the way to Illinois and finished them off. One by one," he added grimly. "I been with special operations ever since I got out of boot." The driver looked up at the sky. "I better be gettin' you back, sir. It's gonna rain pretty soon."

"All right. I'm ready when you are. There certainly isn't anything left to do here."

Thirty minutes later, Ben and his team were airborne, heading bask to the SUSA.

Cecil was waiting on the tarmac when Ben's plane touched down. His team scattered, anxious to start their leave, and Ben got in the car with Cecil.

"Well, Ben," Cecil said. "I've had conversations with the Presidents of the WUSA, the EUSA, and the NUSA."

"So the nation is now officially broken up into four smaller countries?"

"For a time, yes. You know as well as I do a couple of them won't last. We're the only section that will endure and prosper. Maybe the WUSA. That's up for grabs. And . . . I've also had lengthy conversations with the Secretary General of the UN."

"Let me guess: the Eastern United States of America—that bunch of head-up-their-ass liberals wants us to go to Africa as peacekeepers?"

"Right."

"I hope you told them to forget it."

"In no uncertain terms."

"The secretary general?"

"He's unhappy about us going into Africa, 'spoiling for a fight,' to use his words."

"There won't be a shot fired unless we are fired upon. Did you tell him that?"

"Several times. His response was that the Rebels operate with a hair trigger."

"Indeed we do."

Cecil laughed. "Other than that, things are moving very smoothly here. Applicants for residency are flooding in. We're Okaying about three out of ten. Those that we reject just don't seem to fully grasp what it means to live under a common-sense form of government."

"And they never will. Big Brother Liberalism conditioned them too well to look to the central government to solve all their problems. Call it the de-balling of America."

"I did. One wild-eyed feminist who is now the governor of some state back East called me a sexist for that remark."

"Fuck her."

"Not even with your dick, thank you."

That set both men off into a binge of laughter and the driver smiled and shook his head at their antics.

"I wish I was going with you, Ben," Cecil said, wiping his eyes.

"I know, Cec. Believe me, I do. But you're needed here. You're ten times the diplomat I am. You know me: I just kick ass and take names."

"When are you planning on shoving off?"

"I gave the enlisted personnel ten days off. Officers will report back in a week. That will give me time to map out and firm up plans. Then we go."

"Lamar going on this campaign?"

"Would you like to be the one to tell him he can't?"

"No, thank you." Cecil smiled. "And after Africa, Ben? What next?"

"Central and South America."

"You answered very quickly. You must have been giving it some thought."

"Some. Might as well get it done while I'm still fit for the field."

"And then?"

Ben laughed. "I haven't thought *that* far ahead, Cec." Ben gazed out the window for a few miles. "Crops look good."

"Experts say it's going to be a great year. We'll be able to send hundreds of tons up north to help feed the starving."

"While their elected officials sit on their asses and argue

about the finer points of punks, disarming the citizens, and passing more needless laws. The stupid sons of bitches will never learn that in government less is best. You would think that a war would teach them that, but no."

"You want to go to your house, right, Ben? The turn is right up here."

"No. Take me to the BOQ on the base. I'll stay there. And no, I don't want to see Smoot. Smoot's got a good home now, and my showing up would just confuse the animal. I need to spend some time alone."

Cecil looked hard at his long time friend. "She must have been one hell of a woman, Ben."

"She is. And I'm going back some day. Bet on it."

As Ben lay in his bed that night at the BOQ, he dreamed of running wild and free, and of Jenny, sitting on the front porch of the cabin.

Waiting.